IN DANGER'S HOUR

Romulus Hutchinson Book Two

David Clensy

Also in the Romulus Hutchinson Series
For Those In Peril
The Mighty Ocean

IN DANGER'S HOUR

Published by Sapere Books.

24 Trafalgar Road, Ilkley, LS29 8HH

saperebooks.com

Copyright © David Clensy, 2025

David Clensy has asserted his right to be identified as the author of this work.
All rights reserved.

No part of this publication may be reproduced, stored in any retrieval system, or transmitted, in any form, or by any means, electronic, mechanical, photocopying, recording, or otherwise, without the prior written permission of the publishers.
This book is a work of fiction. Names, characters, businesses, organisations, places and events, other than those clearly in the public domain, are either the product of the author's imagination, or are used fictitiously.
Any resemblances to actual persons, living or dead, events or locales are purely coincidental.

ISBN: 978-0-85495-780-4

Dedicated to the memory of all those who suffered or perished as a consequence of Liverpool's May Blitz in 1941.

Eternal Father, strong to save,
Whose arm hath bound the restless wave,
Who bid'st the mighty ocean deep
Its own appointed limits keep;
O hear us when we cry to Thee,
For those in peril on the sea.

O Trinity of love and pow'r,
Your children shield in danger's hour;
From rock and tempest, fire, and foe,
Protect them where-so-e'er they go;
Thus, evermore shall rise to Thee
Glad hymns of praise from land and sea.

William Whiting, 1860

CHAPTER ONE

*Mediterranean Sea,
195 nautical miles east-southeast of Malta,
January 1941*

The two bombs that struck HMS *Southampton* had a delayed explosive mechanism, providing a few valuable moments for the Luftwaffe's Stuka dive bomber pilots — two chisel-jawed aces of the Sturzkampfgeschwader 2 squadron — to turn and lift away from the stricken vessel. In the same moment, eighty-one members of the veteran light cruiser's crew were experiencing the final seconds of their lives — seconds that were filled with the banshee scream of the impact, followed by the sucking of the air from their cabins, the passageways, the staircases and ultimately from their lungs. The world became an explosion of light and heat and energy, before the onset of an eternity of silence.

Sub-Lieutenant Romulus Hutchinson, who had been thrown back onto the deck by the force of the explosion, raised his hand to touch the bloodied tangle of hair where his head had connected with a steel rivet on the edge of the deck. As he got to his feet, he was faced with an apocalyptic vision — the ship was engulfed in flame from the stern to the bridge, and a cloud of acrid black smoke was billowing high into the blue Mediterranean skies.

Rom ran towards the metal steps that led to the pilothouse, taking a deep breath as he steeled himself to launch headlong into the cloud of smoke. Inside, he could barely see anything

— one whole half of the pilothouse had collapsed in on itself, but ahead, inside the chart house, he saw the outline of a man, curled in a foetal position beneath the chart table. Still holding his breath and squinting against the smoke, Rom pulled at the man's ankles, then grappled the limp body up onto his shoulder, before turning back towards the doorway. Buckling under the weight of the body, Rom staggered back down the metal steps and placed his heavy load onto the deck with a dull thud. He looked down at the soot-stained features of a fellow sub-lieutenant, Angus Merriweather — a young man Rom had got to know well in his first few weeks onboard his new ship. He felt for a pulse in Merriweather's neck.

'Thank God,' Rom muttered. 'You're alive.'

Behind him, a group of ratings started to work the winch of a lifeboat. Rom shouted across to them. 'Get this man in the boat!' he commanded. 'He's still alive.'

The men helped Rom to transfer the young sub-lieutenant into the lifeboat. As they did so, Merriweather came to and vomited across his own chest.

'You're all right, Merriweather. Take it easy,' Rom sad soothingly. 'We're getting you to safety.'

Moments later, Merriweather, Rom and the group of sailors were in the lifeboat, edging away from HMS *Southampton* as fire tore through much of the deck above. Around them, clusters of other lifeboats were filled with wide-eyed young ratings, all gazing towards the light cruiser that had become their home and now seemed almost certainly doomed.

By the time Rom's boat was picked up by HMS *Gloucester*, almost the entire deck of *Southampton* was engulfed by the tumbling cloud of black smoke. As Merriweather was taken away to *Gloucester*'s sick bay, Rom stood on the deck and watched *Southampton* as she was consumed by the flames. A sick bay attendant approached to take a look at the wound on Rom's head, but he waved him away impatiently. 'I'm fine, man. See to the others,' he muttered as he watched on, unable to take his eyes off the burning ship for which he had had such high hopes.

After losing his first ship, HMS *Grenade*, at Dunkirk, and being invalided off his second ship, HMS *Havelock*, for a period of psychiatric assessment at an institution near Belfast, returning to active service with a place on the bridge of HMS *Southampton* had felt like a towering achievement and a fresh start. But just weeks after joining the ship, at the height of Operation Excess — a high-stakes convoy mission designed to deliver vital supplies to Malta — the end for *Southampton* had come far more swiftly than he could have imagined. Once again, he found himself without a ship, thanks to the relentless work of the Luftwaffe's merciless dive bombers.

Rom sensed a presence beside him and turned to see the familiar square jaw of Captain Basil Barrington-Brooke, the crestfallen master of *Southampton*.

'Good to see you safe, sir,' Rom said, breaking the silence that hung between the two men. Barrington-Brooke nodded, his eyes fixed on the burning vessel.

'You too, Hutchinson,' the captain said, reaching into the inside pocket of his jacket and producing a silver cigarette case. He offered one to Rom, who took it with whispered thanks. Barrington-Brooke then lifted a silver lighter towards Rom's face with shaking hands. Once their cigarettes were lit, both men inhaled deeply, before almost simultaneously releasing their own little clouds of smoke in the direction of the burning HMS *Southampton*.

'I heard what you did for young Merriweather,' Barrington-Brooke said at last, the nicotine seeming to calm him almost instantly.

'Oh, it was nothing really.' Rom shrugged. 'I couldn't have left him, knowing that he was up in the chart house when the bomb hit. I had to go back for him.'

'I wouldn't describe it as nothing,' Barrington-Brooke said swiftly. 'You saved his life — there can be no debate about that. I shall certainly be recommending you for the Distinguished Service Cross.'

Rom didn't know what to say. He hadn't thought what he had done was an act of valour, just a decision made in the heat of the moment. The idea of receiving a formal honour for it felt a little absurd.

'I only wish I could have saved more men,' Rom said at last. 'We must have lost many of our officers when the bridge was taken out, and God knows how many men below decks.' He started to reel off the names of his fellow sub-lieutenants and lieutenants whom he had not seen since arriving on HMS *Gloucester* and whom he now assumed must have been killed. After a few names, his voice began to break, and he returned to smoking his cigarette.

Barrington-Brooke nodded sombrely. 'Dozens, scores even, no doubt. But whatever the final number, there was one less death, thanks to your actions.' He patted Rom on the shoulder and walked away.

Within a week, Rom and the other survivors of *Southampton* found themselves in Gibraltar, waiting for a place on a troopship to take them back to England. A nurse finally stitched up the small wound to his scalp, as he sat beside an open window in a military hospital overlooking the busy harbour.

'You'll have a bit of a scar, but your hair will cover it,' she said, working gently. 'You should have allowed them to see you sooner.'

'No matter.' Rom smiled. 'It won't be the first scar and it probably won't be the last. Two minutes earlier and I would have been on the bridge — a goner. So, I shan't trouble myself too much about one more scar on my head.'

The nurse nodded. 'That's the spirit,' she said.

'Anyway, it's bought me a ticket to Buckingham Palace,' Rom continued.

The nurse looked suitably impressed. 'Why's that then?'

'I've been awarded the Distinguished Service Cross for gallantry, though I can't entirely work out how I was any more gallant than anyone else that day. So I'm due at the palace for a presentation from King George himself, two days after we arrive back in Blighty — scar or no scar.'

'Two days?' The nurse laughed. 'Let's hope your ship isn't delayed, in that case.'

'I imagine they must be churning them out at the moment, gallantry medals,' Rom said with a laugh. 'Poor King George is probably battling to keep up with the job of pinning things on lapels. He should be the one getting a gallantry medal.'

'Don't undermine your achievement,' the nurse advised him, with a playful frown. 'You chaps are all far too good at doing that.'

Rom nodded. 'I suppose it goes with the territory — mustn't take ourselves too seriously and all that.'

'Well, you say hello to the king from me when you see him.' The nurse grinned as she tied off the thread and stepped back to assess her handiwork. 'There, that should hold it. You can tell the king that you've been a very brave young man indeed.'

Rom laughed. 'Thanks, I'll be sure to let him know.'

*

After months of dreaming about meeting King George, the idea of actually seeing the monarch in the flesh was making Rom nervous. It played on his mind throughout the voyage back and when the troopship docked at Plymouth, he was dismissed affectionately by Captain Barrington-Brooke with a warm handshake and a whispered word of advice. 'Only speak when you're spoken to, and don't forget it's "Your Majesty" the first time you address him, and just "sir" after that. Don't be tempted to overdo it with the flimflam.'

Rom nodded. 'Thank you, sir. I'll remember.'

'Oh, and Hutchinson?'

'Yes, sir?'

'Best of British luck to you with your next ship.'

Rom smiled. 'You too, sir.'

Rom had four hours in Plymouth before his train to London, so immediately set about the mission of finding Charlotte, his childhood sweetheart, who had for the past few months been working as a plotting officer at the Western Approaches Command HQ in the city. Rom had not seen Charlotte since she had joined the WRNS, so he was keen to track her down — even if only for a few minutes.

He went first to the address he had for her, but was told by the landlady that Charlotte had left a few days before. 'Gone back up north, son,' she said pleasantly.

Back up north? That didn't make sense — Charlotte hadn't mentioned it. As he was stepping away from the property, a young Wren came out of the house and called after him in a broad cockney accent, 'You were asking after Charlotte?'

Rom nodded.

'You wouldn't be Sub-Lieutenant Hutchinson by any chance, would you?' she asked.

'Yes, that's me. I'm Hutchinson.'

'Charlotte talked about you all the time — I'm Polly, by the way, Polly Parker.' She reached out her right hand and Rom gave it a shake. 'She's gone back up to Liverpool,' Polly went on, leaning towards Rom conspiratorially. 'We're all going. It's a bit hush-hush, so not a word to anyone, but the whole of the Western Approaches Command is relocating to Liverpool.'

Rom raised his eyebrows. 'Well, I suppose that makes sense, given that so much of the nation's shipping is now going through the Mersey,' he said. 'Charlotte must be thrilled to be going home.'

'She was.' Polly smiled. 'But she would have been more excited to see you turning up on her doorstep. It's such a shame she missed you.'

'No matter. I'll write to her at her parents' house,' Rom said.

'Yes, do that. And maybe I'll be seeing you up in Liverpool one day, Sub-Lieutenant Hutchinson.'

Two hundred and sixty-seven miles to the north, Charlotte Burton was wondering how she was ever going to find the address she was looking for, given the absurdly convoluted instructions she had been given. She took a slip of paper from her jacket pocket as she turned the corner of Castle Street, passing the wall of sandbags that had been built around Liverpool Town Hall. She was to make her way to an unmarked door at the corner of Exchange Flags on Rumford Street.

As a Liverpudlian, she understood the reference to Exchange Flags — it had been the centre of cotton trading in the city for more than a century. Charlotte knew it as a great rambling

Victorian building. However, all of that had been demolished since she had last been in this part of the city centre and replaced with a sleek new Portland Stone building that would have looked more at home in New York. Charlotte approached the unassuming entrance, folding the piece of paper back into her pocket and reaching deeper for her identification papers.

The guard at the front desk checked through Charlotte's papers carefully, before unlocking a door and directing her through it and down a staircase towards the basement. The gloomy lighting in the stairwell made Charlotte feel nervous as she heard the guard close the door behind her with a thunderous clang. But halfway down the stairs she was relieved to meet a familiar face from her training in Plymouth. Duty Commander Jack Walters was a slight fellow, with a shiny bald head and wire-rimmed spectacles. He had a kind smile, which flashed up at Charlotte.

'Welcome to the Citadel, my dear,' Walters said with a flourish. 'We have two entire subterranean storeys down here — a reinforced bunker measuring fifty-five thousand square feet, with so much concrete in its construction that the Germans could flatten the entire city above us and we could carry on working safely below.'

Charlotte raised her eyebrows. 'Thank you, sir. If I wasn't feeling nervous before, I certainly am now.'

Walters laughed. 'Come on down with me. I'll show you around the place. It's not half as bad as you might think.'

Walters led Charlotte along a series of corridors and through a noisy room full of teleprinters. They eased their way along another narrow corridor, passing a busy telephone switchboard being operated by two ladies in the uniform of the Women's Auxiliary Air Force.

'We're a mixed crew — WAAFs and WRNS mostly,' Walters explained. 'Just like in Plymouth, but on a much bigger scale.'

As he said the words "bigger scale", he opened the door on to a cavernous operations room. Convoy plotters were already hard at work on the main floor, some perched on rolling ladders that gave access to the floor-to-ceiling map of the North Atlantic that consumed one entire wall. Opposite the map, on the far side of the operations room, there were a series of windows, through which Charlotte could just make out the figures of men in RAF and Royal Navy uniforms, overseeing the women working below.

'The boss has his office up there, as well as a bedroom, from which he can look out at the convoy map,' Walters said with a smile.

Charlotte raised her eyebrows. She didn't need to ask which boss Walters was talking about. There had only been one man who was referred to as "the boss" throughout her time in Plymouth, and she knew Admiral Martin Eric Dunbar-Nasmith had already made his way north for the transfer of operations to the new headquarters. He was in the process of handing over the role of Commander-in-Chief, Western Approaches Command HQ to Admiral Percy Noble, who was coming in with new ideas about forming established escort groups to build resilient teams that would work together seamlessly without the need to adjust to new escort collaborators every few weeks.

Dunbar-Nasmith appeared to be unconvinced by the idea. He was a distant man, with striking aquiline features and a strong jawline. He had been serving in the Royal Navy since Queen Victoria was on the throne and in his neat admiral's uniform, he seemed the very epitome of the old-school military leader.

'What's he like, the boss?' Charlotte asked Walters. 'He seems such a mysterious figure to us girls.'

Walters paused and looked towards Dunbar-Nasmith's office while he considered the question. 'He's really rather thoughtful, actually,' he said at last. 'Extraordinarily experienced as an officer, of course — he commanded submarines in the last war. I heard a story that he once captured a sailing dhow in the Sea of Marmara and lashed it to the conning tower of his sub as camouflage, so he could go on to capture an enemy ship filled with ammunition, despite only using small arms fire. It was all about the element of surprise, I suppose. That's the kind of mind the man has. He can see problems from different angles and come up with solutions that others would never have thought of. I only hope the new chap will be as good.'

At that moment, Charlotte was alarmed to see Dunbar-Nasmith himself appear, striding across the operations room. She felt a flush of guilt, as if she had been caught talking about somebody behind their back.

'Well, here's your chance to get to know the man himself,' Walters said.

'No, I couldn't,' Charlotte muttered, mild panic rising in her throat and stifling her words before any more could escape.

'Don't worry — he's really rather lovely.' Walters turned to intercept the commanding officer. 'Sir, I wanted to introduce Wren Plotting Officer Charlotte Burton,' he said.

The boss turned his piercing grey eyes towards her. 'Like the actress?' Dunbar-Nasmith said with a smile.

'I'm sorry, sir?'

'The actress — Charlotte Burton. She was in the silent films, before the talkies came along. You must have seen *Polly of the Storm Country*?' The senior officer looked hopefully from Walters to Charlotte, but then dismissed his own question with a shrug. 'Of course not — you're both far too young.' He turned his focus back to Charlotte. 'Are you new?'

Charlotte suppressed a smile. 'No, sir, I've been serving in Plymouth for a few months now.'

'Good, good.' Dunbar-Nasmith nodded.

'Burton is one of our brightest young plotting officers, sir,' Walters put in. 'She has a very quick mind.'

'Good, good,' Dunbar-Nasmith said again. 'We need more women like you, in that case.' He looked as if he was about to move on, but paused and turned back towards Charlotte. 'She married William Russell, your famous namesake. You know the handsome chap — *Cyrano de Bergerac*, *The Twins of Suffering Creek*, *Pride and the Man*, and so on?' The admiral gave an exasperated sigh as he looked once again from Charlotte to Walters, but found no acknowledgement in their faces. 'I used to like the films in those days,' he added in a melancholy tone. 'There was some sort of artistic merit to them. I've never been able to stand the talkies. They do tend to induce a headache, I find.'

Charlotte nodded, before noncommittally adding a formal, 'Yes, sir.'

Dunbar-Nasmith nodded back at her and walked off towards his office.

Meanwhile, across the city, Rom's mother Eileen Hutchsinson was finding some relief in the relative calm that had fallen after the horrors she had witnessed during the final two months of 1940. Bad flying weather had slowed down the Luftwaffe's merciless barrage of Liverpool, and life as a volunteer first aid ambulance driver had become more tolerable. She had been called out to bombing raids on Herculaneum Dock and the Dingle Oil Depot, but casualty figures were light compared to the pre-Christmas raids.

She had been teamed up with another woman for her ambulance work. Bella Templeton was also resurrecting the skills she had learnt as a nurse before leaving the profession to have her children almost twenty years before. Both women had been acutely aware of being a little rusty in the first few months of volunteering, while Eileen also had to get to grips with driving an ambulance — she hadn't driven anything at all since sitting behind the wheel of an old truck on the family farm near Formby as a girl of fifteen. Those were halcyon days, long before she had met her husband William, who was currently somewhere in the Atlantic at the helm of the SS *Robert Holt*, moving vital supplies around the empire and bearing only a passing resemblance beneath the white beard to the fresh-faced young sailor she had met in her late teens.

Before William had come along, Eileen had shown little interest in men — though plenty of farmhands had shown an interest in her. Up in the cab of the farm lorry, with the sleeves of her plaid shirt rolled up to the elbows, she had made for a striking vision. Today, buttoned into her Red Cross uniform, perched primly behind the wheel of the ambulance, she would occasionally catch sight of herself in the vehicle's wing mirror and register a little sadly how her face had aged in recent years — the worry lines that creased her brow a consequence of having a husband and two sons at sea with U-boats roaming the waters of the North Atlantic, sniffing out their prey.

Remus had followed his father into the Merchant Navy, while his twin brother Romulus had opted for the Royal Navy. While Remmie was happy to join up as a deckhand, his more confident and ambitious sibling had put himself through officer training with the Royal Navy Volunteer Reserve and had spent much of the war so far on the bridge of Royal Navy destroyers, taking part in both the evacuations of British forces from Norway and later from Dunkirk and St Nazaire. It was no wonder she had developed such deeply ingrained worry lines, Eileen thought to herself, as she drove the vehicle along the dock road.

'Do you hear much from your Henry?' she asked Bella, who was perched in the cab alongside her, trying to get her hair to sit neatly beneath her cap.

Bella took a hairpin out from between her lips and inserted it determinedly into place. 'I've had a few letters, but not many,' she replied, as she watched the rubble-strewn cityscape passing by through the ambulance window. 'Henry came out via Cherbourg, not Dunkirk, so I don't know if he saw the same sort of horrors as those boys on the beaches. But he is certainly quieter since coming back. They've got him camped on Salisbury Plain, doing some sort of training. When he writes, it's mostly about how gloomy and windswept the Plain is.'

Eileen nodded. At just eighteen, Bella's son Henry seemed far too young to be in the Army. Though her own twins had joined up at sixteen, they somehow seemed more protected within the tight-knit community of a ship. 'Well, it's good that he got back safe and sound and in one piece. It's such a worry, isn't it, having boys out there in the world and having no idea what's happening to them?'

'Sometimes I think it was a small mercy that Frank was taken before all of this kicked off,' Bella said, speaking softly. 'He thought the world of that boy — his only son, and all that. I'm not sure he would have been able to cope with thinking about him out there on the Continent, fighting.'

Eileen reached across and placed a sympathetic hand on Bella's forearm. Bella had lost her husband just two years before the outbreak of war. His lungs had been badly damaged by gas attacks in the trenches during his service in the Great War, and poor Bella had simply woken up one morning to find him cold in bed beside her.

'It can't be easy for you, being on your own at a time like this,' Eileen said sympathetically.

Bella shrugged. 'You do what you have to do, don't you? That's why I volunteered for this work, though — it beats sitting at home worrying about Henry all day long.'

Eileen nodded. 'Same here. Having the three of them out at sea was almost more than I could bear. At least when I'm out of the house, driving the ambulance or helping the wounded, I feel as though I'm doing something to help. I still have plenty to give, even at my age.'

'Oh, forty-five isn't so old,' Bella chided. 'There are women still having children in their forties these days.'

'Hardly!' Eileen laughed.

'There are too,' said her friend, pausing to think of an example. 'Nora O'Malley, the butcher's wife, she's just had her eighth child, and she's forty-two.'

'Eight! Jesus wept!' said Eileen. 'If old O'Malley has enough energy for that kind of thing at his age, he must be keeping all the best cuts for himself.'

The two women erupted into laughter as they drove on along the dock road.

It had been difficult for Remmie to readjust to life on board the SS *John Holt* after the death of his friend, Eric Taylor. One of the ship's stokers, Taylor had been a rough-and-ready brawler who had terrified Remmie at first. But the unlikely pair had got on well, and Remmie had attempted to nurse Taylor on the voyage home from Lagos as the stoker battled the dysentery he had picked up in the West African city. Remmie couldn't have imagined how swiftly Taylor's condition would deteriorate. He had been stunned to find him dead in his bed and watched on with sorrow as his friend was taken off the ship in a coffin when they had finally reached Liverpool.

On days like this, when the ship was some miles south of the Tropic of Cancer, but still far from their destination port, Remmie would spend much of his free time up on deck, leaning on the rail and gazing out at the endless expanse of ocean. He would think of Taylor and wonder whether he knew the end was coming in those final hours in the sick bay, or whether he had simply slipped away, unaware of his own demise even as it happened. He would think of his mother back home in Liverpool, and his father and twin brother out at sea in their own ships, somewhere over the shimmering horizon, more acutely aware than ever of the perilous nature of fate, the thin veil between life and death in these times of war.

Even as a humble deckhand, Remmie felt at home on the ship that his father had once captained — perhaps more truly at home than he had ever felt growing up in the suburban district of Crosby, north of Liverpool's city centre. He gazed out towards the horizon and wondered how many times he would visit the sprawling port of Lagos in this trusty ship.

Remmie's reverie was broken by a flash of something beneath the surface of the water on the port side of the ship. Just a few hundred yards away, the enormous shadow had loomed only momentarily, but he was certain he had seen it, ghostlike at the edge of his vision. Remmie looked closer. The shape had all the hallmarks of a U-boat lurking just beneath the surface. But was he certain enough to raise the alarm? He was, he told himself — that momentary flicker had been more than a figment of his imagination. As he turned to dash towards the metal staircase that led up to the bridge, the shadow flashed beneath the waves once again. Remmie gasped — a combination of awe and relief — as the marble-sheened expanse of whale flesh surfaced, arching and flicking an enormous grey tail in the air, as if in a playful gesture to the ship's crew, before slipping back beneath the waves.

'Did you see her?' a voice called out from behind him.

Remmie turned to see Leading Seaman Tommy Scarisbrick approaching him across the deck at an excited jog. 'I did, Scaggs!' Remmie replied, using the sailor's nickname. 'Christ, she nearly gave me a heart attack — I thought she was a U-boat surfacing for a moment.'

Scaggs laughed. 'No fear,' he said. 'There aren't many U-boats venturing this far south. She's a baleen whale. I saw her earlier this morning too. I think there's a pod following us. I can't be sure, but I thought I saw a couple of calves with her.'

Remmie looked out towards the rough point in the ocean where the whale had submerged, but there was no sign of their new travelling companion. 'Why would she swim alongside the ship like that?' he asked.

Scaggs shrugged. 'Just for kicks, I suppose. There can't be much fun to be had in a big expanse of ocean like this. I suppose we're a bit of a novelty.'

As he spoke, the whale breached the surface once again. This time, she was followed by two calves, cresting the waves like dolphins in their mother's wake.

'There they are!' Remmie pointed. 'You're right, Scaggs. There are two calves with her.'

Scaggs held the deck rail firmly with his large hands and chuckled to himself as he watched on. 'It's good to see a bit of life in these seas. There's been so much death and destruction this past year that to see a bit of life and rebirth, well —' he shrugged his shoulders — 'it makes it all worthwhile, somehow.'

Remmie patted the older man on the shoulder. 'It certainly does, Scaggs,' he said. 'It certainly does.'

CHAPTER TWO

London felt like a more beleaguered city than the one Rom had visited just a few months before. It was clear that the capital had taken a heavy bombardment in the latest Blitz, and the tumbledown wrecks of buildings and rubble-strewn streets told a different tale from the upbeat reportage he had read in the newspapers. The people he passed in the streets seemed different too, with deep frowns and shadows beneath their eyes that betrayed the reality of long, sleepless nights. As he walked across St James's Park, rainclouds hung heavily in the skies above him, and the people rushed by at a restless pace, their collars lifted against the chill.

When Rom reached the gates of Buckingham Palace, he paused, taking in the significance of the moment. This would be a day he would remember for the rest of his life, he told himself. He must stop and take it all in — he mustn't let it pass him by in a blur of activity. He looked up at the familiar facade of the palace. He could see no obvious signs of damage, despite having read about the palace being bombed just a few months before. They seemed to have cleared it up swiftly — important for morale, Rom thought to himself. He walked across to the main gate and showed his pass to a policeman, who ticked his name off a long list of people who were to receive honours that day.

A small, preoccupied-looking man in a morning suit appeared and led Rom under an archway beneath the familiar frontage of the palace and across the quadrangle within. It felt peculiar to see the inner face of the palace, and more peculiar still when the man from the palace directed him through an entrance door and across a lobby, dominated by a crystal chandelier. He felt the soft red carpet beneath his feet and feared slipping in his shiny shoes, so smooth was the surface. The corridors of the palace were busy with guests and Rom followed the man to his briefing, nervous to keep up, but all the while scanning the plush opulence in which he found himself. He passed a grand staircase with shallow steps and ornate balustrades that somehow reminded him of the pretentiously baroque architecture of a cinema.

The ballroom itself was a vast space — laid out with rows of seats, ready for the ceremony. The small man instructed him to join a group of other servicemen on the front two rows, where a more friendly-looking equerry was waiting to brief them on the etiquette for the event.

Rom tried to listen to all he was being told, but found his mind wandering — thinking back to his experiences of the previous months, his training at HMS *King Alfred*, his time at Scapa Flow, the evacuation of British troops from Norway and then from Dunkirk, and then St Nazaire. The waves of Stuka dive bombers swooping in to attack. The thrill of seeing a U-boat crippled by HMS *Grenade*'s depth charges bobbing impotently to the surface; the horror of seeing his best friend Chubby Smith gunned down by the U-boat's machine gunner in a final act of vengeance. As these recollections replayed in his mind, Rom hardly noticed the preamble for the ceremony passing by.

The arrival of King George VI into the room was something of an anticlimax. Rom was taken aback by the slight figure the king cut in real life. He seemed tiny and looked much older than Rom had expected. He was no longer the dashing figure of his most famous portraits. King George looked as world-weary as the rest of London.

When the moment finally came for Rom to step forward and receive his medal, the king leaned forward, and with an unfortunate combination of a lisp and stammer, said, 'We hear you have demonstrated v-v-vigorous v-v-valour in these t-t-troubled times.'

'Everyone is just doing their very best, Your Majesty,' Rom said, gazing up at the deep lines in the king's face. It was a very normal-looking face, Rom realised. He could have just as easily been talking to a bus conductor. The lines of the royal face creased into a smile.

'Y-y-yes, everyone is doing marvellously,' the king agreed, and Rom bowed his head and stepped back, just as he had been told to do.

It was all over in an instant — a surreal whirlwind of an afternoon — and before he knew it, Rom found himself walking back along The Mall, his new medal feeling heavy on his lapel. He walked for a while, trying to take in all that he had experienced that day, but eventually he wandered into a bar off Piccadilly Circus, deciding that a celebratory drink would not go amiss.

He sipped at his pint of beer, standing alone at the bar for a time. He sensed that the old soldier serving behind the beer pumps had clocked the Distinguished Service Cross on his lapel and he fully expected the barman to ask him about it, but he didn't — he just carried on polishing glasses. Eventually, Rom turned away and found a quiet spot near the window. He sat down and studied his pint, taking the occasional sip and feeling brutally alone in this sprawling city of eight million souls.

It was already getting dark when he walked back out of the bar, through the uncharacteristically muted streets of the West End — the theatre lights just as subject to the blackout as everywhere else. Further along Piccadilly, he spotted a small photographic studio. Checking the time on his watch against the opening hours painted on the glass of the door, he reached for the door handle and with a jingle of the bell that was screwed to the doorframe, stepped inside.

'If I asked you to take my portrait, how quickly would you be able to do a couple of prints?' Rom asked the old man behind the counter.

The man took a watch out of his waistcoat pocket. 'I could have them ready for you for nine o'clock tomorrow morning, but you might have to pay a bit extra.'

Rom nodded. 'Fair enough. Where do you want me? Can you get the medal in the shot?'

'Of course.' The man smiled. 'Come on through to the back room. We're all set up in here.'

'I'm going to send one to my mother and one to my sweetheart, up in Liverpool — they don't even know I was going to the palace.'

'You've been to the palace today then, sir?'

Rom nodded.

'How was he? The king?' the photographer asked, as he was setting up the shot and fiddling with the flash gun.

'He looked tired,' Rom said.

'Aren't we all, sir? Now, watch the birdie.'

Rom sat up straight and turned his face to the camera, as the flash burst startlingly into life.

Rom was no sooner off the train at Lime Street Station and breathing deeply the air of his home city, still a little flushed with pride at the Distinguished Service Cross that was now safely stored in his bag, than he had to rush to the docks to HMS *Walker*. He met the captain at the base of the gangplank.

Captain Donald Macintyre was also new to the ship and had arrived off the same train to take his new command.

The two men introduced themselves, pausing at the foot of the gangplank while taking in the outline of the imposing vessel that stood before them.

'Sub-Lieutenant Romulus Hutchinson, reporting for duty, sir,' Rom said, before adding with less formality, 'Everyone tends to shorten it to Rom, sir.'

'Both new boys arriving together then,' said Macintyre with a laugh. He had pleasantly smiling eyes and a warm Scottish lilt to his voice. Rom imagined he must be in his late thirties. 'A nervous morning for both of us, I'm sure,' the captain continued. 'How was your journey?'

'A bit stop-start, sir — we were held up at Crewe, because of an air raid.'

Macintyre nodded. 'Me too. We must have been on the same train. I've heard all about you already, Hutchinson. Aren't you in line for the Distinguished Service Cross?'

'Just received it a few days ago, sir, from the king himself.'

'Well done indeed.' Macintyre smiled. 'From the king himself, eh? That's quite something. It'll be an honour to serve with you, Sub.'

'Thank you, sir,' Rom replied, blushing. 'But really, I didn't do that much to deserve it.'

'I find that hard to believe, but I'm sure your modesty is admirable. I've just been transferred from the bridge of HMS *Hesperus*, which has not, despite its ominous name, met an ill end, thankfully.'

Rom laughed and quoted a passage from Longfellow's poem: *'Such was the wreck of the Hesperus, In the midnight and the snow! Christ save us all from a death like this, On the reef of Norman's Woe!'*

'Most impressive, Sub! You certainly know your literature too.'

'We had it drilled into us at school, sir.' Rom shrugged. 'A few years ago I would have been able to recite the whole thing by rote. But it's faded from my memory.'

'Yes, well, we've all had plenty to keep our minds occupied in recent months, I'm sure.' Macintyre gestured towards the gangplank. 'Come on then, Sub, after you. Let's go and meet our new comrades.'

Rom looked up at the veteran destroyer — built in the last war and still fighting on valiantly in the current one. He suddenly felt a wave of weariness, despite his young age. Another ship, another captain, another crew to get to know. He took a deep breath. 'No, after you, sir, I insist.'

'Thank you, Sub.' Macintyre nodded and led the way onto the ship.

He'll have to put an end to all this politeness soon enough, Rom thought to himself. The first lieutenant and the quartermaster were standing at the top of the gangplank, waiting to meet the new master.

'First Lieutenant Langton, sir.' The officer saluted.

'Langton? Unusual name,' Macintyre commented.

'Yes, sir, it's a village in Yorkshire, sir. My father was a Langton; my mother was a Dumbarton. Which is ironic, as Dumbarton is where HMS *Walker* was laid down back in 1917, I believe.'

'Extraordinary coincidence, what?' Macintyre smiled. 'And you must be the quartermaster?'

'Petty Officer Jacob Thompson, sir,' the quartermaster said. 'Though everyone calls me Wheels.'

Macintyre nodded sagely. 'Yes, I rather thought they might. And can I introduce you all to *Walker*'s other new member?' He turned to bring Rom into the conversation.

'Sub-Lieutenant Rom Hutchinson,' Rom said.

'Delighted,' Langton said, dropping all formality to offer Rom a welcoming handshake. 'Welcome aboard, Hutchinson. Do come with me and I'll introduce you to the other officers on the bridge.'

Rom followed on behind the first lieutenant and looked around at the deck — which could just as easily have been HMS *Grenade* or HMS *Havelock*. *Just another ship*, he thought again to himself.

Charlotte soon grew accustomed to the great chasm-like space of the new operations room. At first intimidating, within a day or two it had started to feel like a second home. Indeed, it might as well have been, given the amount of time she now spent there. The other women were friendly enough — even the officers, though sour-faced Superintendent Agnes 'Nan' Currie was the exception to the rule. She wasn't unkind, but she certainly wasn't friendly — perhaps feeling that her role was to keep the women in check, she was all for prim discipline, her eyes roving across the room for anyone putting a foot out of line. Charlotte thought of her as a headmistress-like figure. At the end of her first week the mood lightened considerably with the arrival of Polly Parker — her old friend from the Plymouth ops room.

'Look at you, Little Miss Efficient!' Polly laughed, her cockney accent transforming the word "little" into a single syllable.

'Polly Parker! Fancy seeing you here,' Charlotte exclaimed, before remembering herself and flicking a cautious look back towards Nan Currie, who thankfully was engaged in giving another young Wren a dressing-down on the far side of the ops room.

Polly strode across and gave Charlotte a quick embrace, before taking her by the shoulders and examining her face carefully. 'You look tired, lovey,' Polly said. 'Have you been getting much sleep?'

'Chance would be a fine thing,' Charlotte replied. 'It's round-the-clock here, you know — we've stepped up a gear since coming up north.'

Polly looked concerned. 'Oh, that doesn't sound like fun.'

'When did you arrive?'

'I'm straight from Lime Street Station. I stopped at my digs enroute, dropped my bag off, and thought I'd come and get the lay of the land before I start work properly tomorrow.'

'I wouldn't spend any longer here than you need to,' Charlotte whispered conspiratorially. 'If you've got a free day, I'd use it to explore the city. There must be hundreds of sailors out there waiting to buy you a drink.'

Polly laughed. 'Speaking of which, I met your chap, Sub-Lieutenant Hutchinson.'

'You met Rom? How? Where?'

'You didn't tell me he was such a dish, you naughty woman,' Polly teased. 'I was rather taken with him. He's quite the matinee idol.'

'Where did you meet him?' Charlotte repeated in exasperation.

'Down in Plymouth, of course. He'd just jumped ship and came knocking on the door of our digs. He was looking for you.'

'Was he?' Charlotte whispered. 'How did he seem?'

'Full of joy,' Polly said wryly. 'He said he'd write to you at your ma's house.'

'When was this? I've not had a letter.'

'Just a few days back. Don't worry, I'm sure it's on its way. I told him you're up here now, so no doubt he'll search you out the next time his ship comes into the Mersey.'

Charlotte became aware of a presence behind her. She turned to see the eagle-like features of Dunbar-Nasmith. He was standing with his hands behind his back, as though waiting in line for a cinema box office.

'Sorry to intrude,' said the commanding officer. 'I just wanted to welcome Miss Parker back into the fold.'

'Thank you, sir.' Polly smiled up at the old man. 'It's jolly nice to be here at last.'

'Yes, isn't it?' he said wistfully, looking around the room. 'How was your journey, my dear?'

'Fine, sir, no problems.'

'Good, good.' Dunbar-Nasmith nodded, before turning his attention to Charlotte. 'And you, my dear. I don't believe we've met. Are you new?'

Charlotte suppressed a laugh. 'No, sir, I served in Plymouth for a few months, before coming up here.' She stood up a little straighter, almost coming to attention. 'Wren Plotting Officer Charlotte Burton, sir,' she said. 'You know, sir, like the actress — you must have seen *Polly of the Storm Country*?'

The boss's grey eyes glinted warmly. 'Absolutely, absolutely,' he beamed. 'I was a great admirer of Miss Burton, back in the day.' He reached out and gave Charlotte's shoulder a friendly squeeze. 'Well, it's lovely to meet a like-minded soul. Somebody who appreciated the cinema before these awful talkies came along.'

Charlotte nodded. 'That's very true, sir,' she said. 'They do tend to give me a headache.' She turned and winked at Polly.

Later that afternoon, Dunbar-Nasmith returned. It was Nan Currie who called for silence.

'Thank you, my dear,' the boss muttered, with a slightly embarrassed smile. Nan Currie moved around the room like an over-enthusiastic sheepdog, shooing personnel towards the far end where Dunbar-Nasmith and Noble were waiting, having managed to clamber up onto wooden chairs. Charlotte and Polly dutifully fell into place at the back of the gathering.

'Thank you so much, ladies,' Dunbar-Nasmith began. 'Now we're all finally here, I just wanted to say a few brief words to thank you for all your hard work. Transferring the entire Western Approaches Command HQ nearly three hundred miles, from one end of the country to the other, was no small feat. So very well done, everybody. Your work is very important. I don't want anyone here to be under any misapprehension about that. On our shoulders now rests the great responsibility of ensuring the safe arrival of our Atlantic convoys upon which our nation's survival now depends. We need to do what we can to get as many ships as possible safely through, despite a critical shortage of escort vessels.

'We lost many Royal Navy ships at Dunkirk. I won't beat around the bush. We're going to have a few very tough months ahead. Fifty American destroyers have been acquired through the Lend-Lease programme, so that will help. Our plan, such as it is, will be to establish robust escort groups that become used to working together. I know what life is like on the bridge of a warship. Captains develop an intuition for what each other are up to, as long as they work together a lot. That's what we want to achieve — that kind of intuition, so the few escorts we do have become somehow greater than the sum of their parts.'

He looked around the room, as if he was waiting for a response from the assembled WRNS and WAAF women and the Royal Navy and RAF men. But they all just looked on.

'Well, there it is,' Dunbar-Nasmith added with a slight stammer. 'Thank you all for listening. Do carry on.'

'Hear, hear,' Noble called out. 'I've nothing particularly to add to that. Only to say that I'm absolutely convinced that organised, regular escort flotillas are the key to success. Keep up the good work, everyone.'

The gathering dispersed swiftly as everyone returned to their posts. Charlotte watched as Dunbar-Nasmith got down from the wooden chair and walked wearily back towards the steps that led up to his office. There was a handshake between the two admirals, and it was clear that she had been listening to a handover of sorts.

A letter was waiting for Charlotte on the kitchen table when she arrived home. She recognised Rom's handwriting on the envelope straight away, but didn't want to read it in front of her mother, so took it with her upstairs when she went to get changed. She sat down on the edge of her childhood bed, carefully opened the envelope and unfolded the paper. The letter was postmarked Plymouth just a few days before.

Dear Charlotte,

I met your friend Polly and she told me you were headed home — so I hope this letter finds you safely there. You'll never guess where I am off to — only Buckingham Palace! I have been awarded a Distinguished Service Cross somehow or other, and by the time you read this, the king himself will have pinned it onto my chest. What strange times we live in!

I'll then be taking the train up to Liverpool, but I'm afraid it will be a mad dash to make my new ship — HMS Walker — before she casts off. So I'm sorry to say I won't be able to see you this time. At least you'll be able to look out for HMS Walker on all those charts. It's always good to know I have my guardian angel watching over me.

Sorry this is so short — I've got to dash to make the train.

Sending you all my love.

Rom x

Eileen had noticed that the ambulance shifts got tougher as the weather improved. With the Luftwaffe able to take to the skies, inevitably the raids over both sides of the Mersey became heavier once again. The Cotton Exchange, the White Star Building, the Municipal Annexe in Dale Street and the General Post Office in Victoria Street were all severely damaged as winter turned to spring. Night after night, she and Bella would drive around the city encountering one scene of devastation after another. They worked long hours. Few Red Cross volunteers could drive back to the base at the end of their shift just because their wristwatch told them to. With more and more civilians being injured and killed all the time, Eileen, like so many of her colleagues, often kept going for hours longer than they were expected to serve.

A particularly heavy raid struck Birkenhead and Wallasey on the night of 12th March. Unusually, Eileen and Bella were sent through the Mersey Tunnel to support the struggling ambulance teams on the Wirral side of the river. No sooner had they made it through the tunnel than they witnessed a parachute mine exploding near the Cammell Laird shipyard. They had seen it falling elegantly beneath its silks, before exploding at roof-level with an almighty blast. Eileen instinctively turned the ambulance towards the blast and raced to the scene.

Upon arrival, they were met with a landscape of utter devastation. A couple of terraced houses were completely flattened, while roofing tiles had been blown off every house for two or three streets. Eileen and Bella got to work, offering what little first aid they could provide.

'I loved that house, but I'll not be able to go back there after this. Everything's ruined,' one young mother muttered angrily, perched on the back step of the ambulance as Eileen patched up her cuts and scrapes. She was a little woman, softly spoken with delicate features. Her two children stood beside her, still in their pyjamas, their eyes wildly scanning the changed landscape around their home. 'I'm supposed to be at work in the morning,' the woman fretted.

'Where do you work?' Eileen asked.

'Factory work — making barrage balloons, just down the road here.'

Eileen nodded and reached into her first aid bag to find a bottle of disinfectant and some cotton wool to clean the woman's cuts.

'What did you say your name was, my love?' Bella asked the woman, as Eileen concentrated on dabbing disinfectant.

'Bridget,' she said, before pointing towards the two children. 'And this is Brenda and Les.' The little girl clung to a well-worn teddy bear, while the boy, who was around seven or eight, stood quietly, taking it all in. 'My eldest, Eileen, has gone to tell my sister.' She tutted under her breath as she gazed around at the devastated street.

'I'm an Eileen too,' Eileen said, as she finished putting butterfly stitches across the cut on the woman's arm. 'You'll be all right, my love. And the two kiddies look completely unharmed, so that's good.' She tousled the little boy's hair as she spoke.

'Thank you both. But I'm all right. It's only cuts and scrapes,' Bridget said. 'Worse things happen at sea. You'd better get off and help those who really need it. I think the next street along got it worst.'

'You've got somewhere to stay tonight?' Eileen asked, as she packed away her bandages.

Bridget nodded. 'We'll go to my sister's. She's only down the road. Wait until my husband sees what they've done.'

'Is he in the forces?'

'Army,' Bridget said. 'He's back safe and sound from France, thank God, but I don't know when he'll get back up here.' She looked back at the neat little house, with its roof torn off and the tiles scattered across the street. 'He loved this house too. He'll be devastated when he sees it.'

'It'll get fixed.' Bella smiled. 'It may take a while, but it'll get fixed.'

Bridget shook her head. 'I don't think I'd be able to go back in there. I thought we were all done for, I really did.' She took a deep breath. 'Well, I'd better go and find a bed for these children.' She took the two children by the hand, one on each side, and walked off along the rubble-strewn street. Eileen and Bella stood for a moment at the side of the ambulance and watched them move off into the darkness.

They drove in silence until they found that Bridget had been right. The next street was even worse, and a large grey blanket had been stretched out across the pavement, with the distinctive shape of a body beneath.

'Give us a hand over here,' a young policeman called across as soon as Eileen and Bella stepped out of the ambulance. He was in his shirtsleeves, using his jacket to stem the bleeding of a woman who was lying on the ground, a gaping shrapnel wound across her neck. Eileen reached down and felt for a pulse, but it was immediately clear to her that the woman was dead. The poor young bobby had been battling to save a life that was already gone. She placed a hand on the young man's shoulder. He looked up at Eileen. 'No good?' he whispered.

Eileen shook her head. 'I'm sorry, Officer, but she's dead.'

The policeman looked back at the dead woman's face. 'I reckon she was still alive when I got to her, but there was so much blood ... so much blood.' He held out his bloody hands, as if to emphasise the point. Bella returned from the back of the ambulance with another large grey blanket to place over the woman's body, while Eileen gently led the policeman to a garden wall, where he sat and she cleaned the blood from his hands.

It was a grisly start to a long night shift in Birkenhead. But by the time they decided to call it a day, some two hours after their shift had been due to end, Eileen had lost count of the number of casualties they had helped.

'That was a good night's work,' she said to Bella, as she dragged herself back up into the driving seat of the ambulance and smiled at her partner. Bella rested her head back against the passenger seat, her body limp with exhaustion. Eileen started the engine and drove through the empty streets. It was that time, just before the dawn, when it seemed as if nobody lived in any of the rows of back-to-back terraced streets. She gave a wave to the driver of a passing fire engine, whose crew were also returning from a long night.

The entrance to the Mersey Tunnel was shrouded in darkness, but once inside, a series of ornate lamps stood out at intervals from the tunnel walls, illuminating the twists and turns of the road as it made its way deep below the river. There was nobody else on the road — the tunnel was clear both behind the ambulance and ahead of them. Eileen yawned. She looked across to see that Bella was already fast asleep, leaning against the doorframe of the cab. Eileen smiled to herself and turned her eyes back towards the road. An Army lorry was approaching head-on. Eileen lurched the steering wheel to the right in an attempt to avoid the oncoming vehicle.

She never even heard the terrible crunch of the impact as the two vehicles collided.

CHAPTER THREE

Following initial orders to "get some sleep", Rom's first few hours on HMS *Walker* were spent snoring in his new cabin — which looked remarkably like every cabin he had ever slept in, only this one had a porthole, which represented something of an upgrade. His cabin mate was a Lieutenant Reginald Thomas, known to all as Tommy. Rom only met him briefly, as Tommy was joining the opposite watch on the bridge as Rom was going to put his head down.

Tommy had a good decade on Rom. In fact, Rom guessed he was probably in his mid-thirties. He wasn't sure if it would be reassuring to have a much older and more experienced officer as a cabin mate, or if he might have had more fun with another of the young subs. But from the brief meeting on the deck, Tommy seemed pleasant enough.

'Make yourself at home, though I have the top bunk!' Tommy called back over his shoulder after a brief handshake and an apology for having to dash as he was running late for his watch.

Rom slept well enough, and woke, as he always did, half an hour before the start of his watch — plenty of time for a wash and shave before donning his uniform and heading up to the bridge. HMS *Walker* had already left the Mersey and was being tossed about by the excited waves of the Irish Sea, which stretched out in an expanse of grey on either side of the vessel.

The bridge of one destroyer is remarkably similar to the bridge of another destroyer, and it was no surprise to Rom to find himself feeling almost immediately at home. As the ship cut through the empty seascape, Rom had an opportunity to speak properly with the first lieutenant.

'How long have you been with *Walker*, sir?' he asked.

Langton looked out at the sea as he cast his mind back, as if the answer might appear out there on the spray blowing off the crest of the waves. 'August 1939,' he said at last. 'It seems a long time ago now.'

'You've seen some action with her then?'

'Yes, we have.' Langton nodded. 'Good times and bad — you know how it is.'

Rom nodded and the two men were silent for a few moments.

'You went to Norway too, I recall? I was there on HMS *Grenade*.'

'Yes, we took some damage from the gentlemen of the Luftwaffe up in Norway, but made it home,' said Langton. 'But you'll know what Norway was like, if you were there on *Grenade*.'

'Yes — dive bombers every way you turned,' said Rom grimly. 'People back in Blighty seem to have forgotten all about Norway already.'

'You've heard about the sinking of the RMS *Andora Star*?'

'Yes,' Rom replied. 'Wasn't she carrying German prisoners of war across to Canada?'

'Germans and Italians,' Langton corrected. 'More than sixteen hundred souls aboard when the U-boat targeted her.'

Rom shook his head. 'I presume they didn't know they were killing their own men.'

Langton shrugged, his eyes still focused on the featureless sea that stretched out before them towards the horizon. 'I don't know about that. But we were involved in the unsuccessful counterattack on the U-boat. The swines got away.'

Rom nodded sympathetically.

'After that, we headed home. We had a fair bit of damage and she was in dock for some weeks undergoing repairs, and then more weeks on her post-repair sea trials.'

'So it feels good to be heading back to the convoy work?'

'As good as it ever can, I suppose,' Langton reasoned, with a dour smile.

The ship was passing Rathlin Island and rounding the northern coast of Ireland before Rom had a real opportunity for a conversation with his new cabin mate. He quickly got the measure of Tommy as a razor-sharp man with a wry wit. He liked him straight away.

'I've not had to share my cabin for some months. I've rather spread my things around,' the older man said apologetically, as he gathered up some of his books and a framed photograph of himself with a man Rom assumed was his brother. Another photograph, this one unframed, featured a close-up of a golden retriever.

'Not a problem,' Rom said cheerily. 'No pictures of a wife, there, I see. You're not a married man?'

Tommy licked the edge of his roll-up. 'No, not my sort of thing,' he muttered.

Rom nodded. 'Confirmed bachelor, eh?'

'Something like that,' Tommy said. 'You don't mind if I smoke?'

'I won't tell if you don't.' Rom smiled.

'Good chap,' Tommy said and offered him the open pouch of tobacco. 'Sorry, you'll need to roll your own, but you're welcome to help yourself.'

'It's all right, thanks,' Rom said, reaching for a packet in his pocket. 'I have my own.'

Tommy checked out the box. 'Senior Service,' he said with a laugh. 'How apt.'

'Oh, you know what we Wavy Navy boys are like — always trying to look the part,' Rom joked.

'You said it, not me.' Tommy grinned, but Rom could see the older man's eyes flash towards the wavy gold insignia of the RNVR — the so-called "Wavy Navy" — embroidered in gold thread on his jacket cuffs, which marked Rom out as an amateur in comparison to the RN officers.

'Your dog?' Rom said, picking up the picture of the golden retriever.

Tommy nodded with a noncommittal gesture. 'Poor old Jackie. Long since dead, I'm afraid. Dear old boy, though.'

Rom picked up the other picture. 'Your brother?'

Tommy snatched the picture out of Rom's hand and put it back on the shelf, then smiled apologetically. 'No, just a pal.'

The two men sat in silence and smoked for a few minutes before Tommy spoke again. 'We lost him back in September 1939, my pal,' he said at last.

Rom raised his eyes from his cigarette. 'Oh, I'm sorry.'

'*Walker* collided with another bloody destroyer — one of our own, I mean. HMS *Vanquisher*.' Tommy watched the smoke from his cigarette curl up towards the ceiling. 'She was well-named, that one — *Vanquisher*. Fourteen of our own men were killed in that collision, and both ships were pretty well mangled. Some of the men were not killed outright, including my friend here.' He pointed his cigarette back at the photograph. 'Our own first lieutenant was compelled to shoot dead the poor souls who were trapped in the wreckage and were already mortally wounded. My pal here was one of those men.'

'Good God,' Rom whispered. 'I'm so sorry.'

A heavy silence hung between the two men as they smoked.

In the early days of the war, Royal Navy escorts only provided protection to Atlantic convoys as far as 15 degrees West. But with German U-boat command now having firmly established bases in France, the subsea menace was able to push further across the Atlantic, which meant the Royal Navy was required to provide escort protection as far as 35 degrees West. By establishing new refuelling bases in Iceland, the British were able to develop a solution that saw them deliver escort duties in relay with the Royal Canadian Navy (RCN) — with the Royal Navy handing convoys over to their RCN counterparts to provide cover for the final part of the voyage.

It was a solution that made sense to Rom. There was nothing quite as dispiriting as knowing that the ships you had protected for hundreds of miles were being left to their own devices. With the Kriegsmarine's U-boat force growing at an astonishing rate and increasingly working in submarine "wolf packs" to devastate convoys, the threat from below loomed larger than ever.

Consequently, it came as quite a pleasant surprise to find that the first journey across the Atlantic was remarkably uneventful for Rom and HMS *Walker*. It was only when the escort left the westbound convoy moving on towards Nova Scotia and paused to take on fuel at an isolated Icelandic inlet, before turning back to meet the new eastbound convoy, that Rom realised just how eerily quiet the crossing had been. Rather than feeling grateful, it made him strangely nervous. What did the return crossing have in store?

The landscape of Iceland itself didn't help to assuage Rom's underlying anxiety. There was something peculiarly ominous about the rocky, volcanic expanses that stretched out from the coastline — flat, mossy places for the first few miles, with clusters of seemingly deserted villages of little wooden houses and red-roofed churches, before the topography lurched up swiftly into snowcapped mountains, with craggy peaks that growled down like rows of sharpened teeth towards the Royal Navy destroyer.

The British had occupied Iceland the previous spring, following the German invasion of Denmark. They had been all too aware of the island's critical importance as a safe haven in the middle of the high North Atlantic. But Rom had no idea how the locals felt about the situation — brief refuelling visits only put the crew into contact with the occupying British Army and Royal Navy personnel in the port. It was almost as if the Icelandic people had slipped back from the coast, exacerbating this ominous sense of being amid a barren and deserted landscape.

Rom watched the refuelling operation from the portside wing of the bridge, an icy wind cutting towards him from the west and flapping the lapel of his overcoat against his jawline.

'Not too long now, Hutchinson,' Captain Macintyre muttered as he joined him to gaze out at the otherworldly expanse that stretched out before them.

'The sooner the better as far as I'm concerned, sir,' Rom said. 'This place gives me the creeps somewhat.'

'How are you settling in?' Macintyre asked, stifling a yawn as he spoke.

'Fine thanks, sir. You know how it is — once you've seen one destroyer, you've seen them all.'

Macintyre nodded. 'Still, I think this is a happy ship, as far as I can tell.'

Rom smiled. 'I'm certainly feeling happier on HMS *Walker* than I ever did on *Havelock*.'

'An unhappy ship?'

Rom shrugged. 'I got the wobbles for a while. I'd seen *Grenade* go down at Dunkirk, then to see the *Lancastria* hit in the way she was... It was tough.' He paused and looked out towards the distant mountains. 'But I'm back on form now, sir, I'm relieved to say.'

Macintyre nodded. 'It can be difficult to come back to this life, if you've taken a break from it. Back in the twenties I spent quite a few years flying in the Fleet Air Arm. I only came back to this life when an injury meant I could no longer fly. But I remember it being tough at first, being back on the bridge. There was quite a thick coating of rust on my navigational knowledge, for instance. I had to relearn things fast.'

'I was only out of it for a few weeks,' Rom said. 'Not long enough to forget the essentials, thankfully.'

'Good.' Macintyre seemed to consider him for a long moment. 'But if you need any help, do let me know. Even if it's just a friendly ear, I'm happy to listen.' He patted Rom on the shoulder, before turning and heading back onto the bridge.

By the time HMS *Walker* had taken to sea, leaving the rocky silhouette of Iceland behind them, Convoy HX112 had already set off from Halifax, ready to meet the bulk of its escort of half a dozen destroyers, as well as some corvettes, cruisers and minesweepers, a few days into the crossing. When HMS *Walker* had taken up her protective place on the portside flank, the convoy consisted of more than forty ships — mostly tankers carrying much-needed fuel across to the British Isles. It made for a splendid sight — stretching out towards the horizon, with its escort ships forming a "wall of steel" on each flank.

The forming-up of a convoy was something that Rom never tired of seeing, and with his own captain as the commander of the escort, it was clear that HMS *Walker* would be taking a prime position throughout. Yet the sense of unease in the pit of Rom's stomach did not lift. Although all seemed well on the surface, something troubled him.

'I don't know what it is — I just have a bad feeling about it,' he confided to the first lieutenant as they stood side by side on the bridge, scanning the horizon through their binoculars.

Langton lowered his glasses. 'If you take my advice, you'd better not trouble our new captain with your bad feelings. He'll have you down as a complete coward.'

'It's not like that,' Rom grumbled, a little perturbed by Langton's dismissive attitude. 'It's just a feeling — like when you sense that somebody is watching you on the deck and then you turn around and find a rating on the far side of the deck with his beady eyes on you. Call it sailor's intuition if you like, but it just feels like we're being watched.'

'By a U-boat?'

'I don't know, but I would have thought that would be the biggest threat.'

'ASDIC hasn't reported anything.'

'There are a lot of propellers out there churning up the water. They could be disguising any sound,' Rom muttered. 'I'm a twin, you know — twins have a sort of sixth sense.'

Langton laughed. 'Perhaps about each other, but not about the location of German U-boats.'

'I'm just saying we shouldn't be too complacent. Just because the Atlantic was quiet last week, it doesn't mean it will be this week.'

Unheard by either Rom or the first lieutenant, Captain Macintyre had rejoined the bridge behind them and was listening to their conversation. 'Nobody's taking anything for granted, I can assure you, Hutchinson,' he said.

Rom spun around. 'Sorry, sir, I was just telling the first lieutenant I had a bad feeling about this one for some reason.'

'That's only healthy, Hutchinson — it's called fear. It's what keeps us all safe — a healthy fear of the unknown.' Macintyre flashed a quick smile at Rom. '*Walker* may be an old ship, but she does have many of the modern scientific wonders that have changed the lot of the professional seaman over the last generation.'

'Yes, sir,' Rom said. But he knew the captain did not understand what he had been trying to convey. He wasn't afraid. He was on edge. Rom trusted his prescience well enough to take it seriously.

Remmie had grown fond of quite a few of the members of the SS *John Holt*'s crew, but none more so than Scaggs. The leading seaman was a hearty, larger-than-life character, who brought his banjo with him on every voyage and would sit on deck when he had some downtime and pluck out twangy little tunes. The song that Remmie enjoyed most from Scaggs' repertoire was an old sea shanty that he and many of the other deckhands would join in with, so catchy was the main refrain: '*For it's cheer up me lads, let your hearts never fail, For the bonny ship, the Diamond, goes a-fishing for the whale.*'

One day, as Scaggs was playing the song idly on the edge of the deck to nobody in particular, Remmie asked the older man what the song was called.

'It's called "The Bonny Ship the Diamond".' Scaggs frowned at Remmie's blank expression. 'You're from a seafaring family, Hutchinson. Did nobody tell you of the *Diamond*?'

Remmie shook his head.

'Well, it's a sad but true tale,' Scaggs said, plucking the tune as he spoke. 'You see, not long after the turn of the nineteenth century, the mildest northern waters were fished clean and whalemen were having to search in more distant corners of the Arctic — places like the inhospitable Melville Bay in northwest Greenland and the Davis Straits. In 1830 a fleet of fifty British whaling ships reached the grounds in early June, a full month before they expected to get there. At first the fishing was good, see? But the same winds that had helped them get there so swiftly, also crowded the bay with ice floes and locked most of the fleet in, including the *Diamond*, the *Resolution*, *Rattler of Leigh* and the *Eliza Swan*. These were famous whalers back in the day.'

Remmie nodded, though he had never heard of them.

Scaggs stopped plucking the strings and turned suddenly icy eyes towards the youngster. 'Twenty-five ships were crushed to splinters, and many brave whalemen froze or drowned in the icy waters,' he said. 'The *Eliza Swan* was among the few that got free and brought the sad news home. My great-grandfather, whose name I share, was among the men who came home on the *Eliza Swan* and this here ballad is a little song that was written to commemorate the men who didn't come home.'

Scaggs played the song once again, though this time Remmie simply listened carefully to the words and didn't join in with the catchy refrain. Rather he looked out towards the expanse of the North Atlantic Ocean that surrounded the SS *John Holt*, and tried to imagine the horrors that had taken place hundreds of miles north, more than a century before. The jaunty song echoed out into the warm winds of the ocean. *'For it's cheer up me lads, let your hearts never fail, For the bonny ship, the Diamond, goes a-fishing for the whale.'*

'I certainly hope I never serve in the Arctic,' Remmie said when Scaggs had finished. 'I can face death all right, but I'd like to die in warm waters rather than cold ones.'

'Careful what you say, my boy,' Scaggs muttered. 'The sea might just hear you, and she's a fickle creature.'

Remmie looked at Scaggs and smiled, but the smile quickly faded when he saw Scaggs's serious expression. Remmie nodded. 'All right then, Scaggs. I'll watch what I say.'

'Good lad,' Scaggs said and started to pick out another tune.

'Do you reckon you could teach me?' Remmie said after a brief pause.

'What? The song?'

'No, the instrument.'

'You want to learn to play the banjo?'

'You make it look so easy, though I'm sure it's not,' Remmie said.

'Oh, I'll teach you, if you've a mind to learn,' Scaggs said. 'Why don't you come here and try it on for size — see how it feels in your hands?'

Remmie sat down beside Scaggs and took hold of the instrument. 'My word,' Remmie muttered. 'I hadn't expected it to be so heavy.'

'A good banjo is a heavy banjo,' Scaggs said, enigmatically. 'Well, go on, have a strum.'

Remmie plucked a few strings, tentatively at first. They sounded oddly flat after hearing how Scaggs had brought the instrument to life, seemingly effortlessly. Remmie shook his head. 'I'm not sure I'd ever manage to pick it up.'

'You just might,' Scaggs said, and reached around to place the youngster's hands into the correct positions. 'Right, let's start with some simple fingering positions,' he went on, settling himself in for the challenge.

Eileen Hutchinson was consumed by confusion when she opened her eyes on the hospital ward. She attempted to sit up, but found her arm attached to an intravenous drip. A nurse approached rapidly, her shoes clipping on the tiled floor.

'How are you feeling, Eileen?' The young woman looked down at her with a smile.

'Bella?' Eileen managed to whisper. The nurse's smile disappeared from her face, which told Eileen all she needed to know.

'I'm sorry, my love,' the nurse said, shaking her head.

Eileen felt the tears running down her cheeks. It was almost impossible to keep up with the horror of the night.

She lay that way, staring up at the ceiling, for some time, feeling hollow and unable to move. Eventually an elderly doctor examined her.

'The other lady didn't make it, but you mustn't blame yourself, my dear,' the doctor said. 'She would have been killed instantly. She wouldn't have suffered. She wouldn't have known a thing.'

'She was asleep. It was the end of our shift,' Eileen said, her voice sounding harsh to her own ears.

The doctor nodded. 'Well, that's good then. She really wouldn't have known anything about it.'

'What about the lorry?'

'It was being driven by a young soldier — his first time through the tunnel in a vehicle of that size. He got the bend wrong and veered straight into your lane. There was nothing that you could have done. It was just a terrible accident.'

'The soldier?'

The doctor shook his head. 'He would have died instantly too, I'm afraid. You were lucky, I think. It sounds like you just turned the driver's side of your cab away from the impact at the very last moment.'

'So I killed Bella?'

The doctor shook his head firmly. 'No, no, you really mustn't think like that. Your reaction was instinctive. It's what anybody would have done.'

CHAPTER FOUR

HMS *Walker* steamed on alongside the mighty convoy in its protection, its crew oblivious to the threat that lurked as a shadow following them beneath the waves. The U-110, commanded by Fritz-Julius Lemp, had been the first to sight the convoy. He had called together the wolf pack of surrounding nearby U-boats — the U-100, U-99, U-37 and U-74. Each of these were merciless killing machines when acting alone; when working together as a pack, they could be utterly ruthless.

The U-100, under the command of Joachim Schepke, was one of the most successful of the Third Reich's new generation of U-boats. Schepke was a star of the Kriegsmarine's U-boat division, with his film-star good looks, his eye for the ladies and his habit of setting his captain's cap at a rakish angle on his head. In August of the previous year he had made his name when he torpedoed five ships in three hours, and in the months that had followed his charisma had ensured his reputation continued in its ascendency back in the Fatherland. Similarly, the U-99 was under the command of Lieutenant Otto Kretschmer, another star captain in Admiral Donitz's submarine fleet. The son of a Silesian schoolmaster, he and his crew had endured a baptism of fire the previous year when their first experience of torpedoing a British convoy had led to a Royal Navy destroyer subjecting them to a relentless depth charge counterattack.

After two hours, the submarine's oxygen supply system had failed, and the crew had been forced to resort to using emergency breathing masks. After six hours, many of his men were gasping like fish out of water, while being pounded by depth charge detonations. They held still, with Kretschmer conscious of the need to avoid making any sudden movements that would give away their location to the British ASDIC rating high above them.

After twelve hours of this torture, the oxygen levels were so depleted in the U-boat that the air had turned yellow and foul-smelling. Finally, after an extraordinary fourteen-hour bombardment, the destroyer's captain finally gave up. But Kretschmer had to guard against a trick and remained stationary on the sea floor for a further five hours. His crew had been down below for nearly twenty hours without an adequate oxygen supply by the time he finally gave the order to surface, and scrambling to open the hatch, the crew members were able to collapse across the deck of the U-boat and breathe the fresh air.

With U-boats of this calibre shadowing them, the convoy was under real threat from battle-hardened submariners. But above on the bridge of HMS *Walker*, Rom, convoy escort commander Captain Donald Macintyre, and the rest of the crew, were blissfully unaware of the threat they faced.

Rom had been standing on the bridge of HMS *Walker*, giving him a grandstand view of the drama as it unfolded before him — *Walker*'s own lookout had been the first to shout, 'Torpedo, two o'clock!' All the officers on the bridge lifted their glasses to catch sight of the swift-moving line of white foam, cutting through the gap between HMS *Walker*'s prow and the stern of HMS *Vanoc* — the veteran, First World War V-class destroyer that steamed on ahead of them on the port side of the convoy.

Captain Macintyre had been working closely with Gerrard, HMS *Walker*'s Yeoman of Signals, to enable him to have a feisty conversation via light signals with the convoy commodore, Rear Admiral Watson, who was aboard the SS *Tortuguero*. The old commodore had access to a radio set, but preferred the old ways. Watson and Macintyre, as escort commander, had been having a heated discussion about one of the ships, the SS *Everleigh*, and her bad station-keeping, which was disturbing the entire formation of the column.

'Sir!' Rom called across, interrupting Macintyre mid-flow. 'Torpedo, sir!' But by the time the words were out, the presence of the torpedo was obvious, as it blasted into the side of a tanker and the middle of the ship was almost instantly engulfed in flames.

Macintyre finished his relayed conversation without another word to the commodore and picked up the speaking tube that connected the bridge with Backhouse, the ASDIC rating on duty. 'Can you get a contact on that U-boat? Keep trying.'

But a moment later, it was the bridge of the *Vanoc* that crackled through on the radio set. 'Good,' Macintyre said, 'you have permission to go hunting, *Vanoc*, keep me updated. *Vanoc*'s ASDIC has a possible contact,' he added to the officers around him, 'bearing zero-six-zero.'

'You're not tempted to join them, sir?' Rom asked.

Macintyre shrugged. 'Our place is here, holding the line,' he said. 'For the moment, at least.' He turned back to Gerrard. 'Get me a damage report from the stricken vessel.'

'Yes, sir,' Gerrard said.

Moments later, after it had been reported back to Macintyre that the fire had been isolated and the captain of the tanker was confident he would manage to get her back to port, Rom watched *Vanoc* moving back into her place in the escort formation.

'If they ever had a contact, they lost it,' Macintyre relayed, the disappointment clear in his voice. '*Vanoc* is equipped with one of these new radar sets, which can help to find a U-boat on the surface. I don't know how effective they are, but it might just come in useful if they attack at night.'

'Yes, sir,' Rom said. 'Any new technology that can help has to be a very welcome thing.'

The convoy steamed on as night began to fall, but the bridge of HMS *Walker* was noticeably tenser, with the knowledge that a U-boat — at least one U-boat — was out there somewhere, probably shadowing the convoy and waiting for its next opportunity to strike.

As evening fell, the forward guns, the prow itself and the mast of HMS *Walker* all began to flicker with an otherworldly glow. Rom stepped out onto the deck to take a closer look at the phenomenon, which appeared to have transformed any protruding tips of the ship into eerie candles of flickering blue flames.

'What the hell is it?' Rom muttered, unable to take his eyes off the mysterious lights. He turned back to the bridge and called to Macintyre. 'We're ablaze!' he cried. 'The mast, the forward guns and the prow are all alight!'

Macintyre grinned. 'Calm down, Hutchinson. We're not on fire. What you're seeing is the phenomenon that the Greeks called Helene — literally a torch. We know it as St Elmo's Fire. It's rare, but I've seen it a few times before out here in the Atlantic. Normally when there's a storm coming. Charged plasma particles.'

'I've never seen anything like it,' Rom gasped.

'I know — remarkable, isn't it? You'll see some strange things at sea, lad,' Macintyre said. 'Still, it's not a good thing to see.'

'How's that?'

'Plenty of seafarers believe St Elmo's Fire is an ill omen. William Bligh, the captain of the *Bounty*, reported seeing it in his log before the famous mutiny. It was also seen just before the Hindenburg went down.' He shrugged his shoulders, as if to rest his case. 'It'll be bringing bad luck for somebody. I just hope it's them and not us.'

Rom nodded pensively and looked out towards the darkening waves beyond the luminous flickering at the edges of the deck.

The phenomenon passed almost as swiftly as it had arrived, leaving a ponderous atmosphere on the bridge. Some considerable time passed before the wolf pack struck again. The two destroyers started firing starshells to light the scene in a desperate attempt to catch a glimpse of a surfaced U-boat. But the unseen U-99 penetrated the convoy from the north, on its port side, striking two more tankers and a large freighter, all in the space of a few minutes, while the convoy's escort watched on impotently, with ASDIC ratings desperately trying to pinpoint the location of the attacker.

The U-boat remained hidden beneath the formation of the central column, and its captain was audacious enough to sink another freighter just fifteen minutes later, before turning to make an escape. Macintyre brought HMS *Walker* around to pick up survivors from the SS *J.B. White*, while the ASDIC rating continued to scan for the U-boat.

Rom, who had been directing the rescue from the deck, returned to the bridge. 'We have thirty-seven crew members and the master aboard, sir,' he said, rubbing his cold hands together. 'She lost two men in the blast. The survivors have blankets and rum is being served to them.'

'Well done, Hutchinson,' Macintyre said. He looked out at the scene of devastation, with burning wrecks in various stages of sinking all around. 'So, we've lost *Ferm*, *Bedouin*, *Franche Comte*, *Venetia* and *J.B. White*!' Macintyre shouted across the bridge, as he attempted to take stock and keep track of the massacre. 'Three tankers and two freighters.'

As he spoke, another torpedo struck another nearby ship, the tanker *Korshamn*, which erupted into a ball of flame before sagging inwards, as if folding itself in two. The officers on the bridge of HMS *Walker* looked on in transfixed horror.

'We had better add *Korshamn* to that list,' Macintyre muttered, lifting his cap and running his fingers through his hair in exasperation.

But then, just after one o'clock in the morning, fortune favoured them once more, with Macintyre himself catching a glimpse of a U-boat on the surface, moving towards the convoy under the cloak of night. The captain gave the order for the ship to move out of formation and immediately bear down on the U-boat.

'She dived straightaway, sir!' Rom bellowed across the bridge, his glasses trained on the speck of darkness from which the U-boat had almost instantly disappeared.

'Yes, I rather thought she might,' Macintyre replied. 'But submerging will slow her down. Prepare the depth charges, Mr Jones!' he shouted, turning towards the chief armourer, who was standing at the back of the bridge, the wind buffeting his collars.

'Yes, sir!' Jones called back, as he in turn picked up the voicepipe that connected him to his depth charge teams on the decks.

'Hit them with a shallow pattern, Mr Jones,' Macintyre commanded, before turning in a flash towards the voicepipe that connected him with the quartermaster below and barking out his next steering direction. 'Wheels, bear zero-five-zero,' 'Bearing zero-five-zero, sir,' the quartermaster repeated back, as the ship turned beneath them.

'Fire at will, Mr Jones,' Macintyre called, and moments later, as Jones relayed the message, the depth charges clattered off the decks and turned the ocean into a bubbling soup of foam.

'Surely to God,' Macintyre said, scanning the water. 'Hutchinson, radio *Vanoc* and give them permission to move back out of formation and come and give us a hand here.'

'Yes, sir,' Rom said and dashed across the bridge to the radio set.

Langton, who was standing on the portside wing of the bridge with his binoculars raised, called out, 'She's been damaged by the depth charges, sir!' There was a certain amount of glee detectable in his voice. 'She is back on the surface and doesn't seem to be able to resubmerge.'

The first lieutenant moved back onto the main body of the bridge and Macintyre lifted his own glasses in the direction of the U-boat. 'It's so bloody difficult to keep track of her, even when she's on the surface,' he growled.

'*Vanoc* has got her on the radar, sir,' Rom said.

'Of course, the radar.' Macintyre allowed a smile to creep across his face. The newly fitted radar set was still considered a relatively experimental technology, but now it might come into its own.

'She's turning, sir, bearing zero-five-eight, mark,' Rom added.

At that very moment, the great hulking portside of HMS *Vanoc* appeared before them, lighting up the night-time seascape and bearing down rapidly on the stricken U-boat. She was aiming her sharp bow straight at the conning tower. The officers on the bridge of HMS *Walker* lifted their glasses as one and watched in silence as the U-boat's hatch opened and men began to throw themselves off the conning tower into the darkness of the waves. Even from this distance, they could hear their screams as they plunged into the icy water.

Walker swept in alongside *Vanoc*, and they could hear a commanding German voice coming from the conning tower: '*Keine panik! Sie werden uns vermissen!*'

'He thinks *Vanoc* will miss them,' Macintyre translated.

'Perhaps *Vanoc*'s orientation is creating an optical illusion for him?' Rom muttered. But *Vanoc* did not miss them, and with the grisly, clawing scream of metal striking metal, the bow of the destroyer impacted the submarine at the very point of the conning tower, throwing more men overboard from the deck of the U-boat with the sheer force of the impact, and horribly mutilating others.

The momentum of the ship continued to drive her forward, with *Vanoc* rising momentarily up over the submarine, before finally grinding to a halt, and drawing clear with another grinding jolt. The U-boat captain, still conscious, thrashed wildly in the Atlantic swell for a moment, before he slipped beneath the waves and was finally silenced.

'Well, he must be feeling a little cut up about the whole thing,' Macintyre said drily, as he lowered his glasses and shook his head as if to settle the collection of violent scenes he had just witnessed into the correct compartments of his brain. The three men moved back to the middle of the bridge. 'Wheels, we'll stand by, while *Vanoc* picks up any survivors,' Macintyre said into the voicepipe.

'Aye aye, sir.'

Macintyre raised the bridge of the other destroyer on the radio. 'Very well done indeed,' he congratulated his opposite number. 'Collect any survivors you can and in a few minutes we'll catch back up with the convoy.' He replaced the radio receiver as the remains of U-100 slowly began to sink back into the ocean, following its master into the icy depths. 'I think a cup of tea might not go amiss,' Macintyre said, turning to a messenger at the back of the bridge.

'Aye aye, sir.' The messenger slipped silently away as he set off on his errand.

'Sir, ASDIC is reporting another contact, possible U-boat, echo to starboard,' Rom called across from the other side of the open-air bridge, where he stood holding the voicepipe.

Macintyre turned with alarm. 'Another bloody one? Surely he must be mistaken?'

'He seems fairly confident, sir. Two hundred yards, bearing zero-nine-zero.'

'It's just off *Vanoc*'s stern,' Langton muttered.

'Order *Vanoc* to withdraw immediately,' Macintyre said, then snatched the radio handset himself. 'Never mind, I'll do it.' He raised it to his mouth. 'You have another U-boat just off your stern, *Vanoc*!' he shouted into the mouthpiece. 'Well, get out of the way then!' He slammed the handset back down. 'Mr Jones, prepare the depth charges.'

'Aye aye, sir.'

Vanoc turned ahead of them and began to move swiftly away. Macintyre gave the order for the depth charges to be scattered in a shallow pattern. Once again, the surface of the sea around them lit up in clusters of watery stars, as if the waves were reflecting a firework display overhead. 'Let's turn for another run, Wheels,' the captain said calmly into the voicepipe.

'Aye aye, sir,' the quartermaster called back. But at the same moment, the radio crackled into life and the operator on the bridge of *Vanoc* reported a sighting of the U-boat.

'*Vanoc* reports that the U-boat has surfaced astern of her,' Rom called back towards the captain.

'We got her,' Macintyre said with a grin.

Rom turned to look across the starboard wing, as *Vanoc* trained the harsh beam of its searchlight on to the stricken U-99. A signal lamp flashed into life from the conning tower of the submarine. 'The U-boat signals to say, "I am sunking",' Rom said, stifling a laugh.

'Sunking? Indeed, well, I think we know what she means.' Macintyre smiled. 'It's about bloody time some of these bastards experienced just what it's like to be sunking in the middle of the Atlantic Ocean. They've done it to enough of our merchant men.'

A machine gun fired wildly from the deck of HMS *Walker* towards the submariners on the deck of U-99. 'Stop them firing,' Macintyre said to Jones. 'I think they have had enough.'

A series of black boxes were thrown from the deck of the submarine into the water. 'They're disposing of their confidentials,' Macintyre said. 'Pull up alongside with caution, Wheels,' he added. 'We will commence rescuing the German submariners. Mr Jones, make sure our guns are trained on the deck of that U-boat, in case they fancy any funny business. Mr Hutchinson, let *Vanoc* know our intentions. They can stand off.'

'Aye aye, sir.'

As a rescue boat was lowered from *Walker*, one of the submariners on the deck returned down the hatch of the conning tower and a moment later the U-boat shuddered as the air was swept back out of the ballast tanks. The U-boat then slipped into the ocean in seconds, the Atlantic waves consuming it hungrily, with the submariner who had returned inside not making it back out in time to make his escape.

The submariners that were transferred onto the deck of HMS *Walker* looked bedraggled, freezing cold and world-weary as they left their U-boat behind — all except their commander, who still somehow cut a proud and neat figure in his uniform. He was the last man to board the destroyer, clinging to the scramble net that had been lowered from the deck, ensuring all his surviving men had made it up ahead of him. He gazed around at the stretch of ocean where his U-boat had been a few moments before. He then looked up at the destroyer and seemed to struggle to find the energy to clamber up the net.

Rom leaned over the rail and saw the German officer's seaboots were heavy with seawater and weighing him down. He reached over and helped to drag the U-boat ace up as Langton on the bridge gave the order for *Walker* to speed up and head back towards the convoy. Macintyre, who was beside Rom, offered a final hand to the heavily weighed-down German officer as he tumbled over the rail onto the deck.

The German gave an ironic little laugh and dragged himself back onto his feet. He stood proudly to attention and saluted Macintyre as a fellow captain — a Kriegsmarine salute, his right hand moving sharply to his cap, palm facing down, not a Nazi salute with an arm outstretched as Rom had fully expected. Macintyre returned the gesture.

'Kapitänleutnant Otto Kretschmer,' the German said, before he looked down and seemed to realise he was still wearing his high-powered Zeiss binoculars on a leather strap around his neck. He reached down and in one fluid movement went to throw them towards the sea. But Rom lunged towards him and grabbed them, before handing them to the captain.

Macintyre weighed them in his hands, as if assessing them.

'Let's call it a gift, for your hospitality, Captain,' Kretschmer smiled, as he regained his composure. 'I'm rather afraid your depth charges had put our engine completely out of action.' Kretschmer turned once again to look at the stretch of sea where his U-boat had last been seen slipping below the surface. 'We had sunk to seven hundred and twenty feet and at that depth the hull was beginning to crack. I had to force air into the ballast tanks, and bob around on the surface most inelegantly — how you say, like a cork?'

Macintyre nodded. 'If you can lead your men inside, please, Mr Hutchinson here will see you are taken care of and relieve you of any side arms.'

'We have none,' Kretschmer said as he followed Rom off the deck. 'But thank you, Captain.'

A thousand miles away, beneath the streets of Liverpool, Charlotte's flushed face was gazing up at the ever-evolving map of the North Atlantic when Polly approached.

'Everything all right, lovey?'

'I think so,' Charlotte said. 'Rom is serving on HMS *Walker* now — I've been following its fortunes very closely.'

'Rom is on Donald Macintyre's new ship?' Polly sounded surprised.

'Is he a well-known captain?'

'Increasingly so,' Polly said. 'He's building quite a reputation as a U-boat killer.'

'I'm not surprised,' Charlotte said. 'Look what his escort group has done in the last few hours — two U-boats taken out of action. The report that's just come in says they've taken the entire crew of U-99 prisoner.'

'He's certainly seeing some action, your fella.' Polly laughed. 'You seem to have found quite the dashing hero in that one. First the Distinguished Service Cross, now this.'

Charlotte blushed a little and looked at the floor. 'I don't care about all that. All I care about is that he makes it home in one piece.'

'He will be fine,' Polly said, placing a sympathetic hand on Charlotte's forearm. 'It sounds as if he is more than capable of looking after himself.'

'I do hope so,' Charlotte replied with a nod. 'I certainly do hope so.'

Remmie stood on the deck of the SS *John Holt*, leaning on the rail, and watching as the new anti-aircraft gun was fitted. It was a simple 4-inch deck gun, which would take its place fairly unobtrusively at the stern, but it still felt like a significant change. A young Royal Artillery gunner from the newly formed Maritime Anti-Aircraft Regiment, Corporal Eddie Crabtree, had been assigned to the crew of the *John Holt* on a semi-permanent basis. It would be Crabtree who would man the gun, if it was ever needed, but the mere presence of the weapon still made Remmie feel strangely nervous.

'What do you make of that?' Remmie asked Scaggs, who was passing along the deck, a cigarette between his fingers.

Scaggs turned to look back towards the new gun at the stern. 'I think I'd rather have it there than not have it there,' he said, after giving the question a long moment's thought. 'At least it gives us some protection — especially when we're sailing outside of the convoys.'

Remmie wrinkled his nose a little. 'I don't much like it. I didn't sign up for the Royal Navy. I'm not sure I like being on an armed vessel. It feels to me as if it might make us more of a target.'

Scaggs shook his head. 'I don't think so,' he mused. 'The Jerries are attacking merchant ships all over the Atlantic. You don't imagine they are picking and choosing, depending on which ones have a stern gun?'

'It makes me nervous, that's all.' Remmie frowned.

'Well, here's the man to put you at ease.' Scaggs smiled and waved across young Corporal Crabtree, who was making his way back along the deck to check up on the work to assemble the new gun.

'Crabtree, have you met Hutchinson?'

'No, I don't believe I've had the pleasure.' Crabtree smiled benevolently and offered a hand for Remmie to shake.

'It's just you then, is it?' Remmie asked. 'Don't take this the wrong way, pal, but you hardly represent much of a protection force, one man and his gun.'

'Well, I suppose it's one more gunner than you had before,' Crabtree said without bitterness. 'At least I can take a few potshots at any German aircraft that gets a bit too close.'

'It might make them think twice,' Scaggs added.

'I suppose so,' Remmie admitted begrudgingly. 'Well, it's good to have you onboard.'

'Thanks, pal. I must admit, I feel a bit all on my lonesome on here — a solitary soldier surrounded by sailors. I feel like a right lemon.'

The three men laughed, breaking any residual tension.

'Well, you're one of us now,' Scaggs said, patting Crabtree on the shoulder. 'It's an honour to have you aboard, young man. Think of all that drill that you won't have to do.'

'That's true enough,' Crabtree said with a laugh. 'But it's the seasickness that worries me.'

Remmie smiled. 'Keep your eyes on the horizon, and you'll be right as rain.'

'Eyes on the horizon — I'll remember that,' said the young gunner with a nod, and he carried on towards the activity at the stern.

'Let's just hope we won't be requiring his services,' Scaggs muttered and took another long draw on his cigarette.

CHAPTER FIVE

Back on the bridge of HMS *Walker*, Macintyre passed "the conn" — control of the bridge — to Tommy, and sent Langton and Rom down to the wardroom to support half a dozen of HMS *Walker*'s more burly young ratings as they led the German submariners through the ship.

'Please, take a seat, sir,' Langton said to Kretschmer. 'We will arrange for some hot drinks to be brought to your men, but firstly, I need to make a record of all of your names. Do you understand?'

'Perfectly well, First Lieutenant,' said Kretschmer, smiling as he took a seat and looked around at the wardroom with its drinks cabinet and paintings on the walls. 'You have a very comfortable place here.'

'We do try to keep things as civilised as possible.'

As Langton and Kretschmer exchanged pleasantries, Rom glimpsed one of the young submariners reaching beneath his jacket and producing a small pistol from the back of his belt. It was a Mauser HSc — a neat little 7.65mm semi-automatic with a wooden handle. It fitted so snugly in the submariner's palm that for the briefest of moments Rom thought he was imagining the weapon. But then the German directed the barrel towards the first lieutenant's head and screamed, '*Für das Vaterland!*'

As he went to pull the trigger, Rom lunged at the assailant, rugby-tackling him to the floor. The shot rang out towards the ceiling. Rom violently turned the submariner over on the floor and punched him hard in the face. The German's nose erupted with blood as Rom snatched the gun from his hand and flung it across the room.

In the same moment, Macintyre entered the wardroom and ran forward to help Rom. Together they wrestled the aggressive young German into submission, but a moment later he slipped out of Macintyre's grip and launched himself back across the room towards the pistol. Once again, Rom was the first to react, his right foot flicking out to trip the submariner. He caught him under the left kneecap and sent him into a tumble. As the German went to get back on his feet, Rom was ready with a raised knee in the young man's already bloodied face. It sent him sprawling back onto the floor at the sea-soaked boots of Kretschmer.

Kretschmer reached down and grabbed the young submariner by the collar, ordering his subordinate in colourful German to behave himself. He turned towards Macintyre, still holding the man by the scruff of the neck. 'I can only apologise, Captain,' he said. 'This young fellow never knows when to give up.'

'Lock him up,' Macintyre said to the group of British ratings who had been watching on, open-mouthed. 'And check all the others for any more concealed weapons.'

'The others will cause you no trouble. I can vouch for them,' Kretschmer said. 'Would you mind awfully if I smoke?' The U-boat captain was already taking a cigar from the inside pocket of his jacket.

'Not at all,' Macintyre said. 'Langton here will organise a drink for you and your men, as long as they behave themselves.'

The aggressive young German was manhandled out of the room, blood dripping from his nose as he went.

'He is — how you say? — passionate, that one.' Kretschmer shrugged. 'You always get one who insists on fighting to the death. It's the romantic nature of Bavarians, you understand.'

Two of the ratings and Langton worked their way around each of the Germans and patted them down, revealing no further small arms. Macintyre did the honours with his opposite number. 'Excellent,' he said, looking visibly embarrassed by the exercise. 'Now, we have some tea being prepared for you all and a tot of rum each, and then we'll show you to your accommodation for the voyage back to Britain. Your aggressive comrade will be under lock and key for the majority of the time, I'm afraid.'

'I think, given that he tried to shoot your first lieutenant, that is only to be expected,' Kretschmer said drily.

A group of stewards came into the wardroom with a tea urn, a tray of mugs and a couple of bottles of rum and began to set up in the corner.

'Ah, you English and your tea-drinking,' said the U-boat captain, laughing. 'You really do nothing to resist the stereotypes.'

Macintyre smiled. 'Well, if we can't be civilised enough to get you all a cup of tea, then what are we fighting for?'

Kretschmer laughed again and accepted the mug of tea that was offered to him. He raised it in thanks towards Macintyre. 'Well, here's to your success, Captain.'

HMS *Walker*'s engineering officer, Lieutenant Osborne, appeared with a collection of reefer jackets and trousers, which he handed out to the prisoners. They stripped and put on the dry clothing.

Once tea was consumed, the U-boat crew were allotted cabins — or at least, spaces with blankets that would act as their cabins, two or three in each space. HMS *Walker* was fully staffed at the time so there was little room to accommodate the captured crew as well as the rescued merchant sailors. As Langton took control of the bridge and manoeuvred *Walker* back towards the convoy, Macintyre led Kretschmer from the wardroom to his own day cabin.

An hour later, at the first lieutenant's request, Rom left the bridge and checked up on the captain's welfare. He found him sitting in his after cabin reading a book. His German opposite number was asleep in the other armchair, snoring quietly.

'I'm fine, thank you, Hutchinson,' Macintyre whispered. 'You know, actually, it's the damnedest thing — I actually rather like the chap. We had a tremendous conversation. Lots in common. In any other circumstances, I'm quite sure we could have been the very best of friends.'

Rom smiled. 'It's a funny old world, sir.'

'He's certainly no Nazi, I'll say that much,' Macintyre continued, as he looked across the cabin and considered the sleeping German. 'He seems like a good egg — a highly professional naval officer, as well as being something of a *bon viveur*. But he does seem rather exhausted, poor chap.'

'Shall I help him to his cabin, sir?'

'No, don't disturb him. He can sleep there in the chair for as long as he likes. He's not troubling me in the least.'

'Right you are, sir.' Rom made to slip back out of the door, but Macintyre looked up and caught his eye before he left.

'Everything all right on the bridge, Hutchinson?'

'Yes, sir, the convoy is steaming along fine. Everything seems to have settled down.'

'Good man. I'll be up in due course to relieve Langton.'

'Yes, sir. Thank you, sir.' Rom left the captain and his sleeping companion to their quiet contemplation and returned to the bridge.

'All going all right with Jerry down there?' Langton asked.

'Remarkably well, in fact,' Rom said.

'Really?'

'The two captains seem to be getting on pretty well, under the circumstances.'

Rom and Langton exchanged an amused glance, before the first lieutenant turned back towards the bow to take in the sight of the convoy steaming on to their starboard side and ahead of them for some distance. HMS *Vanoc* was back in her place immediately ahead of them in the escort group.

'Well, I suppose two commanding officers have a lot in common, whatever flag they happen to serve under,' Langton said at last.

'Yes, it's a funny old world, isn't it?' Rom said, repeating his earlier observation. 'Two chaps can knock seven bells out of each other with their torpedoes and their depth charges and so on, then pass the time of day perfectly civilly as soon as they are in the same room with a steaming mug of tea.'

'Yes, as you say,' Langton mused. 'It is indeed a funny old world.'

As the convoy steamed on through the churning waters of the dark ocean, the two men stood in silence for a while and took in the magnificent sight, quietly considering the nature of warfare and how it could dehumanise even the most well-meaning of men.

The silence was broken by the arrival of the ship's medical officer, Lieutenant Humphries, on the bridge. Rom turned to see that the Welshman's face was ashen.

'I've just informed the captain and now I'm informing you gentlemen,' Humphries said. 'The young German submariner who attempted to shoot Mr Langton earlier has been found dead in his cabin.'

'Dead?' Langton repeated in disbelief.

'He hanged himself with his belt.'

'Dear God,' Rom muttered.

'I suppose he didn't fancy spending the rest of the war as a POW,' Humphries went on. 'It's a damned shame that nobody thought to remove his belt when they locked him in there.'

The three men stood for a while in silence.

'Has the U-boat captain also been informed?' Langton said at last.

'He has,' the medical officer said. 'He was actually rather cut up about it — called him a damned young fool. He was only nineteen years of age.'

The following morning a burial at sea service was arranged, conducted by Macintyre and Kretschmer, with both the German and the British crew in sombre attendance. A Union Flag was not used to cover the body, for obvious reasons, and in the absence of a German flag on board, a simple grey blanket was used. Wrapped up, the body looked just like any British body as it was tipped from its catafalque and slipped noiselessly into the sea.

Macintyre led the British contingent in a rendition of 'Eternal Father, Strong to Save', before the German crew in their turn sang a rousing few verses of 'Der Toten Erwachen'. Their deep baritones harmonised and echoed out across the ocean.

The men stood for a long moment in silence, before Macintyre closed his prayer book and led Kretschmer off the quarterdeck.

'If only the young fool had drowned when the U-boat was sinking, rather than bringing disgrace on my crew in this way,' Kretschmer said to Macintyre. 'Perhaps, as far as the formal record goes, it might be possible to assume he did just that?'

Macintyre raised an eyebrow at the German. 'I certainly wouldn't want to embarrass you unnecessarily, Kretschmer,' he said.

The U-boat ace nodded and looked out across the ocean as he followed the captain back inside.

Later that evening, Rom and his cabin mate Tommy joined a group of officers who were playing bridge with the U-boat captain in the wardroom. Like Macintyre, Rom became quietly amazed by the charisma of the German.

'What a strange time this has been,' Kretschmer said morosely. 'You know, just a few weeks ago, I met with Günther Prien, our best-known U-boat commander — the hero of Scapa Flow.'

'I'm not familiar with the name, but I have heard about his work at Scapa Flow,' Rom said, emphasising the word "work" a little awkwardly.

'If you were a German sailor, you would certainly know his name. He met his death with a battleship and twenty-eight merchant ships totalling 160,935 tons to his tally and the oak leaves to the Knight's Cross of the Iron Cross to his credit. We will never see his likes again. Then, I hear the great Schepke has also now met his fate. Meanwhile, I will spend the rest of the war making baskets on a Scottish island, no doubt.' Kretschmer laughed bitterly. 'We called this last year our "happy time" — our U-boats were the pride of the Fatherland and we were beating you, yes?'

Rom did not speak, but simply listened and took a sip of his own drink.

'But now our greatest U-boat aces are dead and I am captured — the end of our happy time, I think, for sure.'

'You will forgive me if I don't have too much sympathy,' Tommy muttered.

Kretschmer laughed again. 'I wouldn't expect you to sympathise. You men are doing your job, as I was doing mine. But Prien and Schepke, they were great men. It is, I think — how would you say? — a real shame that the war has required them to make the ultimate sacrifice.'

'War is a strange thing, when you think about it,' Macintyre said. He had just entered the room and overhead the last part of Kretschmer's thoughts about his fellow U-boat aces.

Kretschmer nodded. 'I spent some time with Prien, before he set sail on U-47 that final time. A brass band was playing on the quay to see them off. Prien looked immaculate, as ever, with his leather coat as stiff and shining as a suit of armour. A young girl stepped from the crowd and handed him a bunch of camellias. They bloom so early in Britanny, you know, the camellias.'

Macintyre nodded as if to encourage him to go on with his story.

'He smiled at me then and raised the camellias. I shook his hand and said, "I'll be following you in a couple of days. Have a convoy ready." Then Prien leaned forward and said to me, "Just leave it to Papa's nose to smell something out. I have a hunch about this trip. I think it will be a big one for us all." Well, he wasn't wrong. It certainly was a big one for us.'

Rom, Tommy and Macintyre exchanged silent glances. Were they supposed to show sympathy for a fellow mariner under such circumstances?

'You know, it's a funny thing, Captain,' Kretschmer observed. 'The insignia of your ship features a horseshoe. The insignia for my U-boat was also a horseshoe.'

'Ah, but your horseshoe was upside down,' Macintyre said. 'In our culture, we believe that allows all the luck to run out of it.'

Kretschmer laughed. 'Well, that was certainly true for us,' he said. 'All our luck had run out by the end.'

'Well, perhaps not all your luck. The other U-boat captain met a worse end, regretfully.'

Kretschmer nodded sombrely. 'Yes, poor Schepke. He was an honourable man.'

'I'd better get myself back up on the bridge,' Macintyre said after a long pause.

'Of course, Captain.' Kretschmer nodded. 'Thank you for making young Schmidt's departure so fitting.'

'It's certainly been a curious voyage for us all,' Macintyre said. 'But I wouldn't deny the man a Christian burial.'

'Thank you, Captain,' Kretschmer repeated as Macintyre put down his glass and went to leave the wardroom.

'I have made no record of the burial having taken place, Kretschmer,' Macintyre added, looking at the floor. 'As far as I'm concerned, and as far as the official record goes, young Schmidt never made it onto this vessel.'

Kretschmer nodded. 'I appreciate your sensitivity, Captain,' he said. 'The youngster made fools of us all.'

'Well, I don't think it's fair that you need to be embarrassed by one fanatic.' Macintyre shrugged. 'But the incident hardly paints us in a good light. We should have thought to remove the man's damned belt. No, it's best all round that Schmidt was never rescued from the sea. My men will understand as much.'

'My men too, Captain,' the German said.

The following morning, with the coast of Ireland visible on the horizon, the convoy was disbanded and HMS *Walker* headed into the Irish Sea and towards Liverpool Bay.

'It sounds as though Liverpool may have taken another battering in our absence,' Macintyre explained to the officers on the bridge. 'The Gladstone Dock is temporarily out of action, apparently, so we've been redirected to the Prince's Landing Stage.'

'Isn't that usually reserved for rather grander vessels than ours?' Langton asked.

'I rather think word might be out that we have been involved in taking out some of Germany's best-known and hero-worshipped U-boat aces on this trip. I suspect there might be a bit of a welcome party.'

Rom stood on the portside wing, once the ship was up alongside, and took in the view as the city stretched out before him. The harbour was busy with activity and had a fresh smell of morning, crisp in the watery sunlight. Macintyre had been right — there was a welcome party, in the form of Sir Percy Noble and many of his senior staff from the Western Approaches Command HQ. Much to Rom's disappointment, Charlotte was not amongst them. She would still be busily working at the plotting desk, deep below the city.

He watched as Macintyre was piped off the ship to receive the Admiral's congratulations. Tommy appeared beside Rom on the wing and both men looked on as Kretschmer was taken off the ship by a contingent of Military Police ahead of the removal of his men. Kretschmer nodded an acknowledgement towards Macintyre on the quayside, then turned one last time and offered a sombre wave up at the bridge of HMS *Walker*. His own men, the captured submariners, had formed up on the deck of HMS *Walker*, and crisply stood to attention and saluted their commander. A smile flickered on Kretschmer's lips before he turned and stepped into the back of a waiting car.

*

Charlotte didn't mind working on the night shift. After all, there was no real sense of whether it was day or night once you were down in the depths of the Western Approaches HQ and the tiredness didn't bother her, as it did some of the other girls. She could sleep just as well through the day in the little bedroom at the front of her parents' house, where she had slept as a child. Surrounded by her childhood toys, she felt more comfortable there than anywhere in the world — though after a long shift in the operations room, Charlotte was certain she would be able to sleep anywhere.

'The new chap's a bit of a dish,' Polly whispered, nodding towards a square-jawed lieutenant with hair that had been Brylcreemed back tight against his scalp.

Charlotte shrugged. 'He's a bit on the short side,' she whispered back.

'Oh, I don't know, sometimes great things come in small packages.'

'Polly Parker!' Charlotte hissed. 'I really don't think you should be looking at his small package!'

The two women doubled over in a fit of suppressed laughter. When they finally composed themselves, Polly gave out a little shriek. 'Gawd, he's coming over here!'

Charlotte looked across the operation room, and sure enough, the new lieutenant was approaching, his eyes fixed on Charlotte's.

'Good evening, ladies. I sensed you were discussing the new boy, so I thought I'd better come and introduce myself,' he purred with a smile.

Charlotte and Polly awkwardly stood to attention, their faces turning puce with embarrassment.

'At ease, ladies,' said the lieutenant, laughing. 'I'm only pulling your legs.' He paused, took a single step back, and examined the two women's legs. 'And rather fine-looking legs they are too, may I say.'

Polly giggled like a schoolgirl.

'I'm not sure our legs are any of your business, sir,' Charlotte muttered.

The officer laughed again. 'My word, aren't you the feisty one?'

'I'm Wren Plotting Officer Polly Parker,' Polly interrupted, offering a hand for him to shake. He obliged, but didn't take his eyes off Charlotte as he did so. He seemed to be appraising her silently. 'And this is my charming colleague, Wren Plotting Officer Charlotte Burton.'

'I'm Lieutenant Derek Belvoir — that is B-E-L-V-O-I-R, but pronounced "beaver", you see. Don't ask me why. But my friends call me Dirk.' He grinned unpleasantly.

'Lieutenant Dirk Beaver. We certainly won't forget that,' Polly said, giggling.

'I shall be calling you "sir", sir,' Charlotte said, sour-faced. 'Now, if you don't mind, sir, I'm sure you'll understand we have some rather important work to be getting on with.'

'Of course, of course,' said Belvoir, smirking. 'Don't let me hold you ladies up.' He walked back to the other side of the room.

Polly sighed. 'He couldn't take his eyes off you. Why is it you get all the luck?'

'He seemed like a greasy little creep to me,' Charlotte muttered. 'Dirk Beaver indeed. What kind of a name is that, anyway?'

The two women erupted into another bout of stifled laughter.

The sun-bleached streets of Lagos were no longer ominous and exotic for Remmie. After a few visits to the port, it was starting to feel like a second home. He enjoyed the lively bustle of the place. It was so far removed from the ground-down atmosphere of his native Liverpool, which was still suffering regular Luftwaffe attacks. But there was something different about Lagos on his latest visit — a growing contingent of British soldiers on the streets, who changed the general feel of the place with their banter and theatrical Britishness, and, somewhat to the bewilderment of the crew of the SS *John Holt*, there was a growing number of Polish troops fighting as part of the British Army in the Royal West African Frontier Force.

Remmie met a group of these smiling Polish fighters in the Lagos bar that the crew frequented whenever they were given shore time in the city. The three soldiers were dressed in khaki shorts and open-necked shirts, with wide-rimmed slouch hats. For a moment, he had mistaken them for Australians.

'No, we are all from Warsaw, or thereabouts,' one of the soldiers said.

'Walsall? In Staffordshire?' Remmie sounded confused.

'No, Warsaw, in Poland,' the soldier corrected, laughing. He reached out to Remmie along the bar. 'My name is Pawel,' he said, shaking his hand. 'And this is Filip and Bartek.'

'Good to meet you all,' Remmie said. 'But what in the hell are you doing out here?'

Pawel leaned back a little on his bar stool. 'We were all soldiers in Poland, before the war. After the Nazis invaded, we got out and made it to London,' he explained. 'From there, we volunteered to join the British Army — to help to fight back, you understand?'

Remmie nodded.

Pawel took a sip from his beer glass. 'But the British put us into the Royal West African Frontier Force, so we find ourselves stationed out here, of all places — under the hot African sun.'

'So, you're defending Lagos from what? The Germans?'

'Hopefully that won't be necessary,' Pawel said. 'Mostly, we're going to be involved in recruiting West African men to join the British Army. Once we get the numbers up, who knows? They'll send us where we're needed. Somewhere equally hot.'

'It's a funny old business, this war,' Remmie said, as he swirled the dregs of his beer around the bottom of his glass. 'You soldier types are getting everywhere. We even have a Royal Artillery squaddie onboard our ship now.'

'You are a sailor on a merchant ship?'

Remmie nodded. 'Yes. We carry a lot of cement, but our cargo can be anything — even fruit occasionally. We're mostly on the Lagos run, but sometimes we go to Douala too.'

'You're brave men,' Pawel said, slapping Remmie on the shoulder. 'Sailing up and down the Atlantic, with all those U-boats out there looking for a chance at a little target practice.' He made a gun-firing gesture.

'Well, we all do what we have to do,' Remmie said. 'There is a war on. You know that as well as anyone — you poor folks have had your whole country taken away from you.'

'Ah, but we will get it back some day,' Pawel said with a knowing nod. He reached for the end of a chain that was hanging around his neck and pulled out a little silver saint who was hanging from it. He kissed the pendant. 'Good will always overcome evil,' he went on. 'Sometimes it takes a while, but we will get our country back some day, I'm sure of it.'

The two men sat in thoughtful silence for a moment.

'Who is it? On your pendant?' Remmie asked.

'Ah, Saint Wojciech. He's a very important saint back in Poland. He was martyred by being beaten to death with the oars of a boat. So you see —' Pawel gave another of his hearty laughs — 'there have always been dangers at sea. You are far better off on the land.'

Remmie grinned and ordered a round of drinks for his new friends.

A few minutes later, as they sipped their beers, Pawel removed the chain from around his neck. 'I have been thinking very carefully, my friend,' he said. 'And I want to give this to you. It will protect you from all those U-boats.'

'I can't take this,' Remmie said, taken aback by the gesture.

'You need it more than me. After all, when will I next get on another ship? We're supposed to spend the next few months in the jungle here, going from village to village, recruiting the locals. I will be a long way from the sea.'

Remmie considered pointing out that the jungles of West Africa might well contain as many threats as the regular passage from Lagos to Liverpool, but seeing the sincerity in the young Pole's eyes, he realised he couldn't refuse. 'Thank you, Pawel,' he said at last, conscious of the lump in his throat, and he carefully fastened the silver chain around his own neck. 'It means a lot.'

CHAPTER SIX

Much to Rom and Macintyre's horror, they later heard a report that the U-boat crew had been met with a barrage of abuse and aggression from the widows of the city's lost merchant sailors, as the captured men were marched to Lime Street Station, where they should have been put on a train to London. In fact, the mob that had gathered became so large that the Military Police had to divert the Germans to spend the night at Walton Gaol, for fear the submariners might otherwise end up strung up from the streetlights of the dock road. They were finally marched back to the railway station at first light, when the angry locals were still in their beds.

Macintyre had only snatched a few minutes on the quayside at the Prince's Landing Stage. He had to be back on board the ship as she was turning around almost immediately. Rom never even made it ashore. HMS *Walker* was to be hauled up at Southampton for a refit later in the year and most of the crew, Rom included, had been granted a full week's shore leave while she was in for an initial assessment of the vessel. Consequently, Rom had the frustrating experience of accompanying the ship to the south coast only to catch a train back north to Liverpool.

It was an uneventful journey around the Welsh and Cornish coastlines, but as he was packing his bag to head back up to Liverpool, Rom was called to the captain's cabin.

'How are you, Hutchinson?' Macintyre asked as he offered Rom a chair and a cigarette.

'I'm well, sir, thank you,' Rom replied, moving the cigarette to the lighter flame being offered by the captain.

Macintyre sat down and lit his own cigarette. 'Jolly good — looking forward to a well-earned rest, no doubt.'

'Absolutely, sir.'

'Now listen, I don't want to beat around the bush,' Macintyre said, brushing away a fleck of ash that had fallen on his lap. 'I was damned impressed by the way you handled yourself when that Jerry pulled a gun on us in the wardroom.'

'I don't know what you mean, sir,' Rom said. 'That particular Jerry never even made it on board HMS *Walker*.'

Macintyre nodded sagely. 'Quite right, old man,' he said, smiling. 'Still, between you, me and the gatepost, I was damned impressed.'

Rom shrugged. 'Anyone would have done the same — I just happened to be the one who saw him reach for the weapon.'

Macintyre shook his head. 'I don't think that's necessarily true. Not everyone has that ability to make a quick decision and act on it. As I say, I was damned impressed. So much so, I took the liberty of recommending you for promotion to lieutenant.'

'Thank you, sir.'

Macintyre waved it away. 'Not at all. Anyway, there can't be many sub-lieutenants walking around with a Distinguished Service Cross. It's about time you were promoted.'

'Thank you, sir,' Rom said again and took a draw from his cigarette. 'I won't let you down.'

'Well, here's the thing,' Macintyre added, rubbing at the stubble on his cheek. 'The request for your promotion was warmly received, as you might imagine. But the Admiralty had a slight issue. They felt we were a bit top-heavy on officers, while other ships were running a bit light. The upshot is, they want to promote you to lieutenant on another ship. We'll get you replaced by another fresh sub-lieutenant, straight out of training. It's a damned shame for us, but hopefully it will be good news for your career.'

Rom nodded. 'That's a little disappointing, sir. I have been very happy serving on this ship.'

'I know,' Macintyre said. 'You're a good chap. But I'm sure you'll get on just as well on your next vessel, which is HMS *Defender* — so another veritable old destroyer, though not quite as old as *Walker*. You'll be missed, Hutchinson. I hope we will serve together again someday.'

Rom nodded. 'Thank you, sir. Still, I've had more ships than Cammell Lairds. It hardly looks good on my service record.'

'It's just the nature of serving in wartime, Hutchinson. You mustn't worry about it. After your week's leave, you are to report to Plymouth next Sunday morning, where I'm told you'll be able to hitch a ride on a minesweeper that is heading out to Gibraltar. You will spend a few days there, before you can catch a ride on another ship that is heading for Malta, where you will rendezvous with *Defender*. It's all written down here.' He handed Rom a slip of paper. 'You may have a week or so at Gib, but there are worse things — you'll see a bit more sunshine down there than we ever saw in Iceland.'

'I spent some time in a Gibraltar hospital back in January, sir, after *Southampton* went down.'

'Ah, well, it'll all be familiar to you then.' Macintyre smiled and held out a hand for Rom to shake, indicating that the meeting was over.

Rom stood and shook the captain's hand. 'It's been an honour, sir.'

'Good man,' Macintyre said and watched as Rom walked out of the cabin.

He met Tommy on the quarterdeck.

'I'm being moved on,' Rom said with a shrug. 'I'm being promoted, but I'm also being moved to another ship.'

'Well, congratulations on the promotion, Lieutenant Hutchinson, but I'll be sorry to see you leave us so soon.' Tommy smiled. 'You're the tidiest cabin mate I've ever had.'

Rom laughed. 'I'm not good with clutter. Tidy room, tidy mind and all that.'

'So when do you go?'

Rom looked down at his double-faced wristwatch. 'Pretty much now, I believe.'

'It's a tough business, this bloody war. It's like one long exercise in not getting attached to other people.'

Rom nodded and reached out a hand. Tommy shook it with both his hands. 'You take care of yourself, won't you, Tommy?'

Tommy nodded. 'You too, Rom. I hope our paths cross again someday.'

The train journey north dragged on for hours, with a severe hold-up at Birmingham, where the train crawled through the city as work was being carried out to repair tracks broken up by the Luftwaffe's heavy bombing a couple of months earlier. Rom watched the charred remains of Birmingham passing by through the window and wondered what images of devastation would be awaiting him in his home city.

By the time he emerged from the platform at Lime Street Station, Liverpool was shrouded in darkness — with the gloom heavily reinforced by the blackout. There were certainly a few more bombsites in the city centre than when he was last home, but all Rom was interested in was finding his way onto the Crosby train. He walked through the city, passing the Town Hall and wondering how close he was to the Western

Approaches Command HQ where Charlotte spent so many hours. He could be walking over the operations room even now, he thought as he headed towards the Overhead Railway.

He found himself in a carriage alone and sat back in the darkness, gazing out at the docks — each of them in turn with their numerous merchant ships and a little way beyond, the familiar sight of a couple of destroyers up alongside the quay at Gladstone Dock, which must be back in service, Rom thought to himself.

It was nearly midnight by the time he made it to Crosby — the familiar garden path and the house itself, like the rest of the city, was shrouded in darkness. He began to wish he had telegrammed ahead, so his mother would be waiting for him. He knocked and it took her some minutes to get to the door. But her face lit up with a smile when she opened it to see her son standing on the doorstep with his bag strapped over his shoulder.

'Rom! You're here!' said Eileen, embracing him on the doorstep, before stepping back and ushering him into the hall. 'Come in, come in, we'll have the ARP Warden shouting at us for breaking the blackout.'

As she stepped back into the light of the hallway, Rom saw the bruising to her forehead and her heavy black eye. 'Mother, what the hell happened to you?'

'I'm fine. Don't fuss,' she said, brushing away his concerns. 'I crashed the ambulance — in the Mersey Tunnel, of all places.'

'Dear God, Mother, are you all right?' He took a closer look at her injuries.

'Just cuts and bruises — nothing worth worrying about, Rom — but they kept me in hospital for a few days. Your father was home, so that worked out well. I was glad to see him.'

'He's back on the ship now?' Rom asked.

'He is, but he got me settled before he had to go back.'

'So what happened?'

'Head-on collision with an Army truck. It was bad, Rom.' Her hand began to shake as she spoke.

'Come and sit down,' Rom said, dropping his bag and leading her into the sitting room.

'I'm all right, but Bella, the woman who was with me in the ambulance, was killed.' Her eyes filled with tears as she spoke. 'So was the soldier who was driving the lorry. He would have been killed instantly, they told me.'

'I'm sorry, Mother,' Rom said, sitting down opposite her. 'I'm the one who's supposed to be in the wars, not you.'

Eileen raised her eyes to the ceiling and laughed. 'We're all in the wars, I'm afraid, my dear.'

'I'll put the kettle on.' Rom headed to the kitchen.

'How long's your leave?' she called out to him as he filled the kettle.

'A week!' he shouted back as he struck a match to light the gas hob. 'I'm heading to the Med, joining HMS *Defender*.' He walked back into the sitting room while he waited for the kettle to boil.

'Another ship!' Eileen laughed. 'You've had more ships than…'

'Cammell Lairds, I know. It's just the way of things, with the war on a knife-edge. They're shuffling people around all the time.'

'How was the last convoy? Iceland, was it?'

Rom nodded. 'Eventful. You certainly never get bored in this job.'

The kettle began to whistle in the kitchen and he headed back out to turn off the stove. 'I didn't wake you, did I?' he called. 'I thought the train was never going to get here.'

'No, love, I was in bed reading my book,' Eileen said. 'I've been having trouble sleeping since the accident.'

Rom handed her a mug and took his own to the settee, where he settled himself down and took off his hat. 'Well, it's certainly good to be home.'

'It's good to have you home, love,' Eileen said, gazing at him through the steam rising from her mug.

'So have you given up the ambulance, then?' Rom asked.

Eileen shook her head. 'You can't give up something like that. I'll get back to it, once I've recovered a bit and the bruises have gone down.'

'Well, you take care. We can do without you getting into scrapes,' Rom said. 'It sounds like we're very lucky that you're still here.'

Eileen smiled weakly. 'I suppose it just wasn't my time quite yet,' she mused.

Rom nodded. 'I suppose not. Any word from Remmie?'

'Remmie's back and forth to Lagos. Sometimes I see him, when he's back in port. More often than not, though, they're straight back out. They've got him working around the clock, no doubt. But he seems happy enough.'

'And Father?'

'It's the same for him — busier than ever, as far as I can make out. You should see the number of ships in and out of the docks each day. It's incredible.'

'Aye, they're keeping the country fed,' Rom said. 'Everyone's doing their part.'

Eileen nodded. 'That's true, very true. Everyone's doing what they can.'

*

It had been a long shift and Charlotte had been dozing on the bus home as the sun rose over the suburban streets — only just waking up in time for her stop. When she got home, she opened the front door and threw her hat onto the little bureau. 'It's only me!' she shouted to her mother, as she slipped off her shoes. 'I'm completely exhausted.' She shuffled into the sitting room and was surprised to find her mother was not alone. A man was seated on the settee opposite her. He turned and she was met by Rom's smiling face. He put down his teacup and saucer and got to his feet.

'Surprise!' he said and held out his hands.

Charlotte gave a little squeal and dashed across the room and into his arms. 'You didn't say you were coming home!' she remonstrated playfully.

'I didn't know until the very last minute. It's good to see you, Charlotte.'

She leaned in and held him tightly. 'It's good to see you, too, Rom.'

Charlotte's mother gave an embarrassed little cough and got to her feet. 'Well, I'd better make some more tea,' she said quietly and slipped discreetly out of the room.

'You're in one piece?' Charlotte asked, leaning back from his embrace to check him over.

'I am,' he said.

'We were monitoring you when you came up against that U-boat,' she said. 'My God, Rom, you were lucky.'

'You don't know the half of it,' Rom said, but then paused as he saw Charlotte's pretty blue eyes filling with tears. 'What's wrong?'

'There are just so many times when I think I'm never going to see you again,' she said, struggling to prevent her voice from breaking.

Rom continued to hold her. 'I'm here now, safe and sound,' he said. 'Now, what are you doing tomorrow?'

'Working, of course.'

'Oh, I thought we might be able to do something — go for a walk on the beach, perhaps.'

'Maybe we could go for an hour or so, before I get changed for work? I'm working nights. Why don't you come back here for three o'clock and we can do something for a couple of hours?'

'Sounds good,' Rom said. 'You get some sleep.'

Five hours later, Rom was back knocking on Charlotte's door.

'You're certainly keen, young man, I'll give you that,' her mother said as she let him into the hall. Charlotte appeared in moments, ready to leave.

'Did you get much sleep?' Rom asked.

'Enough,' Charlotte said. 'Let's go.'

'Have a nice walk, you two,' her mother called from the kitchen.

Once outside and walking along the street, Rom leaned in for a kiss. Charlotte obliged, but then made a comment about "the neighbours".

'I'm sure they've seen worse,' said Rom, laughing. 'Shall we jump on the train and go up to Formby for a change of scenery?'

'Yes, all right, as long as I'm back here for five o'clock to get ready for work.'

'That gives us plenty of time,' Rom said, with a glance at the double-faced watch he wore on his wrist — a gift from his parents so he would always know the time at home, as well as the time wherever he was in the world.

The train was just pulling in when they arrived at the station, and they were at Formby within minutes — with its tranquil coniferous woodland stretching down to the sand dunes and the promise of the sea beyond.

They walked hand in hand down the lane and talked in a relaxed and carefree manner as they continued along the springy woodland path, occasionally stopping to gaze up at the high canopy above them, with the summer sunshine breaking through.

Beyond the woodland, the sand dunes began, enormous crumbling mounds, twisting and turning into countless passageways, marked out with wiry grass that whispered in the breeze. Climbing the last of the dunes, Rom and Charlotte stopped to catch their breath and looked out towards the glittering sea.

'You will keep coming back to me, won't you, Rom?' Charlotte said, her cropped hair dancing in the breeze.

Rom touched her cheek. 'Of course I will. How could I not keep coming back to you?'

They embraced. Rom could feel the sun on his back and Charlotte's soft lips against his own. There wasn't anywhere else in the world he would rather be in that moment. He moved his head back and took in the beauty of her smiling face.

'You're rather lovely, you know,' he said.

'Well, you're rather lovely yourself.' Charlotte laughed.

Rom took her hand and led her back into the dunes, where they could find a quiet corner to lie down.

The world was all sand and sky and wiry grass as they nestled in the little elbow of the dune, without another soul around for miles.

'I've never…' Charlotte paused. 'I've never done anything like this before,' she said at last.

'Don't worry,' Rom said. 'Neither have I.'

'Do you really think this is such a good idea?' Charlotte muttered, her fingers already unfastening his belt.

'My love,' Rom gasped, taking her face in his hands. 'I think it's probably the best idea we've ever had.'

High above them, a single gull circled and cried out mournfully as it glided on the summer thermals.

Rom and Charlotte returned to the same place — secluded and tranquil — three times over the course of the week. It felt like one of the few places where they could be truly alone to explore each other's bodies and minds fully. The physical exploration came naturally enough for both of them — gentle and sensual and somehow strangely elemental, Rom thought, as though they had blended magically with the blue skies and the white sand dunes, the whispering grasses and the richly aromatic pine needles. Exploring deeper into each other's minds came afterwards, as they lay in the dunes looking towards the sky, watching the clouds as they reshaped themselves against the blue dome of the heavens.

Rom asked Charlotte things he had never even wondered about before, gradually building up a picture of how she really felt and thought about the world and her place in it. Charlotte did the same with Rom, picking at the threads of his life that she knew so well and drawing out unexpected memories and passions: the things he loved and the things he hated. He told her about life at sea, revealing more about his fears and traumas than he had ever told anyone. He spoke about the good friends he had lost to this relentless war, and the petty enemies he had made along the way. He even told her about his breakdown — the nights he had spent sleeping on deck because the walls of his cabin had closed in on him until he cried out in terror.

By the end of the week, Charlotte and Rom were closer than they had ever been. Their souls had intertwined during those long summer days on the beach, like a spliced rope, unravelled and rebound together.

Late on Saturday afternoon, Rom shouldered his long, canvas Royal Navy holdall, kissed his mother on the cheek and smiled back towards her as she waved from the doorstep. He had said his goodbyes to Charlotte before the start of her evening shift, with a final walk — this time along the open wet sand of Crosby Beach. Rom had grown accustomed to her shorter hair, but its auburn strands still danced in the breeze blowing up from the estuary, just as it always had. It seemed to him that Charlotte always looked at her most beautiful whenever he had to say goodbye.

Rom made his way towards the battered old Royal Navy minesweeper, which would provide him with a passage to Gibraltar ahead of his rendezvous with his new ship.

CHAPTER SEVEN

The main operations room at the Western Approaches HQ was never quiet. It was always bustling with activity as teams of plotters kept track of the convoys and their escorts passing back and forth across the North Atlantic. But the network of corridors surrounding it, deep underground and firmly reinforced with thick slabs of concrete, were always eerily quiet at any time of the day or night.

Charlotte had a message for the Chief of Staff, Commodore John Mansfield, who had an office behind the main operations room. She knocked and entered, but he wasn't there. Then she heard his voice, calling her through to a small lobby area between his office and his bedroom, where he had a sofa and a reading lamp.

'Good girl,' he said, taking the memorandum from her. 'Carry on, my dear.'

Rather than returning through his office, she chose to leave by the second door that led from the far side of the lobby space into the so-called "power corridor", not as in the "corridors of power" where the big decisions were made, as Charlotte had mistakenly assumed when she'd first arrived at Derby House. It was called the "power corridor" for the rather more prosaic reason that it contained the main power board and fuses for the whole facility. Surprisingly, given that it was the hub for power in the command centre, this was the darkest corridor in the whole place. It was an isolated corner of the complex, with three-foot-thick walls that no sound would pass through. It was the last place where you might want to call for help. Which was why Charlotte's stomach churned so horribly when she looked up to see Dirk Belvoir walking towards her in the gloom. He stopped, looking over his shoulder, before he turned back to engage with her, giving Charlotte his usual teasing smirk that she hated with such a passion.

'Good evening, my dear,' he said, sneering.

It had been Charlotte's intention to walk past with only the formal acknowledgement of "sir". But Belvoir had other plans. He put his right arm out across the corridor to block her path.

'You're looking particularly beautiful tonight, Wren Plotter Burton,' he murmured, licking the spittle from his lips as his eyes scanned up and down her body.

'If you'll excuse me, sir, I'm expected back at my post.'

'Now, now, Burton, there's no need to be unfriendly.'

He moved closer to her in the darkness and she felt his left hand reach out and rest on her waist, almost casually.

'Listen, I know you've been fighting it, as have I, my dear,' Belvoir said. 'But I rather think we're attracted to each other, aren't we?'

'I need to be back in the operation room.'

Belvoir tutted. 'There's no point putting off this kind of chat,' he said, raising his right hand to run a finger down her left cheek. 'Passions will always spark in these kinds of close confines between a man and a woman.'

Charlotte looked at the floor. She could feel her breathing quicken and her face flushing.

'Sooner or later, my dear,' he added, leaning his lips towards hers, 'I'm afraid we just have to give in to it. We're all just animals, you see.' His lips made contact and Charlotte's head flinched back to escape him, but his clutch tightened, with his right hand moving to grip the back of her head and pull her towards his spittle-flecked lips.

Charlotte whimpered — a terrified little noise — and then began to struggle. But the more she struggled, the tighter he gripped.

'Damn this for a game of soldiers,' he said suddenly. He grabbed her by the scruff of the neck and dragged her into a neighbouring service cupboard. It was filled with fuse boards and various kinds of gauges and switches. He flung her forcefully towards a metal cabinet and closed the door behind him. The only light in the cupboard was coming from a single flickering bulb, which was designed to light up the fuses.

'Don't you dare!' Charlotte cried out as she lay sprawled against the cabinet. But Belvoir was already unfastening his leather belt and the buttons on the front of his trousers.

He drew his pants hurriedly down to his ankles and reaching forward, grabbed Charlotte's face between his thumb and middle finger and squeezed tightly. 'And don't you dare even think about struggling,' he said, banging the back of her head against the metal cabinet.

She struggled to catch her breath, feeling suddenly dizzied by the blow to the back of her head, and somehow she just couldn't find a scream within her as he dragged her legs apart, manhandling her like a ragdoll, before tearing away her underwear and plunging himself into her.

When it was over she folded herself up into the corner and sobbed, while Belvoir hurriedly put his trousers back on. 'Not a damned word to anyone, you hear?' he growled, before walking out of the cupboard and slamming the door shut behind him.

Charlotte stayed there in the darkness for some time, before finding the strength to stand up, straighten her skirt and run to the sanctuary of the ladies' toilets.

*

Charlotte didn't tell anyone about Belvoir's attack — not out of fear of him, but out of a searing, horrendous sense of shame that seemed to envelope her.

For two whole shifts she didn't mention it, not even to Polly. She kept retreating to the toilets when she felt she needed to cry and when she got home she went straight to bed and sobbed into her pillow, finding it impossible to rid her mind of the image of Belvoir lunging towards her. Then on the third day, after two further sleepless nights, something changed. She realised she had found the strength deep within to speak out. She simply couldn't let that bastard get away with it.

Charlotte considered approaching Walters and then thought again. He was too nice a man to trouble with this kind of thing. She knew that Sir Percy Noble himself was in his office, so she walked up the steps and went straight in without knocking.

Noble's office overlooked the operations room, with a window giving him constant sight of the floor-to-ceiling map of the North Atlantic where she normally spent her entire shift, moving the plotting markers across the ocean as news was radioed home from far out in the Atlantic. He was in his early sixties, but he looked much older. With his puffy eyes and deeply wrinkled forehead, one might have been forgiven for imagining he was in his mid-seventies. He was just finishing a call and placing the telephone receiver down as she walked in. He looked up, apparently confused by her presence. 'Yes?' he muttered.

'Sir, there is something I wanted to talk to you about.'

'Not now, my dear.' He waved her away. 'I'm sorry, but I've just received some terrible news.'

'Sir?' Charlotte took a step forward. It was clear the man was upset.

'It's Lieutenant Belvoir. He's dead.'

'He's what?' Charlotte felt the breath stop in her throat.

'Dead. Died instantly, they said. Driving in the blackout last night, drove into a lamp post at some speed.'

Charlotte's eyes dropped to the floor. 'I'm sorry for disturbing you, sir,' she said, turning back towards the door.

'No, please come on in, my dear.' Noble bustled to his feet and waved her back inside. 'What was it you needed to talk to me about?'

'Nothing,' she muttered. 'It doesn't matter anymore.'

She turned on her heel and left the office, her hands shaking.

Rom had the best part of a week to wait at Gibraltar, bedding down in a Royal Navy shore establishment that was comfortable enough at night, but was no place to spend a whole day. He took to wandering Gibraltar town itself. After a couple of days enjoying the warm sunshine and the occasional pint in Gibraltar's back street hostelries, he stumbled across the Trafalgar Cemetery — a long-abandoned graveyard outside the old city walls. It was a particularly hot day, with the sun beating down on him. His head was swimming a little and he thought he might find a little shade in the old graveyard.

Rom wandered in and took momentary refuge beneath a yew tree. He pulled back the ivy on one of the nearby headstones. It recorded the life of Lieutenant William Forster: *Late of His Majesty's Ship Colossus. Died of the wounds he received in the glorious battle off Trafalgar, the 21st Day of Oct. 1805. Aged 20 years.*

'Nothing much changes,' Rom muttered to himself and moved deeper into the cemetery. He pulled back the undergrowth to reveal another headstone: *To the memory of Captain Thomas Norman of the Royal Marine Corps & late of His Majesty's Ship Mars, who died in the Naval Hospital of this place on the 6th day of December, 1805 in the 36th year of his age after having suffered* *several weeks with incredible patience and fortitude under the effects of a severe wound receiv'd in the great & memorable Seafight off Trafalgar.*

Rom stood a while and looked down at the grave, then realised there was a further inscription beneath, completely covered by a tangle of ivy and wiry grass. He reached down and pulled the strands away and brushed at the dirt with the palm of his hand until he could read the words below: *His brother officers on this station have consecrated this humble but sincere testimony of their sense of his distinguished merit and of their regret for his premature fate.* Beneath that there was a Latin inscription: *Militavit non sine gloria nec paucis flebilis occidit.*

Rom became suddenly aware of a presence behind him. Then he heard a voice, speaking very close to his ear.

'He fought not without glory, nor did he die to be mourned only by a few.'

Rom turned his head and there beside him, in the shade of the yew tree, was his old friend Chubby Smith. He was looking resplendent in his full RNVR uniform, with just a few beads of sweat on his ample cheeks and across his forehead where his cap rested above his knitted brow. All in all, Rom thought to himself, Chubby was looking remarkably chipper for a man who had been dead for over a year.

'I believe it's from Horace,' Chubby added. 'You see, old man, all that education didn't go completely wasted.' He smiled and turned his eyes away from the headstone to meet Rom's eyes. 'How are you, old bean?'

Rom shrugged. 'I go from one ship to another, Chubby. You've no idea what it's like. From one battle to the next. I'm living on my nerves, if I'm honest.'

Chubby nodded sagely. Rom gazed at his dearly departed cabin mate. He had watched as Chubby was gunned down on the wing of the bridge of HMS *Grenade* as a U-boat surfaced in the sea off Norway more than a year before. It wasn't the first time this apparition had returned to him during those twelve months. But somehow out here, on the edge of Europe, with the North African coast glimmering on the horizon, he hadn't expected Chubby to make another appearance.

'It's funny, you know,' Rom said. 'In stories, people are always terrified when they see a ghost. But it's always reassuring to see you.'

But Chubby was no longer there.

A week after arriving at Gibraltar, Rom joined a cramped little flower-class corvette as a passenger heading for Malta, where he would ultimately meet HMS *Defender*, which had been in dock undergoing a swift refit on the proud little island.

The Mediterranean Sea was as eye-wateringly blue as Rom remembered as the little vessel made its way between the Spanish and the North African coastlines — what the ancients thought of as the Pillars of Hercules, he thought to himself as he leaned on the deck rail of the corvette, slowly smoking a cigarette and enjoying the sea breeze and warm sunshine on his face. He could taste the salt from the waves tingling his lips and felt a surge of liberation as the ever-present threats of the Atlantic Ocean disappeared into the wake of the little ship. He closed his eyes and inhaled the warm Mediterranean air. The very moment he opened them, a dolphin breached the surface of the water, relishing the foaming sea being drawn up alongside the ship's bow. In another moment, two more appeared, then a fourth — sleek and stone-grey, glistening in the sunlight and turning acrobatic arcs amid the waves. Rom smiled to himself and turned back for one last look at the Rock of Gibraltar, looming in the heat haze behind him.

'Onwards and upwards, eh, Chubby?' he said to the buffering air around him. 'Onwards and upwards, old chum.'

It took the best part of three days to reach Malta, with the indomitable little ship doing around sixteen knots for most of the journey. Rom barely saw another ship during the entire time. The corvette's small crew was friendly enough, and meals were sociable affairs. But he was alone on the deck and in his cabin for much of the day. By the time they arrived at Valletta, Rom couldn't wait to board a destroyer once again and actually have a job to do. He'd had more than enough of being a tourist. But as he gazed out at the fawn-coloured, flat-roofed cityscape, with its occasional church dome or tower to break the monotony, it was difficult to feel any enthusiasm for being back in Malta.

When he had left behind the smoking wreckage of HMS *Southampton* at the beginning of the year, he never imagined he would be back on this side of the Mediterranean so soon. It felt a little ominous, the idea of serving here again — as if this whole stretch of coastline held some kind of curse for him. Rom shook his head silently and lit a cigarette. He was becoming more superstitious the longer he was in the service. There was something about life at sea that made men prone to superstitious thoughts, and Rom was no exception.

Once the corvette was up alongside, he hurriedly said his farewells to the crew and thanked them for their hospitality, then shouldered his bag and marched across the quayside to where he could already see the distinctive outline of a destroyer some way in the distance. But as he approached, he quickly realised it wasn't HMS *Defender*.

He walked up through the Grand Harbour, with his bag weighing heavily on his shoulder in the heat. He found a group of young naval ratings playing cricket on a patch of barren earth, with a petty officer and a single Royal Marine fielding. They pointed Rom in the direction of the Royal Navy headquarters on the island, where an exasperated ginger-haired lieutenant rifled through countless files before finally setting Rom on the right track.

Defender, it seemed, had been moved to Greece following intelligence of Italian manoeuvring off the coast. A place was organised for Rom on a minesweeper leaving for the port of Piraeus in a little under thirty minutes. He grabbed his bag and the sheet of paper that had been given to him by the ginger lieutenant, and dashed back down to the quayside. Within minutes he was on the deck of yet another ship, steaming out of Valletta on a course for Greece.

The following morning, after a restless sleep he lumbered wearily down the gangplank and looked around at the busy quayside of Piraeus. HMS *Defender* loomed large just along the harbour. He marched along the quay with a spring in his step, relieved to have finally met her.

Rom's new captain was hovering around on the quayside at the end of HMS *Defender*'s gangplank, as if he was waiting for a messenger. Rom approached, put down his bag, stood to attention and saluted. 'Sub-Lieutenant Romulus Hutchinson, reporting for duty, sir!'

'No you're not,' said the captain, grinning and looking Rom up and down, as if to assess him.

'Beg your pardon, sir?'

'You're not Sub-Lieutenant Romulus Hutchinson. You're *Lieutenant* Romulus Hutchinson, reporting for duty, sir!'

Rom glanced down at the double wavy line on his cuff. 'My goodness, sir, you're right.' Rom blushed. 'I've only just been promoted, you see.'

The captain laughed loudly and slapped Rom on the shoulder. 'Good man! Happens to the bloody best of us! I'm fairly certain I'm Lieutenant Commander Gilbert Lescombe Farnfield, incidentally.'

Rom smiled. 'Good to meet you, Captain.'

'Come on up. I'll show you around,' Farnfield said, leading the way up the gangplank with long, energetic strides. 'It's going to be a bit of a quick turnaround, I'm afraid, Hutchinson,' he added as he led the way along the deck. 'The boffins back home have intercepted some intelligence on the location of the Italian fleet off the Greek coast. HMS *Formidable* is heading out there.'

'The aircraft carrier?' Rom asked.

Farnfield nodded. 'Along with three battleships — *Barham*, *Valiant* and *Warspite*. They will be accompanied by the Tenth Destroyer Flotilla — HMS *Greyhound* and *Griffin* and the Australian destroyer HMAS *Stuart*. As if all that wasn't enough, they are also taking with them the Fourteenth Destroyer Flotilla — HMS *Jervis*, *Janus*, *Mohawk* and *Nubian*.'

'Good Lord, they certainly mean business, sir.'

'There will be plenty more besides — the likes of HMS *Hotspur*, *Havock*, *Ajax*, *Gloucester*, *Orion*.'

'It sounds like a full-scale naval battle. I've never served with a full battle fleet like that. I've been mostly involved with convoys.'

'Don't worry, Hutchinson. It's only the bloody Italians.' Farnfield grinned mischievously. 'Could be a hell of a showdown, though. The significant thing is that the Germans are poised to invade Greece any day. The Eyeties have essentially been told to get the Regia Navale out there, making a demonstration of force on the western coast of Greece to try to hamper the flow of British reinforcements from Egypt.'

'And what about us, sir? What are our orders?'

'Fleet screening duties. Currently, our orders are to get to the Kithira Channel and wait there to support the fleet in any way we might.'

Rom nodded. The two men had just arrived at a busy pilothouse and there was a shuffle of saluting among the officers at the arrival of the captain.

'Everybody, this is Lieutenant Romulus Hutchinson, who is joining us,' Farnfield said, before turning back to Rom. 'Apologies — there'll be time for proper introductions later on. We need to get the bloody hell out of here.'

'Of course, sir.'

'Messenger!' Farnfield shrieked and a young rating appeared at the back of the pilothouse. 'Show Lieutenant Hutchinson to his cabin, would you?'

'Yes, sir,' the messenger responded, before turning to Rom. 'Could you follow me please, sir?'

'Drop your bag off and come back to the bridge. We can talk properly once we're out of this bloody harbour and heading out to sea,' Farnfield said.

'Yes, sir.' Rom saluted casually, before picking up his bag and following the messenger out of the door.

There was a tropical storm brewing and it was expected to be so severe, the SS *John Holt*'s departure from Lagos had been delayed by twenty-four hours. With a skeleton crew kept aboard the fully laden ship, Remmie and the majority of the men had the unexpected pleasure of an extra night on the tiles in the humid, sticky bars of the city. Remmie favoured a bar called Igba-Egwu, which the larger-than-life landlord had once told him meant "dancing bar" in the local native Igbo language.

The landlord, who went by the name of Joseph, was a terrifying presence — standing at six foot four and seeming almost as broad as he was tall. His knuckles were heavy with gold rings and his teeth had almost as much gold in them. It seemed that Joseph was making a decent living from serving drinks to British sailors.

His eldest daughter, Adanna, helped her mother in the kitchen, and would occasionally appear in the bar to deliver a plate of roasted plantain or the delicious Ofada rice and stew, which reminded Remmie of a sort of spicy version of the Scouse he had been brought up on.

Adanna wore brightly coloured headscarves, lavish pendant earrings and multiple beaded necklaces in bright yellows and reds. Her appearance in the bar always seemed to make the place light up — and not just because of her colourful clothing. Remmie had been watching her for the past few visits to the port, studying the contours of her face — her arching eyebrows, her high cheekbones, her smiling eyes and smooth brown complexion.

Had he imagined running a finger down those smooth cheeks? Touching the smiling lips with his own? Had he in his daydreams on board the ship unfastened the colourful dress and allowed it to slip down to reveal the flawless body beneath? Possibly. But he wouldn't admit it to anybody. Until that day, he had never even spoken to the girl. The electrical storm was crackling in the skies above the city and a strange wind was blowing off the sea, sending the stray dogs scampering from the streets in search of the shelter of an alleyway. Something in the air seemed to fuel Remmie's bravery. The four pints of beer he had consumed in the previous hour and a half also helped to rid him of his timidity.

As Adanna appeared in the bar, a plate in each hand and using her ample behind to open the swing doors that led from the steaming kitchen, Remmie raised his hand at the girl to indicate that one of the stews was for him.

'Thank you, Adanna,' he said as she placed the food before him.

'You know my name?' Adanna smiled, revealing two pristine rows of shining white teeth.

'I'm Remmie.'

'Remmie.' Adanna tried the name on her tongue. 'That is a good name.'

'Not as nice as Adanna,' Remmie said, his eyes fixed on the face before him. He thought he had never seen anything quite so beautiful.

She smiled again. 'It means "the father's daughter",' she whispered.

At the mention of her father, both Adanna and Remmie became suddenly conscious of Joseph's eyes monitoring the conversation suspiciously from behind the bar. Remmie looked quickly down at his plate.

'Enjoy your food, Remmie,' Adanna whispered and moved swiftly away to deliver the second plate to another hungry British sailor.

Remmie ate his food quietly, wondering to himself what his mother and father would say if he turned up back in Liverpool with Adanna on his arm. After his meal, he felt a little uncomfortable about Joseph's gaze from behind the bar. Remmie knew he should probably be heading back to the ship anyway. He would be expected to be back aboard the *John Holt* if the storm continued to worsen.

He slipped quietly from the bar and into the dark street outside. Adanna was waiting in the shadows beside the kitchen door, which was at the side of the building, hidden down a blind alley. 'Goodnight, Remmie,' she whispered, her smile glinting in the moonlight.

Remmie looked up sharply. 'Goodnight, Adanna,' he whispered. 'That was a great stew.'

'Thank you. I'll pass on your compliments to my mother.' She took a few steps towards the street, so he could see her face properly in the amber glow of the streetlamp. *Dear God, she's beautiful,* Remmie thought to himself. She smiled shyly, almost as if she could hear his thoughts. A bolt of lightning crackled in the sky above the city, arcing from cloud to cloud and momentarily bathing her beauty in a vivid white light. She stepped back towards the darkness.

Eileen decided she had recovered from her physical injuries sufficiently to get back to serving in the Red Cross. But the thought of getting back behind the wheel of an ambulance consumed her with a terror that made her feel sick. She spent long nights alone in the house, sitting up in bed with the lamp on, staring at the wallpaper and wondering if she would really be able to do it.

Finally, in the early hours of a Monday morning in late March, she climbed out of bed, sat down at her dressing table and started to slowly brush her hair, fixing her eyes on her reflection. She put on her uniform and reported back to the Red Cross headquarters.

'Good to see you back, my love,' the duty commander said with a warm smile. 'Now, let's get you sorted with an ambulance.' He started flicking through paperwork.

Eileen had expected an interrogation — how was she feeling? Was she up for getting back to work? But there was no time for such niceties in a city under near constant aerial attack.

Within half an hour, she was sitting behind the wheel of an ambulance with a new partner — an earnest little woman called May, with thick-rimmed spectacles and a nervous little laugh.

'Back to it then,' Eileen muttered to herself, pulling out the choke and revving the engine a little, before moving away into the city streets.

CHAPTER EIGHT

On 27th March, Vice-Admiral Pridham-Wippell — with the cruisers *Ajax*, *Gloucester*, *Orion* and *Perth*, and a number of destroyers — sailed from Greek waters for a position south of Crete. Admiral Andrew Cunningham, Commander-in-Chief of the Mediterranean Fleet, left Alexandria to meet them with the aircraft carrier *Formidable* and the battleships *Warspite*, *Barham* and *Valiant*. On the bridge of HMS *Defender*, the tension was rising throughout the day. Rom struggled to sleep at all that night, so primed was he for action. But when he rejoined his watch the following morning, news reached the bridge that the Italians had been sighted and their battleship *Vittorio Veneto* had launched a terrifyingly accurate volley at a range of sixteen miles. The damaged HMS *Gloucester* dropped back as HMS *Hasty* shielded her with a smokescreen.

Within hours, though, the tables had turned and HMS *Formidable*'s Albacore torpedo-bombers scored a hit against *Vittorio Veneto*. The wounded Italian battleship turned for home. A second strike scored another hit, but she managed to steam away at twelve knots with a protective circle of Italian cruisers and destroyers that made the chance of the British launching a destroyer attack impossible.

Farnfield paced the bridge of *Defender*, muttering to himself as they followed the battle from the radio chatter. Rom knew what he was going through, because he too was feeling like a spare part in all this action.

As darkness fell, *Formidable*'s aircraft scored another hit, this time on the heavy cruiser *Pola*, with a single torpedo. Finally, Cunningham unleashed his destroyers — with the 2nd and 14th destroyer flotillas called into action under Captain Philip Mack on board HMS *Nubian*. The main wave of British destroyers took up an attacking position to the north. A third aerial attack against both the Italian battleship and the *Pola* came as the sun set. But as the battle unfolded somewhere over the horizon, the officers on the bridge of *Defender* were simply left to seethe with frustration. It was the early hours of the following morning when the order came through for *Defender* to proceed to Suda Bay for escort duties.

'Well, chaps, I think we may have come very close to witnessing one of the great sea battles of this war,' Farnfield said drily, as he set a course for Crete.

The following morning *Defender* and *Hasty* escorted the transport ship *Dumana* back across to Piraeus, with the atmosphere still verging on depression on the bridge.

'It's peculiar,' Rom said to Farnfield. 'You'd think we would all want to keep out of the action and just survive this bloody war. But every man on this ship seems disappointed to have been on the sidelines.'

Farnfield shrugged as he cast his binoculars across the horizon. 'It's just human nature, I suppose. We none of us want to spend the rest of our lives feeling as if we've missed out on something big.'

Rom continued his work in silence, the tension somehow having been broken by acknowledging the absurdity of their gloom.

The following morning, as dawn broke on April Fool's Day, all the officers were secretly feeling a little foolish for their petulance as *Defender* returned to its day job — escorting a convoy of merchant ships on an uneventful three-day crossing to Alexandria.

*

Rom stood on the quarterdeck of HMS *Defender*, smoking meditatively and watching the great clustered mass of Alexandria emerging out of the early morning heat haze as the convoy neared its destination. He had been thinking back to a time when he and Remmie must have been about eight or nine years of age and their father had taken them for a walk along the river, pointing out countless ships he knew as they went. They had stopped at Mann Island, with the Royal Liver Building looming behind them, and sat down to eat a paper bag of warm chestnuts their father had bought from a costermonger on the corner.

They'd watched the ferries making their way backwards and forwards across the river and talked as they rarely did — father and two sons. Rom had said something, awkwardly trying to articulate his fears that he might never achieve the things his father had achieved in his life — a captain of the line in his early thirties.

'You don't need to worry about what you do or don't achieve in this life,' William Hutchinson had told them sagely, as he picked at the chestnuts. 'All this life is really about is kindness and unkindness. Like that fella back there with his chestnuts, we just have to find our place, set up our stall and trade in kindness. As long as you're putting out more kindness into the world than unkindness, it doesn't matter whether you're a ship's captain, the King of England, or a bloke selling chestnuts in paper bags. Whatever you do, be kind, and that way you can't fail to go to your grave having lived a fulfilling life. Trust me, lads, I know what I'm talking about.'

That sun-kissed day all those years before, looking out at the gulls circling over the Mersey with the taste of chestnuts on his tongue, had never left Rom. It was this deeply ingrained sense of "doing the right thing" that had directed him through life, shaping his pronounced distaste for bullies of all kinds, and giving him the drive to go that little bit further to help the underdog in every situation. It was why he had felt so determined to join the Royal Navy rather than following in his father's own footsteps and joining the merchant service. He had listened to the radio. He had seen the Pathé newsreels. He had read the newspapers. He didn't like what Hitler and his Nazi hangers-on were doing across Europe. He didn't like the idea that there were people out there who were putting out more unkindness into the world than kindness. It didn't sit well with him at all. If he could do nothing else, he could try to rebalance the deficit a little with his own actions.

Rom wasn't particularly religious — he had never been drawn to churches. With their embroidered altar frontals, proliferation of candles and twee little knitted prayer kneelers, they had always felt like a woman's environment more than a man's, but he was confident that he did know the difference between right and wrong. Out here, with the ocean around him and the blue sky arching overhead from horizon to horizon, he was in his own sacred place.

As he watched the ships of the convoy, he got a little kick from knowing he had been a small cog in the great escort machine that had brought them all safely to their destination — the SS *Brattdal*, SS *City of Karachi*, SS *City of Windsor*, SS *Comliebank*, SS *Dumana*, SS *Ulster Prince*, SS *Port Halifax*, SS *Settler*, SS *Thermopylae* and SS *Thurland Castle*. There was a broad smile on his face as he stood on the deck, his cigarette between his fingers, and one by one he counted each of them into the safe haven of Alexandria.

*

It had been a little over a month since Charlotte had last seen Rom. After everything that had happened since, she longed for him to come home — to envelope her in his arms. She felt more alone than she had ever felt in her life, despite the fact that she was surrounded by a busy crowd of Wren plotters. She had felt exhausted throughout the busy night shift and was desperate to get home to her bed. But she knew she had to soldier on for at least another hour.

'You look a little peaky, girl,' Polly said to her with a concerned frown.

'I'm just tired, Pol,' Charlotte said. 'I'll be all right.' But no sooner had she said it than she felt the rising nausea in her stomach. 'Cover for me, would you please, Pol, just for a moment?'

'Of course,' said Polly. 'But you'll need to tell Nan Currie, if you leave the room.'

She dashed across to the superintendent, who was seated behind her usual desk, her beady eyes following all the plotters as they climbed up and down the ladders, recording the movements of each ship. 'I'm sorry, Superintendent, could I be excused for a few moments? I feel as if I might be sick.'

Currie eyed Charlotte suspiciously, before nodding her head in the direction of the door. 'Go on, but don't be long.'

Charlotte dashed across the room as surreptitiously as she could manage and just reached the ladies' toilets in time to lift the seat and vomit copiously into the bowl. She stood for a while, resting her elbow against the partition and trying to catch her breath. Her throat felt raw and she coughed and spat into the toilet bowl, her hand shaking a little as she reached for the toilet roll to wipe her mouth. There were tears in her eyes, and she carefully wiped them away, using the tips of her fingers to avoid her mascara. A little makeup was encouraged, in a bid to ensure the Wrens didn't "lose their femininity" despite working in a male environment. But Charlotte found it a dreadful incumbrance. After all, she had never bothered with makeup during the course of her civilian life, with her pale freckled skin and red hair giving her face more than enough natural colour contrast.

She flushed the toilet and stepped outside the cubicle with a deep breath, pausing at the basin to wash her hands and examine her face in the mirror. It must have been that dreadful chicken her mother had cooked the day before — a scrawny gift from their neighbour Mr Williamson from his allotment. It had been an old hen that had long since stopped laying, and it was as tough as old boots.

When she had to dash to the ladies' toilets to vomit again during the next night's shift, Charlotte knew she could no longer blame Mr Williamson's poor old hen.

Remmie was on the deck of the SS *John Holt*, sitting against the rail, the Atlantic glistening over his shoulder. Scaggs sat beside him, frowning with concentration as he closely checked the movements of Remmie's fingers along the neck of the banjo. He plucked his way nervously through the jaunty little tune he was learning under Scaggs's watchful tutelage.

'You're getting there, Remmie lad,' Scaggs said. 'Christ knows you've more of an aptitude for the instrument than I ever had. It took me years to get to the level you've reached in a few months.'

'Ah, but I've got the best teacher,' Remmie said.

Scaggs laughed. 'Oh, but you do say the nicest things, young fella,' he crooned.

'My fingers are in shreds,' Remmie said, suddenly stopping and examining his fingertips. 'It's going to hurt like hell when I'm on deck-scrubbing duty tomorrow.'

'You have to accept a little bit of pain for your art. Here,' Scaggs said, taking his banjo back from Remmie. 'Let me show you how it's really done.'

Scaggs's fingers moved so quickly on the neck of the instrument that Remmie realised he couldn't even see them anymore; they had become a blur, and the quick-paced English folk song he played, 'The Labouring Man', now seemed to have more individual notes in it than any music he'd ever heard. Scaggs began to sing along: *'You Englishmen of each degree, A moment listen unto me: From day to day you all may see, The poor are frowned on by degree. To please you all I do intend, So listen to the lines I've penned; By them, you know who never can, Do without the labouring man.'*

A group of giggling deckhands approached the two sailors who were spending their downtime with the banjo, but the laughter stopped when they got closer and listened to Scaggs's extraordinary playing.

Scaggs sang on as the tropical ocean rolled along behind him. *'Some for soldiers they will go, And jolly sailors do we know, To guard Old England day and night, And for their country boldly fight. But when they do return again, They're looked upon with great disdain; Now in distress throughout the land, You may behold the labouring man.'*

The group of sailors, who had been all ready to tease the couple of musicians in their midst, were so taken aback by Scaggs's performance that when he plucked out the final notes, there was a long silence as the men stood transfixed for a beat, before erupting into heartfelt applause and wolf whistles.

'Get out of here, you cultureless bunch,' Scaggs said, laughing. 'Get back to mopping the deck.'

Remmie laughed and patted the older man on the shoulder. 'That was brilliant, Scaggs,' he said. 'Bloody brilliant.'

Remmie found his mind constantly wandering back to the girl in the back streets of Lagos as he worked on the SS *John Holt*. Adanna — such a pretty name, he thought. Then he studied her once again in his mind's eye — such a pretty face, he added silently to himself. That smile. Those big brown eyes.

'You wouldn't be daydreaming when you're supposed to be holystoning the decks, would you, lad?' a Liverpudlian voice growled at him. He looked up. It was Anderson — the grim-faced bosun, who still had freckles across his nose despite being in his mid-thirties.

'No, sir,' Remmie muttered.

Anderson grunted and walked on. Remmie went back to scrubbing the deck, backwards and forwards, backwards and forwards — an action that took almost no thought and so left his brain available to wander. Oh, but that skin. So smooth and silky, and a deep copper colour like a sunset through an autumn canopy. How would it be to rest his sallow cheek against that burnished skin, he thought. He imagined the warmth of her, the texture of her long ringlets of hair, which bobbed a little as she walked as though it were dancing, and only kept its peace when wrapped in that colourful headscarf.

Remmie's mouth felt dry and he realised he had stopped scrubbing once again. He raised himself up from his scrubbing position, which might have been prayerlike if it wasn't so painful. He felt his muscles grind and grumble as he straightened his spine, with one hand reaching around to massage his lower back. He took a moment to look out at the miles of sea that stretched out beyond the rail of the deck. The glistening waves diminished into a distant haze, like a mountain range slipping back into the clouds.

He took a step to the right, moved his metal bucket with his foot and, grasping at the wooden handle of his scrubbing brush, he returned to his godless prayer position on the deck.

CHAPTER NINE

Another day, another Mediterranean convoy for Rom and HMS *Defender*. It seemed a surprisingly benign occupation compared with escorting convoys in the wind-ravaged Atlantic. Convoy AC3 was almost at its peaceful conclusion, with the great hulks of the troopships *Ulster Prince* and *Thurland Castle* coasting through the sapphire waters. The port of Tobruk stretched out before them — a British and Australian troop garrison since the start of the year, it was under increasing pressure from Rommel and his Afrika Korps, who had the city all but surrounded and cut off by land. Once the two troopships were up alongside and releasing a steady flow of soldiers along their gangplanks, Farnfield gave the order for *Defender* to be moored for refuelling to the east of the two ships they had escorted all the way from Alexandria.

Rom took the opportunity to step down onto the quayside and feel the novel sensation of solid ground beneath his feet. His fingers occasionally moved backwards and forwards to his mouth to reach for a phantom cigarette he was not allowed to smoke during refuelling.

'Heading straight back out then?' a voice asked from the nearby wall, where a single soldier was sitting, cleaning his rifle meditatively. The voice sounded familiar, but when Rom turned he didn't recognise the face. Rom realised the impression of familiarity had been caused purely by the accent, which seemed to have the soft intonations of the Mersey in it, much like his own.

'We're here overnight and straight back out to Alex in the morning,' Rom said.

'Lucky swine,' the other soldier grinned. 'What I'd do to be getting out of this hellhole of a city right now.'

'Is it that bad?'

The soldier nodded grimly. 'It's getting worse by the day.'

'That sounds like a familiar accent,' Rom said.

'So does yours.' The soldier laughed a little. 'We Scousers get everywhere, don't we?'

Rom smiled and held out a hand. 'Rom,' he said.

'Ernest,' the soldier replied, shaking the proffered hand firmly. 'Good to meet you.'

'Likewise.'

Rom looked towards the dull, distant sound of mortar fire that seemed to be coming from the featureless expanses that stretched beyond the urban sprawl of the city. He caught sight of an aircraft moving along the coast further to the east and watched as it turned and moved back in the direction from which it had come. 'One of theirs?' Rom asked.

Ernest glanced towards the plane and seemed undaunted. 'It's just a spotter plane. They're coming over all the time.'

Two figures appeared in the distance along the quayside. Rom could tell by the distinctive silhouettes of their headgear that one was a British soldier and the other an Australian.

'Come on, lad!' the British silhouette called out. 'Stop chatting up the sailors.'

There was a little flurry of laughter from the Australian.

Ernest waved. 'Just coming, Sarge,' he called, as he stood and shouldered his rifle. 'Good to meet you, Rom. Good luck out there,' he added with a glance towards the sea.

'Good luck in here,' Rom said. 'See you round, pal.'

Ernest gave a slight nod and a smile by way of goodbye, before walking along the quayside towards his friends. Rom turned back towards the distant sound of heavy weapons that echoed through the urban landscape with an ominous rumble that made the hairs on the back of his neck stand on end, before he returned swiftly back up the gangplank.

By Sunday morning, they were back at Piraeus, preparing to take another convoy across to Alexandria. The monotony was broken only by the fact that it was Easter Sunday, so Captain Farnfield led a brief service on the deck, with all the ratings and officers standing to attention while they listened to a Bible reading about Christ's resurrection. Rom thought of all the men he had seen killed in the past year, who had gone to watery graves, and considered the promise of eternal life being made, echoing down to him through two thousand years. He thought particularly of his old pal Chubby, who now seemed so reluctant to accept death as an end. He gave an involuntary shiver, still unsure whether Chubby's own resurrection had been a trick of his battle-addled brain or something more. Had he really come back? Would he see him again?

Farnfield continued reading from 1 Corinthians, his words almost swept away by the Cretan breeze: *'But now is Christ risen from the dead, and become the first fruits of them that slept. For since by man came death, by man came also the resurrection of the dead. For as in Adam all die, even so in Christ shall all be made alive.'*

Rom thought of the Liverpudlian soldier he had met in Tobruk. What would become of him in this war in which lives were thrown into a great global tombola? He thought of his mother back home and her close call with death deep beneath the waves of the Mersey in a screech of brakes and metal striking metal. And what of his father and brother on their merchant ships? Would any of them live to see the end of this conflict, or would they too join *"them that slept"*?

He shivered once more and was glad when Farnfield finally closed his Bible and put aside the trappings of Easter Sunday to allow the crew to get back to their positions and return to the rather more practical business of escorting the convoy out to Alexandria.

After weeks of monotonous convoys backwards and forwards across the Mediterranean, the action came swiftly when it arrived. First came a gathering of the battle fleet off Malta. *Defender* was somewhat late to the party, having fouled her mooring buoy. It had been a frustrating couple of hours, as the crew worked to untangle the rope from the propeller.

'Makes us look like a bunch of buffoons,' Farnfield raged as he paced the deck, watching the untangling operation. 'Prop wrap might be an accepted annoyance on a little launch, but on a damned destroyer, it's nothing short of negligence.'

He blamed himself for the error, and even after the rope was untangled and the destroyer was speeding across the sea towards the massing battle fleet, his deep frown betrayed his own embarrassment.

The battle fleet was circling and swaying around off Malta for much of the next day, as the powers-that-be awaited the optimum moment to strike with the planned bombardment of Tripoli. HMS *Defender* would only be a bit-part actor in this great drama — that was clear from the outset. But their role set back from the main battle struck Rom as a small mercy once the fleet edged into position off the coast of italy's North African colony of Libya. The big guns finally began to burst into life and even a couple of miles back from the action, Rom was struck by the unleashing of hell that the opening salvos brought.

'Dear God,' he muttered. 'That's quite a firework display.'

Farnfield grinned as he continued to gaze through his binoculars in the darkness towards the "front line" of HMS *Warspite*, HMS *Barham*, HMS *Valiant* and HMS *Gloucester*, which were bombarding Tripoli at a range of 11,000-14,000 yards. Between this front line and HMS *Defender*, a second line of destroyers was providing a screen in the form of HMS *Jervis*, HMS *Jaguar*, HMS *Janus*, HMS *Juno*, HMS *Hasty*, HMS *Havock*, HMS *Hereward*, HMS *Hero* and HMS *Hotspur*. A "big day for the Hs and Js" as Farnfield had quipped.

The submarine HMS *Truant* was serving as a navigational beacon during the approach, and aircraft from HMS *Formidable* provided illumination of the target area by dropping flares. The night was clear but after a few minutes of firing, the rising dust and smoke from the distant city made it difficult to see the results of the bombardment.

A few times the distant harbour glowed with a hellish upsurge of flame as a fuel tank was hit, and Rom could only imagine how many Italian ships moored in the harbour must be caught up in the onslaught. The city took a full twenty-five minutes of being battered by the big guns of the Royal Navy's battleships, before the Italians managed to get themselves organised enough to activate a coastal defence battery and open returning fire. But even then, their feeble defence proved toothless.

The battle fleet finally turned and departed the scene intact and headed northeast as one unit travelling at their maximum speed.

The following evening, the fleet briefly came under attack by two JU-88s, but Fulmars from HMS *Formidable* quickly put paid to the attack and sent the two enemy aircraft spiralling down into the glistening waters. As the fleet departed for Alexandria, *Defender* peeled away to head back to Tobruk once more.

It was briefly back to regular convoy duties for the ship, but within days word came through that Operation Demon was getting underway — the evacuation of British forces from Greece — and *Defender* was sent to the Kalamata region to protect the troopships that were steaming in to get the cornered British soldiers out.

Defender moored alongside at Kalamata, with the troopships on the quayside ahead of them gradually filling with the lines of weary-looking soldiers. Rom waited with Captain Farnfield on the deck to welcome a group of Greek diplomats, accompanied by a small guard of armed Royal Marines. The diplomats wore dark sunglasses that hid their eyes and carried a series of cases, which Rom and a group of young ratings were charged with taking straight to the captain's cabin. The cases were stored in the corner of the cabin, with a guard placed as sentry on the door.

'What the hell is it, sir?' one of the cheerful young ratings asked Rom.

'It's the Yugoslav crown jewels,' Rom whispered. 'But keep that to yourself.'

'You're kidding me, sir?'

'Would I do that?' Rom shrugged. 'We've been charged with transporting them to Alex — keep them out of the Germans' hands.'

'Jeepers creepers,' the young rating whispered, wide-eyed. 'Now I understand the armed guard.'

Rom gave him a wink and tapped his nose in a "keep mum" gesture, and the youngster returned to his less glamorous duties on deck.

*

The jewels were still in the captain's cabin and Rom was back on the bridge of *Defender* when disaster struck the following day. He was watching the transport ship SS *Costa Rica* cutting its way efficiently through the Sea of Crete as the convoy formed up when the German dive bombers appeared like shadows overhead. He watched as two bombs dropped through the blue skies towards the ship. They seemed almost to glide for a moment, before dropping like a pair of hunting cormorants. They contacted the edge of the ship's hull and blew an almighty hole in her side, just above the waterline.

Farnfield cried out for somebody to get a damage report from the bridge of the *Costa Rica*, before bellowing his next manoeuvre down to the quartermaster. 'We could be required to get men off that ship quickly,' he muttered, examining the blast site through his binoculars.

Moments later a report came back from the damaged vessel. Its captain seemed confident she could be towed safely back into the harbour. 'It's blown a hole in its engine room and Number Four hold,' Rom recounted across the bridge to the captain, with the radio handset against his ear.

'Very well, we can try to take her in tow,' Farnfield said calmly and set about the operation.

The slightly better-equipped HMS *Hero*, which had been alongside throughout, was quickly chosen to lead the towing mission, but just moments after the towing line was in place and the destroyer began to pull the troopship in its wake, *Costa Rica* started to take on more water. It became a race against time to get the men off the sinking ship.

HMS *Defender*, HMS *Hereward*, the cruiser HMS *Phoebe* and the now untethered HMS *Hero* worked frantically, taking turns to come up alongside the stricken ship and allow men to leap across onto the decks of the destroyers. Miraculously, not a single man was lost, and Rom was left panting on the quarterdeck, unable to conceive how they had managed to achieve such an operation without a single fatality, when the troopship gave the groan of its final death throes, before listing perilously to port. Another moment passed as Rom, the crew of *Defender* and the scores of rescued troops gazed down at the grim sight of the proud transport ship slipping gracefully beneath the crystalline waves.

Rom made his way back to the bridge, pushing through the crowd of soldiers, feeling deep down that something truly remarkable had just been achieved.

Even without the daily vomiting and alarming twisting and turning of her emotions, it had been long enough now for Charlotte to know that she was pregnant. A new life was forming deep inside her body. She felt sick at the thought that it might not be Rom's baby. She held a hand to her still-unswollen belly as she lay in her bed, watching the spring breeze fluttering the curtain in the morning hush of Easter Sunday.

Her eyes darted from one side of the ceiling to the other as she thought through her options. "Honesty is the best policy" — that was what her mother always said. But was she right? Could unburdening herself be an unconscionable cruelty for Rom?

'Poor, dear Rom,' she whispered into the empty room, and the tears came again. She folded her body and turned her face into the pillow with a deep, shoulder-heaving sob.

The following evening, Charlotte heard bombs overhead, peppering the city, as she approached the relative safety of the bunker-like Western Approaches HQ. She remembered what she had been told when she'd first arrived there earlier in the year — that the whole city could be flattened above them and they would remain unscathed deep in the reinforced network of corridors, offices and telegraphy rooms. The chasm of the operation room was the most protected part of the whole complex. She knew she couldn't be in a safer place, but still the regular booms and dull thuds around them left her hands shaking as she stood on the wooden ladder and moved the plotting markers on the great map of the North Atlantic.

It was all she needed, Charlotte thought, given everything she was already going through. She descended the ladder and stepped back towards the desk, with the cacophony getting worse overhead.

'Sounds like they're tearing something down,' Jack Walters said with a reassuring smile. 'Probably a gable end left standing perilously after an impact. Don't worry, they'll get everywhere all tidied up by the time we get back up top. Everyone's just getting on with their own job. It's marvellous, really, when you think about it. All we need to do down here is to get on with ours.' He placed a hand gently on Charlotte's wrist and somehow it stopped her hands shaking. 'Don't worry, my dear,' he added, with a glance up at the reinforced ceiling. 'This place is as safe as houses.'

Charlotte nodded and laughed a little, conscious of the dark irony of the expression, given what was actually happening to houses across the city. 'Thank you, sir. I'll be fine,' she said.

'Good girl.' Walters gave her a paternal pat on the shoulder before walking back off towards his own desk.

When Charlotte finally did emerge from the HQ at the end of her shift, a sombre dawn was breaking across the city. The clean-up operation was well and truly underway, with activity everywhere she looked, and fire crews still hosing down the charred wreckage of office buildings all around. She was winded for a moment by the sheer shock of seeing the city centre utterly transformed from the one she had left behind when she'd descended into the basement of Derby House the night before.

The Liverpool Corn Exchange had been completely destroyed, replaced by a steaming pile of rubble. Brokers and merchants were conducting their business in the street, promising each other that detailed paperwork would follow at the first opportunity. There was almost a jollity to them — manic amid this new wasteland. She turned a corner and saw a row of bodies lying motionless beneath grey woollen blankets, and an Army lorry parked alongside, with two soldiers gradually working to stretcher the corpses up into the vehicle with little ceremony. She looked away and walked swiftly towards the station, uncertain if trains would be running but desperate to get to the safety of her own home.

The attack was similar to those that Eileen had seen before — destructive and frightening, with some loss of life around the city, but the bombers really ramped up their campaign the next night, shortly after Eileen had begun her shift behind the wheel of the ambulance. A swarm of bombers began dropping their deadly loads at around 10.45pm and the bombardment went on with little pause for four hours solid.

It was immediately clear that the Germans were targeting the docks. The Dock Board and White Star Buildings were again set on fire, but the administrative office of the diocese of Liverpool was also gutted. The biggest shock was the peppering of bombs across the district of Bootle to the north of the city, where whole streets were flattened and two hundred people were rendered homeless in a single night.

Much of Eileen's shift was spent in this part of the city, helping rescue teams to pull the most severely injured from the rubble and rush them to the city's frantically over-burdened hospitals. Then she would return back to the same streets to help, knowing that more critically injured people would have been dragged from the wreckage in the time they were away. Their ambulance was one of many that scurried around the city like busy ants on that cold May night.

At the end of their shift, Eileen and May stood beside their ambulance with cups of tea and cigarettes in their hands. After witnessing another night of horrors, they were both at breaking point and needed to talk about all they had seen before returning to their homes. Another two-woman Red Cross ambulance crew joined them. Janie and Betty were also at the end of a long night. One of the women from the second crew was crying as she recalled the things she had seen.

'St Andrew's Hall in Bootle, a Rest Centre, was hit by a high-explosive bomb,' she said bitterly. 'A Rest Centre, for Christ's sake. The entire team of WVS workers were killed. We pulled twelve of them out of the rubble. All dead.'

Eileen nodded sympathetically. 'It's the worst night yet. The Town Hall was hit, and the gasworks. You can imagine how that went up.'

Even as they spoke, a nearby air-raid siren cranked into life and within moments the women could hear the distinctive rumble of bombers overhead. Eileen looked across at the row of parked ambulances standing outside Mill Road Infirmary. 'Should we get to the shelter?' she asked May.

May looked up towards the cloudy skies, listening as the rumble got louder and louder. 'Yes,' she said. 'Let's go.'

All four women threw down their mugs of tea on to the grass verge and began to rush towards the shelter on the far side of the hospital. But a moment later, the distinctive whistle from overhead filled their ears, then the first blast struck, rocking the entire hospital in an explosion of light and noise.

The women tumbled together into a ditch that marked the outer edge of the hospital grounds. They piled on top of each other amid the mud and nettles, consumed by a smell of stagnant water and earth. But a moment later a cacophony of explosions came almost as one — with a blast that whistled above the ditch, sending rubble and sheets of corrugated metal flying through the air high above them. The explosions couldn't have lasted for more than six seconds, but for Eileen, down there in the water-soaked ditch, it felt like a lifetime. Then, all went quiet.

The women lay still in the ditch for a moment more, before Eileen spoke. 'Is everybody all right?'

'Yes,' May said, retrieving her thick-rimmed spectacles from the mud and wiping them on her clothing.

The other two women uncurled their bodies from the tangle and nodded, breathing deep, slow, deliberate breaths as they worked to regain their composure.

Eileen climbed out of the ditch first and was met by a scene of devastation. It looked like one whole wing of the hospital had been hit directly, and many of the ambulances that were lined up at the side of the building were on fire, the flames licking up heavenward, reaching almost as high as the main hospital building.

Flurries of nurses, doctors and patients were emerging from the main entrance of the hospital, people helping each other to get to safety however they could. There were people carrying each other's drips, or walking with their arms around another's back to offer them support in their fragile state. Nurses and doctors were helping patients, but equally, there were patients helping the nurses and doctors. It was like a tableau depicting the very best of human nature, set against the burning fires of this new hell.

'Come on, ladies,' Eileen said firmly, turning to help the other three women to clamber out of the ditch. 'It looks like our shift isn't going to end just yet after all.'

There could not have been a worse moment for the SS *John Holt* to steam back into the mouth of the River Mersey. As the ship turned sharply to port and allowed the incoming tide to spin her around to face the Gladstone Dock, the city reared up in the cold light of morning — a scene of utter devastation. Smoke rose at intervals in great plumes and met in an ominous black cloud that hung over the entire city centre.

As the ship approached the docks, Remmie could see a variety of fire engines speeding along the dock road beyond the Alexandra Dock, each clearly marked with the insignia and names of different regional brigades — Scunthorpe, York, Wakefield, West Hartlepool, Derby, Doncaster, Huddersfield and Leicester. Liverpool was alight and it appeared that most of England's firemen were rushing to dampen down the blaze.

None of the crew of the *John Holt* said a word. They just stood side by side on the deck and gazed out across their home city, each of them feeling the same pitiful sensation — that the end had come, and they were witnessing the final destruction of all they loved and cherished.

Once they were up alongside, Captain Cecil Gordon Hime stepped away from the bridge and joined his men on the deck. Hime was a thoughtful character, tall, almost gangly, and with a worry-wrinkled face and grey beard that made him look far older than his years. He too stood for a while in silence, before finally speaking in a voice that was loud enough to ensure that all the men gathered on the deck would hear him. 'The good news is that there is hardly any wind. The fire brigade should get control over the fires without them whipping up into a fire storm.'

'Thank heaven for small mercies, sir,' Chief Engineer Stanley Clensy agreed.

'Liverpool will rise again, men,' Hime said, puffing out his chest a little as he looked out across the city. There was something distinctly Shakespearean in his bearing.

Remmie wondered whether the old captain had a history of amateur dramatics in happier times.

'You can be certain of that, men — Liverpool will rise again. A phoenix from the flames. Stronger, bigger and better than before. Remember the old city's motto: *Deus Nobis Haec Otia Fecit. God has granted us this ease.* This city is our God-given endowment, and it will not be taken by force as long as the Liver Birds are standing strong. This city is mine by right. This city is each of yours by right. And this city is for all of our children and our children's children, by God-given right.'

Hime allowed the men a moment to look out across the city in silence. 'When we turned into the dock a moment ago, do you know what I did? I took a look through my binoculars. Do you know what I saw?'

The gathered crew members looked up at him, wide-eyed, and shook their heads.

'I saw the Liver Birds up on the domes of the Royal Liver Building,' Hime said. 'Still standing. Still strong. So, all our work can wait for a few moments while we give thanks.' Hime cleared his throat and began to sing in a deep baritone.

Remmie was surprised by the tears in his eyes. Gradually the captain's voice was joined by those of the other officers, then the chief engineer, and then all the crew were singing as one towards the ravaged city below: '*Eternal Father, strong to save, Whose arm hath bound the restless wave, Who bid'st the mighty ocean deep, Its own appointed limits keep; O hear us when we cry to Thee, For those in peril on the sea.*'

A group of dockers who had gathered on the quayside to begin the business of unloading the ship's cargo removed their caps and lowered their heads in solemn observance of the scene.

CHAPTER TEN

Amid the crystalline waters of the Mediterranean, the bridge of HMS *Defender* was bustling with activity. With German paratroopers landing in force, Crete had fallen swiftly, albeit with heavy losses to the Axis forces as they stormed the island from the skies. The Mediterranean Fleet was quickly called in to begin the rapid withdrawal of British troops from the Cretan ports of Heraklion and Sphakia, but HMS *Defender* had played only minimal parts in these operations — the usual frustrating distant screening patrols. But now they had been charged with delivering vital supplies of ammunition from Alexandria to the troops defending the retreat at Suda Bay. For once, Rom felt as if he was at the heart of the action.

As *Defender* came alongside at the quay in Suda Bay, Rom could see the rising smoke of battle high on the island's rocky hillsides, just a few miles away. It was a stunningly beautiful natural harbour, with shallow waters that sparkled like sapphire. The ammunition was busily unloaded and transferred under the beady eye of an imposing British Army captain, who stood on the harbour directing operations, occasionally giving out a series of clipped orders, his hands clasped calmly behind his back.

Rom stood on the portside wing of the bridge, removed from the operation, but taking in the spectacle, and conscious of the distant booms echoing around the hills.

'It's rather good to be doing something solid for once, isn't it?' Farnfield muttered as he joined him in the bright Cretan sunlight.

'I'd say so, sir,' Rom agreed. 'It's the first time in a long time that it's felt like we've made a positive contribution to this damned war, if you'll forgive me for saying so. No offence meant.'

Farnfield laughed a little bitterly. 'None taken, Hutchinson,' he said. 'I know exactly what you mean. All these damned patrols and screening operations can leave a chap feeling a little out of the action. But it's all an important contribution, nonetheless. Sometimes you have to accept your role as a simple cog in a much larger machine.'

Rom nodded. 'Yes, I suppose so, sir.'

Another explosion rumbled across the bay from a nearby hillside. Both men flinched briefly, before swiftly recovering their composure.

'Still,' Rom added, 'it is good to see some action.'

'Don't wish it on us too readily, Hutchinson — too much action can be a rather dangerous thing in a war.' Farnfield cast his eyes up towards the blue skies and the distant rumble of an aircraft. 'Come on then, Lieutenant, the sooner we can get in and out of this place, the better.'

It had been weeks since Remmie had been in Lagos. But the city stretched out ahead of him, reassuringly familiar in the shimmering light of dawn, as the SS *John Holt* slipped noiselessly into the shelter of the lagoon. They passed Ogogoro Island with its scrappy lines of waving palms and its thin skirt of dirty sand, before beginning the steady turn into the harbour. By the time they were up alongside the quay, a heat haze was already rising across the city's dusty network of streets and the sounds of the day were emerging — the barking of stray dogs, the rumble of lorries on the dock road.

Across the lagoon Remmie could see the distinctive boxy outline of the still incomplete Cathedral Church of Christ — a ramshackle section of scaffolding marking the place where work was theoretically continuing on the building, nearly seventy-five years after the foundation stone had been set. Remmie had visited the cathedral on one of his previous visits to the port. He had found the dark wooden pews of the choir stalls and the muted colours of the stained-glass windows curiously reminiscent of home — a little island of Anglicanism in the midst of this distant, sprawling continent.

Just like at home, the dockers were already waiting on the quay, eager to set to work on stripping the ship of her cargo. Within a couple of hours, Remmie and many of his fellow deckhands had been dismissed for their precious few hours of shore leave, while the dock workers took on the burden of the unloading and reloading of the hold. He walked alone through the crumbling backstreets, heading straight for Joseph's Bar — the place that had become a home away from home.

Despite the early hour of the morning, he knew it would be open and food would be being served. God willing, it would be being served by Adanna. He told himself that he must not appear too keen. The girl may not even remember him. After all, he had only had anything like a proper conversation with her on the one occasion. How many ruddy-faced English sailors must she have served since then? He thought about the smooth outline of her face, her beaming eyes and her springy curls enclosed within her colourful headscarf.

He quickened his pace at the thought of being close to her. But turning the final corner, he was greeted by a sight that made his stomach drop. Where the bar had stood was now a charred pile of rubble and soot-stained timbers. A few of the outer walls were still standing, but it was clear that the bar had fallen victim to some unimaginable violence. Given all that was happening back home, his first thought was that the place must have been destroyed in a bombing raid. But he quickly told himself that there was no aerial bombing in Lagos — no Luftwaffe bombers to shadow these tropical skies.

He moved a little closer and stopped at what would have been the front door, but was now a drunken heap of concrete and bricks. The inside walls — those that were left standing — had been coloured an inky black by smoke and the place had a pungent smell. A breeze fluttered the ash as Remmie gazed at the scene, uncertain of his next move.

'They did quite a job with it, eh?' a croaky voice muttered.

Remmie turned to see a frail old man leaning on a stick, his wrinkled face made concave by the absence of teeth.

'What happened?' Remmie asked.

The old man raised a palm, as if to indicate that he knew nothing.

'Who did this?'

'I dunno. Old Joe had some enemies, that's for sure. Could have been any one of the gangs.'

'Gangs?'

'He owed a lot of people money.' The old man sighed. 'He was a bad gambler, was old Joe.'

'What happened to Joseph? What happened to his family?' Remmie demanded.

'Poor old Joe and his wife were both killed in the fire,' the old man said. 'It was the middle of the night. I guess they wouldn't have known a damned thing about it. There was so much smoke, you see. So much smoke, you wouldn't have been able to breathe in there.'

'What about Adanna?' Remmie felt sick. He almost didn't want to hear what her fate had been.

The old man gave him a quizzical look.

'Adanna — their daughter.'

'Oh, their daughter.' The old man nodded. 'She's a beautiful girl.'

'Is she alive?'

'Yes, I think she got out. Her and that niece of Joe's, Ayotunde. They both got out. It was them that raised the alarm. Then the niece ran back in to try to wake up the rest of the family. Then, crash!' He made a queer little shadow puppet show with his fingers. 'Them walls came a-tumblin' down. She was a brave girl, Ayotunde, but she didn't stand a chance. She must have been crushed beneath the roof beams, see?'

Remmie gazed at the scene. 'But Adanna survived?'

The old man nodded.

'Where is she?'

'She left, I guess. If I was Adanna, I wouldn't hang around here, having seen what her father's enemies were prepared to do. You can only imagine what they might do to her now she's all alone.' The old man raised his eyebrows suggestively.

Remmie's cheeks flushed. He felt a wave of anxiety crash through him. 'I need to find her,' he said firmly.

Finding Adanna was easier than Remmie had imagined. The moment the old man left him, shuffling off towards a nearby house, Remmie heard a whimpering coming from the scrubland beside the burnt-out remains of the bar. He knew even before he approached the bushes that Adanna was hiding behind them. But she looked more wretched than he could ever have imagined. Her resplendent beauty, her unblemished perfection, was crumpled and cowed, as she crouched behind the bush, clinging to her scuffed knees. Her eyes were red with tears, her face caked in soot stains and dried blood. Her once bright dress and floral headscarf were gone. She wore only a muddied night gown, torn around the hemline. She slowly raised her head towards Remmie and for a moment seemed not to know him. But then recognition made her eyes sparkle, and she twisted herself up and in a single, desperate movement threw herself into Remmie's arms, sobbing deeply into his shoulder.

'They killed them all, Remmie!' she groaned. 'They burnt us out and killed everyone. My whole family is gone!' For a moment the sobs overtook her speech, and her breathing quickened.

Remmie rubbed comfortingly at her bare shoulders and made quiet, reassuring comments, which eventually calmed her enough to allow her to speak again.

'I'm alone, Remmie, all alone,' she gasped. 'What am I going to do?'

'No, you're not,' Remmie said, taking Adanna's face in his hands and looking into her eyes. 'You're not alone. I'm here.' He embraced her once again and she wept into his chest.

When she was finally able to speak, she looked up at him. 'You're here now, Remmie, but you won't be here long. When the ship blows its horn, you'll be away back to the port and swept thousands of miles away.'

Remmie held her gaze. 'I'm not going anywhere. Not until we've got you sorted with somewhere to stay — somewhere safe.'

'Nowhere is safe.' Adanna shook her head and looked despondently towards the floor. 'My father had many enemies. They will find me and God knows what they will do to me.'

'What more can they do to you?' Remmie raised his voice in exasperation. 'They've burnt down your home. They've killed your mother and father and your cousin. They've wiped out your entire family — what more can they take from you?'

'They would take my honour,' Adanna said. 'Then they would take my life.'

They were both silent for a long time, before Remmie spoke. 'Why would they do this?'

'My father fought his way up. He fought to own this place. The gangs rule here in Lagos. You don't understand. My father wouldn't join any of them. He wanted to go it alone. None of the gangsters liked that. They told him that if he didn't pay for their protection, he would be at risk from the other gangs. Then they said if he didn't pay, he would be at risk from them too. They left him with no choice but to pay. But when he did pay, they wanted more and more, until there was no money left. So, they did this anyway. He gave them everything he had worked for and they still burnt down his bar. They still killed him.'

'We need to go to the police.'

Adanna gave a bitter little laugh. 'The police! They are in the palms of the gangs too, Remmie. We can't go to the police. Not here. The police aren't interested.'

'This is the British Empire, Adanna. I'll take it to the Colonial Office. I'll go to the Governor General himself, if I have to.'

Adanna laughed at Remmie — her face flickering into a sad smile for the first time. 'You silly sailor,' she whispered, reaching up and stroking Remmie's cheek. 'The Colonial Office isn't interested in helping a young African girl like me.'

'I'll do something,' Remmie insisted, desperation edging into his voice. 'I'll do something to get things sorted out for you.'

Adanna reached up and kissed his lips. Their eyes met for a long moment.

'Stay here,' Remmie said, launching himself into action. 'I'm going to get you something to eat and some water. Then I'm going to go and speak with the captain. He'll know what to do.'

He left Adanna in her hiding place in the scrubland with some food and drink, then ran back towards the port. Captain Hime, who had been on the deck, had spotted him running along the quayside and met him at the top of the gangplank, concerned by the young deckhand's frightened eyes.

'What is it, Hutchinson?' Hime asked. 'Whatever has happened?'

'It's a girl, a local girl, Adanna, sir,'

Hime sighed theatrically, raising his eyes to the heavens, and began to walk away. 'What have I told you about fraternising with the natives, Hutchinson?'

'No, you don't understand, sir,' Remmie called after him. 'There was a gang and they burnt down the bar her father ran. They killed her family — all of them. Now she is all alone and living on the streets. I dread to imagine what will happen to her. I don't know what to do, sir. I've got to help her.'

Hime turned on his heel. 'You don't *have* to help anybody, Hutchinson,' he said sharply. 'If we start doling out charity at every port, where would that leave us? We're just here to bring in the goods and take out the goods. The local affairs are, well, they're their own affairs.'

'You don't understand, sir,' Remmie insisted. 'She's not just any girl. I'm in love with her, sir.'

'Stop this foolishness at once,' Hime hissed at him, his temper flaring. 'Get to your cabin and have a wash and shave, for God's sake. She's not your concern. You can't fall in love with every whore you bed.'

'She's not a whore, sir, and I've not bedded her!' Remmie raised his voice at Hime's back as he walked away across the deck, but the captain did not respond. Without another word, Remmie turned and ran back down the gangplank and disappeared into the streets of the city.

When the SS *John Holt* repeatedly blew an angry horn that evening, Remmie was lying in the scrubland with Adanna clutching at his chest. He ignored the sound echoing up from the harbour and closed his eyes on the descending African night.

The following morning, Remmie held Adanna closely in the surprising chill of first light. He could feel her breathing steadily within his embrace. When she awoke, he fetched more food and water from the nearest shop and sat with her, breaking a loaf into pieces and picking at it between them. He handed her a leather purse, which contained all the cash he had — a combination of sterling and US dollars that served his needs in most ports. 'Take it,' he said. 'You're going to need to rent somewhere — a room, perhaps, something small and cheap. But it's a start. With a room, you can get clean. There should be enough left over to buy a new dress. Then a pretty girl like you will soon find yourself a job. There are plenty of bars out there that will be looking for serving staff. Or a shop, maybe. You could serve behind a counter in a shop as well as anyone.'

Adanna nodded and took the purse from him, smiling gratefully. 'I'll pay every penny back to you, just as soon as I can,' she said.

'You don't need to worry about that. I just need to know you're safe.'

She nodded. 'I will be with this. I'll get somewhere to sleep, God willing. But what about you, Remmie? You'll be in such trouble. Your ship has sailed.'

Remmie shrugged. 'Any punishment they give me will be worth it, knowing you're going to be all right. I've also put a scrap of paper in that purse with my home address on it, back in Liverpool. When you find somewhere to live, send me your new address, then I can send you more. Do you understand?'

She leaned towards him, her lips meeting his, and they submitted wordlessly to their rising passions.

The sight of the SS *Robert Holt* standing proudly at the mooring that her sister ship had departed just two days before made panic rise in Remmie's chest. 'Oh, dear God, the old man's here,' he muttered, making a mental note to keep clear of the port.

He headed to a down-at-heel bar on the far side of town. He knew the landlord vaguely and thought he might be open to offering Adanna work. After all, she had years of experience of serving behind her father's bar. The formerly cheerful publican, however, dismissed the idea with a wide-eyed shake of the head.

'No way,' the man said, leaning away from Remmie as if he might somehow be contagious. 'There's no work for that girl here. I'm not getting involved. No way.'

Remmie turned away from the bar in disgust, but as he walked towards the light of the doorway, he noticed a man in a merchant navy officer's uniform sitting with a drink in the darkness. The man eyed him carefully, making Remmie feel particularly uneasy. All the way back to Adanna, he sensed he was being followed but was never quite able to catch sight of the man from the bar in the crowd. Perhaps it was simply his imagination, he told himself.

But within the hour, it became clear that he had been followed back to the scrubland. A more familiar figure appeared — tall and imposing in the uniform of a ship's captain, white beard glinting in the evening light. William Hutchinson gazed down at Remmie lying beside Adanna. Without saying a word, he reached down and grabbed his son by the scruff of his neck. He dragged him through the streets of Lagos, back towards the port, where he pulled him kicking and screaming up the gangplank of the SS *Robert Holt*.

'If you're going to make a fool out of me, I'll make a fool out of you!' William Hutchinson roared, as he finally released Remmie from his grip in the safety of his own cabin. He turned the lock on the door behind him and took a seat at his desk. 'What on earth do you think you're doing, Remmie? I got a message through from the John Holt company head office to say my son had jumped ship at my next port of call, and would I mind finding him and bringing him back? My own son! Do you know how humiliating that is for me?'

'I'm sorry, Father, but you don't understand,' Remmie said.

'Oh, I do understand. I saw that girl you were lying with up there in the scrubland like an animal. I understand well enough what you've been up to.'

'It's not like that, Father, not at all,' Remmie protested. 'I love Adanna.'

William Hutchinson laughed harshly. 'You love her, do you?'

'A gang killed her parents and burnt down her home and now I'm all she has in the world.'

'Well, Remmie lad, you can discount yourself from that equation,' his father said, with a glance at the clock. 'Because in roughly fifteen minutes, the SS *Robert Holt* will be sailing and you can start considering what tale you'll be telling the misconduct board when you get back to Liverpool.'

A quarter of an hour later, the ship was untethered and its great engines burst into life deep below Remmie's feet. She rumbled away from the quayside and turned towards the open sea.

Charlotte decided that directness was the only option when it came to dealing with her mother. She made them both a cup of tea and took a seat opposite her at the kitchen table, where her mother was peeling potatoes.

'I'm having a baby, Mother,' Charlotte said, as she placed the two mugs of tea down on the table.

The older woman paused midway through her task, a spiral of potato skin hanging limply. She stood still for a long moment, as if frozen in time.

'I've spoken with Polly, who I work with, and we're going to set ourselves up with a little flat in the city centre — just the two of us. It'll be so much easier for getting into work, and she's in a horrible little bedsit at the moment in Bootle,' Charlotte went on. 'I knew you'd want me out of the house, at least once it starts showing, so it would probably suit everyone, wouldn't it?'

After what seemed to Charlotte like an eternity, her mother blinked, as if waking from a trance, and returned to her work, her eyes turning down towards the potato in her hands.

'Yes, dear, that would be best for everyone, wouldn't it?' her mother muttered, before dropping the peeled potato into the bowl. She carried on peeling in silence for some time, before finally speaking. 'It's Romulus Hutchinson's child, I suppose,' she said, as she picked up another potato and sliced into it with the knife.

Charlotte picked off a miniscule piece of fluff from her clothing and brushed her fingers together.

'I'm assuming he will marry you?' her mother went on, without making eye contact with her daughter.

'I don't know, Mother. I've not told him.'

Her mother looked up at Charlotte's face for the first time. 'Well, don't you think you ought to let him know what he's done?'

'I'll wait until he's next home,' Charlotte whispered, her bravery suddenly ebbing. 'It's not the kind of thing you can put in a letter.'

Her mother paused. 'Thank goodness your father is dead and buried and didn't have to hear of this,' she said, tightening her lips.

CHAPTER ELEVEN

HMS *Defender* cut an elegant V-shape through the still waters of the Mediterranean, pointing towards the Lebanese coast, which was marked out as a straight, flat line on the horizon. Captain Farnfield replaced the radio receiver and walked across the bridge towards the officers standing beside the chart table.

Rom looked up. 'Everything quite all right, sir?'

'It's more than all right, Hutchinson,' Farnfield muttered. 'That was Commander Biggs on HMS *Hero*, passing on the news that the Home Fleet sank the *Bismarck*.'

'They've done what?' Rom asked incredulously.

'They've taken out the bloody *Bismarck*.'

'Dear God,' First Lieutenant Johnson whispered. 'How the hell did they manage that?'

'She was an absolute leviathan of a battleship,' Farnfield said. 'I had the misfortune of seeing her once, and she put the fear of God into me.'

'How the hell did they manage it?' Rom said, repeating the first lieutenant's question.

'The Admiralty was determined to get its revenge for the sinking of HMS *Hood*,' Farnfield said. 'I suppose it was just down to pure bloody determination.'

The officers burst into a flurry of cheers and back-slapping celebrations.

'Surely, this changes everything doesn't it, sir?' Rom asked excitedly. 'If we can take out *Bismarck*, we might even start winning some battles in this damned war.'

'Maybe, Hutchinson, maybe. God knows we've all spent long enough on the back-foot, evacuating our chaps from every damned corner of Europe. It feels rather good to give the Jerries a bloody nose for once, doesn't it?'

'I'd say, sir,' Rom, said beaming. 'I only wish we'd been part of the Home Fleet for that particular job rather than being tied to the humdrum of these damned Med convoys.'

Farnfield slapped Rom on the shoulder affectionately. 'You're always looking for more action, aren't you, lad? You'll learn, as you grow a bit older and wiser, that the best thing is to keep out of trouble if you can, not to go dashing into it.'

Rom grinned. 'You sound just like my father, sir.'

The captain nodded. 'I bet I do, Hutchinson. I bet I do.'

Rom was on the bridge as HMS *Defender* escorted another convoy towards Tobruk. Shadowing them on the far side of the convoy, the Australian destroyer HMAS *Waterhen* looked almost like their mirror image. Older even than *Defender*, *Waterhen* was a veritable museum piece — launched close to the end of the last war, and looking a little rough around the edges, she still cut a fine figure against the Mediterranean sparkle.

Rom had grown fond of his Australian counterparts. They were a comical bunch, seeming to take life far less seriously than anyone he served alongside on *Defender*. So it came as something of a jolt — like watching a good friend being punched in the face — when a pair of Italian Picchiatello dive bombers, JU-87 Stukas in all but name, appeared in the blue skies overhead and began their ominous descent towards *Waterhen*, like angry wasps defending a nest. The anti-aircraft gunners on both destroyers had barely fired off a single round when the bombs were released, igniting a demonic fireball across the deck of the Australian ship.

The aircraft turned and made a second approach, this time turning their attentions to *Defender*. Rom looked up and to his horror, realised the two aircraft had been joined by a dozen more. 'Dear God,' he muttered. 'There's a whole swarm of them.'

'Right full rudder!' Farnfield cried down to the quartermaster, sending the ship lurching violently beneath them. The officers on the bridge battled to keep their footing, but by the time they had steadied themselves, it was clear the evasive action had been successful and the two bombs destined for *Defender*'s decks splashed harmlessly into the sea.

The planes circled immediately back, and this time the two lead planes plunged once again towards the already damaged Australian ship. When the smoke cleared, a gaping wound was revealed that ran across the deck and the upper half of the hull amidships, almost meeting the waterline. It was impossible to say at first if it was the sort of wound a ship of *Waterhen*'s size could survive, or whether she would be on the seabed within minutes.

The Italians clearly thought they had done enough for the moment, as Rom caught a sight of the two leading planes turning away to the north, their wings glinting in the sunlight. They banked in close formation and headed towards the dozen-strong swarm of aircraft that had already departed the scene amid the chaos of the anti-aircraft guns finally clattering into a useful defence.

HMS *Defender* was manoeuvred delicately alongside the damaged destroyer, leaving the convoy to steam on towards Tobruk. Farnfield had a brief radio conversation with his opposite number on the Australian vessel.

'The final attack brought damage to their engine room, the engineer's cabin and the central store,' he explained as he put down the radio receiver and took his place back at the middle of the bridge. 'Lieutenant Commander Swain has made the decision to abandon ship, so we will come alongside to remove everyone on board.'

Rom was one of the officers sent to oversee the successful evacuation of the stricken ship, rescuing seventy soldiers that had been aboard as passengers heading for Tobruk, as well as the ship's surviving crew members. The Australian captain remained onboard with a small crew to oversee a towing operation, as a line was placed between the two destroyers.

'Christ only knows if it'll work,' Swain called across to the deck of HMS *Defender*. 'But it's about the only chance we've got of saving her now. Aren't they a right bunch of bastards?'

'They certainly are, Lieutenant Commander,' Rom called back, before adding with a glint in his eye, 'Shall we see if we can get her back to Mersa Matruh then, sir?'

'Fingers bloody crossed,' Swain agreed.

Rom dashed back to the bridge. Farnfield gave the order and the engines deep beneath them growled as the towing line tightened and *Defender* attempted to drag her fellow destroyer to safety. Rom stood on the wing of the bridge, his binoculars raised to his eyes.

'I'm not sure it's looking good, sir,' he reported sheepishly. 'She's taking on far more water, even at this speed.'

Farnfield attempted to slow down the towing, but it seemed to make no difference to the wake that was bubbling up and entering the void now running along the waterline of *Waterhen*'s hull. Farnfield stood alongside Rom on the starboard wing and raised his own glasses. A moment later, they could see Captain Swain moving to the wing of his own bridge. He looked equally gloomy. Farnfield radioed his opposite number.

'I'm afraid this isn't going to work, is it?' Farnfield said down the line.

Rom could hear the Australian groaning through the radio, as he looked across the glistening waters, the evening sun bathing the death throes of the Australian ship in a warm orange glow.

'Jesus,' the Australian captain said on the radio. 'She's going to go down, isn't she?'

Rom took the glasses away from his face and nodded sombrely.

'I'm afraid so, old boy,' Farnfield muttered into the receiver.

'You'd better get us off and uncouple her, Captain,' Swain said with a sigh. 'Before she drags *Defender* down with her.'

Moments later, Swain and the towing crew were removed and the stricken ship was uncoupled. Swain made his way up to *Defender*'s bridge, where Farnfield gave his fellow captain a commiserating handshake.

'It's good to get you all safely aboard,' Farnfield said.

'Thank you for your hospitality, Captain,' Swain said with a sad smile.

The two captains watched as *Waterhen* slowly slipped into the sea. She held on longer than anyone had imagined, and it was almost two o'clock in the morning before she gave her final groan and slipped beneath the waves.

Although the eyes of the Wren plotting officers were on the floor-to-ceiling map of the Atlantic and its intricately laced lines of convoys, all chatter was focused on the east, where the Germans had launched an ambitious invasion force heading towards Moscow and the defending Soviets had formally joined the war on the Allied side.

'It'll change everything,' Duty Commander Jack Walters said pensively, standing with his arms crossed and his eyes looking over the progress of the ships on the map.

'Were the Russians on the Germans' side before, though, sir?' Polly asked, with a confused frown.

'Don't forget they invaded Poland from the east back in thirty-nine in coordination with the Germans invading from the West. But I think the relationship might be what you would call an uneasy peace. The Russians must have known that Hitler's attention would turn further east in due course.'

'So, what's going to happen?' Polly asked, as if Walters had all the answers. 'How will it change the war for us?'

'Well, that all depends,' Walters said, rubbing the shadow of stubble that had appeared across his cheeks after a long night shift. 'If the Germans take the Soviet Union successfully, the power of the Third Reich becomes immense. Then we just have to hope that the Yanks come in on our side. But I wouldn't jump to any conclusions too quickly. Even Napoleon had his eastern advance halted by the Russian winter, and perhaps our boys' defence of Greece slowed down the Jerries and forced them to delay their Soviet invasion. Perhaps it was long enough for winter to play her part once again. All the same, it'll hopefully take Liverpool out of the Luftwaffe's target sights for a while.'

'Well, that would certainly be good news,' Charlotte said, as she stepped back down from the wooden ladder serving the Atlantic map and gazed up to take in the progress she had charted with her latest pinpoints. 'I'm not sure how much more of a battering this city can take.'

Polly eyed Charlotte, who was standing with her right hand supporting her back. 'Are you feeling all right?'

'Why wouldn't she be?' Walters frowned and turned to Charlotte. 'You're not feeling ill, are you?'

'No, I'm fine,' Charlotte said. 'I just twisted a muscle earlier, trying to reach Iceland.'

'Good,' Walters said. 'We can't afford any of you ladies getting ill right now.'

He walked back towards his desk and Charlotte frowned across at Polly.

'Don't look at me like that,' Polly whispered. 'I didn't say anything out of place. Anyway, you've got to be nice to me, now we're roommates.'

Charlotte reached out and gave Polly's arm an apologetic squeeze. 'I'm just terrified of them finding out.'

Polly grinned down towards Charlotte's already burgeoning bump. 'Well, they're going to find out soon enough. But it's not Walters you need to worry about. You could be nine months pregnant, and he wouldn't notice. It's old Nan Currie who'll spot it first.' She flicked her eyes towards the dour-faced superintendent who was seated at her desk with her spectacles perched on her nose, working through a document with pinched precision.

'Honestly, Poll, I don't know what I'm going to do,' Charlotte said, her voice quavering with rising emotion.

Polly put her hand on Charlotte's back and gave it a reassuring rub. 'Let's just take it one day at a time.'

Charlotte nodded, anxiety etched across her face.

Remmie walked down the steps of the John Holt & Co. headquarters building and paused to light a cigarette, cupping his hand around it against the sharp breeze gusting up from the river. He had been docked a full month's pay, which would hurt, but all in all, he couldn't help but feel he had got off fairly lightly. Some of the stories he had heard about punishments for merchant navy deserters who had jumped ship were extraordinarily draconian. But they were often in place to dull the allure of adopting a new life in New Zealand or Australia. As the chairman of the misconduct board had told him a few minutes earlier, you'd have to be mad to jump ship in Lagos in search of a better life. Remmie was fairly sure the appearance of his own father as a witness against him ironically played in his favour. The board could see from his father's irate, brooding presence that Remmie had probably already been punished enough in the family home.

'Let's just put the whole thing down to a temporary moment of insanity, brought on by the excessive heat and the dark eyes of a sultry native,' the chairman had said to him, with a not unkind smile, even while his own father could be heard muttering, 'He's a damned disgrace,' under his breath.

Well, that's the easy part over with, Remmie thought to himself as he took a long draw on his cigarette and turned down Water Street towards the river. *Now there's the small issue of the captain.*

The SS *John Holt* seemed to loom menacingly when he arrived at Gladstone Dock. It was still being loaded, with flat-capped dockers craning the bundled cargo from the quayside into the hold. Remmie sauntered nervously up the gangplank and headed to Captain Hime's cabin. He knocked on the door and waited for a response. It was just like being back at school, waiting outside the headmaster's office. After what seemed like an interminable pause, Hime finally responded with a muffled, 'Come in!'

Remmie opened the door and stepped inside.

'Ah, Romeo, Romeo, wherefore art thou Romeo?' Hime quipped at the sight of Remmie, cap in hand and eyes turned shamefacedly towards the deck.

'I wanted to apologise, Captain,' Remmie muttered. 'What I did was wrong. That's been made very clear to me by the misconduct board and my father. But I wanted to say that I did what I did for all the right reasons.'

Hime put down his pen and sat back in his chair, his eyebrows raised, as if keen to hear Remmie's explanation for abandoning his post and allowing the ship to sail without him. 'You're not going to tell me you're in love with one of the locals again, are you, lad?'

'No, sir,' Remmie said. 'But it strikes me that if this war teaches us anything, it's that there really is evil in the world. And if there's a force of evil, then there must be a force for good, or what hope is there? I was just desperate to do the right thing by Adanna, Captain. I wanted to do some good.'

Hime got to his feet and walked towards the porthole as he stuffed tobacco from a pouch into a pipe, pushing it down with dextrous fingers, before searching his pockets for his lighter. 'What you need to learn, Hutchinson,' he said at last, 'is that in a war like this — a battle between good and evil, as you put it — none of us are capable of achieving anything alone. One young man trying to "do good" in a world of a million miseries is about as much use as an ashtray on a motorbike. Do you understand what I'm telling you?'

'I do, sir.'

'So, there'll be no similar nonsense of this kind in the future, Hutchinson?' Hime asked, lighting the barrel of his pipe and releasing a pungent cloud into the cabin. 'I mean, if I allow you shore leave again in the future, you're not going to make a fool of me by jumping ship again, are you?'

'You can trust me, sir,' Remmie said. 'Quite apart from anything else, my father would kill me with his bare hands if I put another foot wrong.'

Hime took the pipe from his mouth and laughed. 'Good old Bill Hutchinson, that's what I say! An iron fist in a velvet glove, and all that, what!'

'You can say that again, sir,' Remmie said. 'I've never been so glad to get away from a ship as I was to get away from the *Robert Holt* with my father at the helm.'

'If it's any consolation, I've just heard that your father is being relocated away from the *Robert Holt*.'

'Again?' Remmie said. 'What's he being given?'

'I'm really not sure you'll believe me.'

'Try me, sir,' Remmie said.

'He's being given command of the SS *Remus II* — it's a step up in the world for him, but quite a coincidence, eh?'

'It certainly is, sir,' Remmie said, with his hand to his brow. 'He won't take his mind off me, now he's commanding my namesake.'

Hime walked around his desk and placed a reassuring hand on Remmie's shoulder. 'Well, don't let me or your father down again, young man, and let's just put this one down to experience, shall we?'

Remmie nodded. 'Thank you, sir.'

'Thank you, Hutchinson. Now, go and report to the bosun, there's a good chap.'

Remmie replaced his headgear, stood to attention and saluted, before leaving the cabin. He closed the door behind him and paused to let out a deep breath as his anxiety eased. He walked out onto the deck and looked across the river. He would keep his nose clean, he thought to himself, but Adanna was now his only real care in the world. Every penny he could save would be sent out to her. This damned war couldn't last forever, and one day, he told himself, he would be free to walk through the streets of Lagos and then Liverpool with Adanna on his arm. 'One day, Adanna,' he whispered, 'one day.'

Remmie walked gloomily along the main deck of the SS *John Holt* as she manoeuvred her way back out of the Mersey and into Liverpool Bay towards the Irish Sea — a landscape of grey water set against grey sky. He would work for the next month with no pay, unable to send anything to Adanna to support her while she looked for work. He only hoped the cash he had given her would be enough to keep her safe for now.

Even when he did have spare money, he wouldn't be able to send anything to her until she wrote to him with her new address. With the current voyage skipping Lagos to call at Port Harcourt and Douala, before returning to Liverpool, it would be weeks before he would even get back home to find any letters she sent.

The chief engineer was walking along the deck towards him with a grin and a cigarette hanging from his lower lip. 'So you saw fit to rejoin us, Hutchinson?' Clensy said.

'Yes, Chief,' Remmie said.

'I'm guessing you've already had a decent earbashing,' Clensy went on, taking his cigarette from his lips. 'So all I'll say is, I hope you won't be so bloody stupid as to do anything like that again.'

'I won't, Chief,' Remmie muttered, but Clensy was already walking on along the deck towards the engine room.

Remmie continued along the deck and found Scaggs, who was plucking at his banjo in a corner of the fo'c's'le.

'Fancy a go?' Scaggs said, offering him the instrument.

Remmie took it and began to pluck at the strings, the sea breeze lifting his fringe as he concentrated on his playing. He gradually started picking out a tune that Scaggs had been teaching him before he'd jumped ship.

'"Cripple Creek,"' Scaggs said. 'That's one of my favourites.'

Remmie nodded but was concentrating too hard to speak.

'You know,' Scaggs went on after a while, 'I think you're playing better.'

'Do you reckon?' Remmie said, lifting his face towards his friend and stopping his performance.

'Definitely,' Scaggs mused. 'They do say you need a few heartbreaks before you can play the banjo with any real passion.'

'Is that right?'

Scaggs nodded. 'It can be a surprisingly sensitive instrument. People think it's all plucky little jigs, but some of the banjo ballads would break your heart.'

'Go on then,' Remmie said, handing the instrument back to him. 'Break my heart.'

'All right,' Scaggs said, rubbing at the stubble on his cheek. 'This one is an old Irish folk song.' He began to pick out the tune on the strings.

Remmie listened, wide-eyed. It might have been the most mournful song he had ever heard. He got to his feet and looked out towards the Irish Sea, feeling tears welling in his eyes. Perhaps it was the music, perhaps it was the sombre ashen skies hanging overhead, or perhaps it was the unrelenting greyness of the sea itself, but in that moment Remmie somehow felt more desolate than he had ever been. What was to become of him now, he wondered? What was to become of any of them?

He wiped at his eyes with the heel of his hand and tried to ignore the unnerving sense of foreboding that was coursing through his veins.

CHAPTER TWELVE

Rom was standing in his usual place on the bridge of HMS *Defender*. He was in good spirits. The sun was shining and the ship was cutting neatly through the sparkling sea, with another Australian destroyer at her side — HMAS *Vendetta*. Together, they made for quite a spectacle as they moved north, leaving Tobruk behind in their wake.

The sun was low in the western skies, giving the scene an almost unreal glow. Rom moved out onto the starboard wing and breathed in deeply. He closed his eyes and thought of Charlotte back home. He wondered when he would next see her as he pictured them lying together in the sand dunes of Formby. He opened his eyes and looked towards the *Vendetta*. She was a handsome ship. Then he noticed it — high above the *Vendetta*'s quarterdeck, an aircraft appeared.

Rom turned back towards Farnfield, who was standing at the centre of the bridge. 'This might be Jerry on a reconnaissance flight, sir.'

Farnfield looked up and frowned. He collected his binoculars and strode over to the starboard wing alongside Rom. 'It certainly looks like it,' he said, directing his binoculars towards the distant speck, which seemed to be rapidly growing. Rom could hear the throb of the aircraft's engines as it approached. 'It's a JU-88, German, not Italian. Right, come on then, Lieutenant,' the captain went on. 'Raise our friends on *Vendetta* and warn them of the threat.'

'Yes, sir.'

Farnfield turned to the chief armourer. 'Let's be ready to give her back a little of her own medicine, should she get much closer.'

'*Vendetta* is readying for action, sir,' Rom said, replacing the radio receiver.

Farnfield walked back to his place at the middle of the bridge and lifted his binoculars again. 'She's headed straight for *Vendetta*,' he said. 'Last thing we need is to lose another of our Australian destroyers.'

But at that moment, the aeroplane changed its course. Twisting in the skies like a snake on a stick, it began its dive — but it was not heading for *Vendetta*. It was looming immediately towards *Defender*.

'Tell them to fire at will as soon as the damned thing is within range,' Farnfield muttered.

The chief armourer relayed the message down a voicepipe. A moment later, the gunners' fingers connected with their triggers, sending sparkling reels of bullets skyward.

'Right full rudder!' Farnfield shouted down to the quartermaster.

The ship lunged. But the German pilot seemed unperturbed, continuing his steep dive like a guillemot. Time seemed to slow for a moment, then sped up once again. The plane suddenly loomed large and Rom watched, eyes wide with horror, as it released its deadly load.

The pilot began to pull up sharply, dancing the plane between the threads of anti-aircraft ordinance. But the bomb continued to fall resolutely towards *Defender*'s starboard side, where it met the ship's steel hull just above the waterline, close to the engine room. The violent shudder of the ship, the roar of the explosion and the flash of brilliant light all seemed to arrive at once, sending Rom and the other officers on the bridge tumbling.

Rom managed to clamber back to his feet just in time to see the attacking plane turn and bank back, as if to inspect the damage to the ship, before turning to the north and moving away with what Rom could have sworn was a little celebratory wiggle of its wings.

'God damn you to hell,' Rom growled as he watched it go. He moved back towards the starboard wing and could see a thick plume of black smoke barrelling skywards from the middle of the ship.

The first lieutenant was already at the voicepipe and relaying a damage report from the chief engineer. 'The engine room is flooding rapidly, but there are no known casualties!' he shouted across to the captain.

'Well, that's something,' Farnfield muttered. 'It sounds like the shock has broken the ship's back.' He reached for the radio and began to speak to his opposite number on *Vendetta*. 'I'm afraid this time we will be the ones requiring the tow,' he said into the receiver.

It was, indeed, Rom thought, an uncanny replay of the attack on HMAS *Waterhen*. The same procedure was followed, with Farnfield and a skeleton crew remaining aboard to oversee the tow, while the majority of the crew, including Rom, were ordered across to the safety of the Australian destroyer.

Rom watched *Defender* lumbering in the water, his hands shaking with delayed shock. He reached into his pocket for a cigarette to calm his nerves. It was all depressingly familiar. He held absolutely no hope that the tow would be successful. As far as he was concerned, it was now just a matter of waiting for *Defender* to succumb to the waves.

For a few hours, they tried to save her. She didn't barrel over and slip away as peacefully as *Waterhen* had done. But the ship's superstructure was breaking up with every attempt to move her. Even though the idea of towing her back to port had to be quickly abandoned and Farnfield and the skeleton crew were brought onto *Vendetta*, it appeared that the mortally wounded British destroyer wouldn't go down without a fight.

It was now well past the middle of the night, and soon the dawn would appear and light the sea around them, revealing the distant landscape where Egypt met Libya on the horizon and increasing their vulnerability to another aerial attack. All the officers gathered on the bridge of *Vendetta* were growing nervous, feeling like sitting ducks in the drifting vessel.

'I think you know what needs to be done, Captain,' Farnfield said to his opposite number.

The Australian captain nodded. 'I believe so,' he said quietly, before turning to his own chief armourer. 'Mr Ramsay, could you prepare the torpedoes, please?'

'Aye aye, sir,' a burly Australian officer barked back.

Rom and the crews of both ships watched the macabre performance in bitter silence as poor *Defender* felt the full force of the friendly torpedoes.

As dawn finally broke, with nothing remaining of HMS *Defender* except a few bubbles still shimmering the surface of the sea, HMAS *Vendetta* turned and headed back for Tobruk.

Rom returned to Britain as a passenger on an almost empty troopship. She had delivered hundreds of fighting men to Tobruk and was returning through the Straits of Gibraltar, up the coast of Portugal and across the increasingly treacherous Bay of Biscay with a few injured men aboard who were being invalided back to Blighty. Rom knew that he, too, was being invalided back. The rest of the crew of HMS *Defender* had been redistributed among Royal Navy vessels serving in the Mediterranean Fleet. But Rom was different — having already served time in a psychiatric institution following a previous sinking, the Admiralty seemed keen for him to be brought home for a proper period of rest and recuperation, before undergoing yet another "assessment".

He was seething with anger about the whole thing. It had been almost a year since he had taken to sleeping outdoors on the deck for fear that his cabin walls were closing in on him, and he felt almost entirely recovered from all that. Now only very occasionally did he get a momentary hit of that suffocating panic that had once so nearly consumed him. He never admitted to anyone that he still felt any such anxiety, so why the hell couldn't they just treat him like all the other officers and put him straight onto another destroyer in the Med?

Still, there would be some benefits, he acknowledged to himself as he walked across the empty deck of the ship and thought about spending time with Charlotte once again. It had been four months since he had been with her last, in the sand dunes of Formby.

When he did step back onto British soil two days later, it was at the gloomy docks of Southampton — with a long day of further travelling ahead of him on the railways. It was nearly midnight when he finally got back to the achingly familiar front door of his childhood home. His knocks produced no response, so he had to scrabble around in the bottom of his kit bag to find his house key. He let himself in and found the house dark and empty. His mother must be working a night shift on those damned ambulances, he thought, before heading into the kitchen and finding some bread and cheese.

As he ate the last crumbs from his plate, he looked down at his distinctive twin-faced wristwatch. There was no point waiting up for his mother — she might not be home until the next morning. He wearily climbed the stairs — how small they seemed now — and threw himself onto his childhood bed. He fell asleep, still fully clothed, within moments.

Rom awoke to the sight of his mother placing a mug of tea on his bedside table. She looked completely different in her Red Cross uniform — not like his mother at all. Younger, somehow.

'Welcome home, Rom,' she said, perching on the edge of the bed. 'I'm sorry I wasn't home when you got here last night. What are you doing sleeping in your uniform?'

'I was too tired to get undressed,' he said, as he sat up in bed and reached for his tea. 'You're looking pretty exhausted yourself, Mother.'

'Three weeks of night shifts,' she said with a shrug. 'Somebody has to do it. Now listen, give me half an hour. I'm going to see what I can get out of that miserable old butcher on the high street and I'll be back to cook up some breakfast.'

'Thanks, Mother,' Rom said, snuggling back down onto his pillow. 'That would be fabulous. I could eat a horse.'

Eileen laughed. 'Careful what you wish for. I've seen what that butcher dishes out. You might end up getting it.'

An hour later, Rom had eaten his sausages gratefully without a second thought for whether the meat in them was porcine, bovine or equine.

'How long are you home for?' Eileen asked.

'Not long, I don't think. They just want to assess me again — check I'm fighting fit, before they assign me another ship.

I'm up before the medical board on Friday, and I reckon I'll get my orders a few days after that.'

'So, I've got you home for a week or so then?' she said. 'And if I'm on the night shift, it means I'll actually get to see a bit of you each day.'

'Don't forget you need to sleep yourself, Mother,' Rom said. 'But don't worry, I'll occupy myself.'

'No doubt,' she said, removing Rom's plate and carrying it to the sink. 'Maybe you could catch up with Charlotte too, while you are home.'

'Maybe,' Rom said nonchalantly, as if he hadn't considered it. 'I might wander over there this morning, see if she's at home.'

'Good idea,' Eileen said.

The sun was shining on his unform, making him sweat a little around the collar, as Rom strode eagerly across Crosby towards Charlotte's home. He stood outside the front door for a moment and straightened his blue jacket, took a deep breath — he had been away for so long, he felt strangely nervous — then knocked on the door. For a long time, there was no reply. He knocked again and caught the flicker of an upstairs curtain. On the third knock, the upstairs bedroom window opened a little and Charlotte's mother appeared in the gap. She stared down at him, looking strangely cautious.

'Hello, Mrs B!' Rom said, lifting his cap in greeting. 'I'm home! For a while, anyway. Is Charlotte at work?'

'I don't know where Charlotte is,' she snapped, looking uncharacteristically sour-faced.

Rom was taken aback. He replaced his cap, wondering if there had been some sort of falling-out between Charlotte and her mother. 'I would like to see her — I might only be home for a few days.'

'Aye, well, you can do a lot of damage in just a few days. We know that much from experience.'

Rom gazed at the woman in bemusement. 'Have I done something wrong?'

'That's between you and your conscience, isn't it?' Charlotte's mother muttered, pulling her cardigan tightly around her.

'Have I done something to upset you, Mrs Burton?'

'You'll not find Charlotte here, so you can stop your knocking. She's moved into a flat with one of the other Wrens.' She shut the window with a brusque slam.

'What the hell's got into her?' Rom said, before retracing his steps back across Crosby.

He walked down to the beach, uncertain what his next move should be. He had only been walking for moments along the wet sand, his heavy uniform jacket swung over his shoulder, when Charlotte appeared from out of the heat haze. She was wearing a long green cardigan, despite the warmth of the day. She was looking out to sea wistfully, smoke rising from her cigarette to create a little patch of fog around her head.

'You look as if you're waiting for a sailor,' Rom said as he approached.

Charlotte turned with alarm. 'You're here? I was just thinking about you — and you're actually here!'

'Sometimes you have to be careful what you wish for, Charlotte.' Rom grinned. 'But thank God I've found you. I've just called at your house and your mother seems to have it in for me, for some reason.'

'I'm living with Polly. We've got a little flat above a pub on Dale Street — The Mitre. It's handy for work. I can almost fall out of bed and be at the ops room.'

'Did you have a falling-out with your mother then?'

Charlotte turned back towards him and nodded. She untied the cord on her long cardigan and revealed the first hint of a bump. 'It's complicated, Rom,' she said, her green eyes glistening.

Rom stood and stared for a long moment. 'We're having a baby?' he said at last, dropping his jacket onto the sand.

Charlotte raised her cigarette and took another calming draw. 'Would that be a good thing or a bad thing?'

'Jesus, Charlotte. Are we having a baby?'

'Like I said —' she turned back towards the sea, her hair fluttering in the breeze — 'it's a bit complicated.'

'Complicated how?' A smile crept across Rom's face. 'We're going to have a baby. A baby, Charlotte!'

'Oh, Rom.' Charlotte sighed.

'Don't worry,' he stammered, taking her left hand, while she lifted the cigarette away from him in her right. 'You don't need to worry, Charlotte. I'll do the right thing. We'll get married. We can get married tomorrow, if you want. Whenever you're ready. I know we're young, but it'll be fine. We'll be all right.'

'Oh, do shut up for a moment, Rom,' Charlotte muttered, turning away from him and biting nervously at her lip.

'What is it? What's wrong?'

'You're not listening to me,' she said, turning sharply to face him once again. 'Why aren't you listening to me? I said it's complicated.'

'How?'

'I don't know,' she said, her voice quavering as her eyes caught his, 'whether you're the father.'

They stood silently for a moment, the breeze dancing invisibly around them. Rom looked at the sand and then directed his stare back towards Charlotte. 'There have been other men?'

'Hear me out, please,' Charlotte said, as Rom turned to pick up his jacket. 'There was a man — one of the senior officers at work,' she began, but he was already walking away. 'Rom, I need to tell you what happened!' she called after him.

But he marched back up the beach, his back turned to the coast.

After the tedious, drawn-out calls at Port Harcourt and Douala, where the dockers had taken forever to unload and reload the ship, Remmie had faced up to the final indignity — a return to Liverpool without any shore leave. He had stood on the deck, looking out at the most recent bomb damage to the fringes of Gladstone Dock, and seethed quietly. But now it felt as if his fortunes were shifting, as the SS *John Holt* moved out of the river into Liverpool Bay, on its way once again to Lagos. If he kept his nose clean for the next week, there was just a chance, he told himself, that the captain might allow him to go ashore at Lagos, even if it was just for a few hours.

He put his back into his work, scrubbing the decks with a renewed vigour, and even volunteering for some of the more laborious tasks and unfavourable watches. Eventually Able Seaman Freddie Miller, the ship's new bosun, who had recently replaced Anderson, got the idea. He was considerably more accommodating than his predecessor would have been.

'All right, all right, Hutchinson, don't kill yourself,' he said, laughing. 'I'll have a word with the captain. Tell him you're a new man and see if we can get your revoked shore leave back.'

'Thanks, Bosun,' Remmie said, beaming. 'That would be great. I'd just like to see my pals in Lagos, even if it's just for an hour or so.'

'Aye, we were none of us born yesterday, Hutchinson,' the older seaman laughed. 'We all know who you're wanting to catch up with. Just make sure you're not catching anything else from her while you're at it.'

Remmie turned his eyes back to the deck he was scrubbing.

Lagos was limbering itself in the early morning light, like a stretching cat recently woken from her slumber. Remmie stood on deck as the *John Holt* slipped into the lagoon and moved silently towards the main harbour. After days at sea, the sight of the city never failed to give him a flutter of excitement. But he had never felt it so profoundly. He could barely contain himself as he waited to come alongside. With permission to take a few hours of shore leave, he would finally be getting to see his beloved.

But first, he had to find her. Instinctively, he walked to the site of the now derelict ruins of her father's bar. It had barely changed since he was last there. But there was no sign of Adanna. He slipped across to the patch of scrubland where he had last been with her, weeks before. But again, he was met only by her absence. Stepping back towards the road, he saw the old man in the house opposite. Remmie approached him.

'You looking for my beautiful neighbour, again?' the old man said.

'Yes, I'm trying to find Adanna,' Remmie replied, his hand raised to his forehead to block out the glare of the morning sun. 'I don't suppose you know where she's living?'

'No, I don't know,' the old man said. Remmie nodded and started to walk away. 'But I do know where she's working.'

Within half an hour, Remmie had got himself across the city to Oyingbo Market. Crowds of shoppers shuffled through every conceivable space, housewives stopping to examine the fruits and vegetables that were laid out in pots and piled up on blankets around the traders — mostly women, seated on the ground or squatting, before taking people's cash in their outstretched hands.

As well as the housewives, the central thoroughfares of the market were crowded with clusters of men, who seemed to be standing around, chatting and joking with acquaintances, swinging strings of beads absentmindedly as they mingled.

'How in God's name will I find her among this lot?' Remmie muttered to himself. He leaned down towards one of the traders and attempted to describe Adanna. But the woman just shook her head and shrugged her shoulders. The next trader gave him an identical response. After a while, he gave up asking and set about simply wandering the aisles of the outdoor market, keeping his eyes peeled for Adanna.

He glanced at his double-faced watch. He couldn't afford to be late back to the ship again. After a while, every young woman began to trick his eyes for a moment, with facial features morphing into brief flashes of Adanna.

Remmie was close to giving up the search when he finally spotted her. She was handing two mangoes to a robust-looking housewife. 'Thank God,' Remmie muttered, and slipped between the shoppers to reach Adanna's stall.

He stood for a moment in front of the stall before Adanna noticed him.

'Well, I do have to admire your mangoes,' Remmie said cheekily.

Adanna looked up and her face was transformed by a beaming smile. 'You're back!' she shrieked, rising to her feet.

'It's so good to see you. I've thought of nothing else for weeks. And you've got a job,' Remmie said, smiling back at her almost as broadly.

'Yes, it doesn't pay much, but with the money you gave me, I was able to rent a room, like you said. I have a home, Remmie!'

'That's fantastic. You're a fighter, Adanna — a real fighter!'

'Well, it was more luck than anything, getting the job. I managed to convince one of the stallholders on the other side of the market that she would make twice as much money if she split her stock across two pitches. So even though she's paying me to run it, she's still in profit. Everyone wins!'

'That doesn't sound like luck,' Remmie said. 'That sounds like you've been pretty smart.'

Adanna turned her dark eyes to the ground with a bashful flicker. 'Or maybe someone was on my side. That's how it felt,' she said. Her eyes turned back to his. 'I feel my father's presence. He's with me all the time. Does that sound crazy?'

'No, it doesn't sound crazy at all,' Remmie said. He rested a hand against Adanna's face. Her eyes glistened with emotion.

'Not here,' she whispered, glancing nervously towards the traders. 'People will talk.'

'I needed to see you so much,' Remmie said.

'I know. I've longed to see you too, Remmie.' Adanna sighed. 'I finish at five o'clock. We can do something then. You can come to see my room.'

Remmie looked at his watch. 'I've only been given three hours of shore leave. I think the captain is afraid I might try to jump ship again.'

'I suppose that's understandable, given what happened. People are starting to look,' Adanna whispered anxiously.

'I'll buy a mango.'

Adanna laughed. 'Would you like to choose one?'

Remmie reached into his pocket and pulled out a pen. He handed it to Adanna, together with a mango from the pile. 'Write your address on it. I'll write to you. I'll send you more money as soon as I can. I would have sent more before now, but they stopped my wages as a punishment for jumping ship.'

'They didn't!' Adanna gasped. 'Oh, Remmie, I'm so sorry.' She took the pen and mango from him and began to write down her address. Handing them back, she added, 'But I can't take any more money from you.'

'Keep the pen,' he said. 'You can use it to write back to me. And you can take my money, and you must. I'm going to look after you, Adanna. Just like I promised I would.'

Tears welled in her big brown eyes once again. She held out her hand. 'You need to pretend to pay me for the mango or the other traders will notice.'

He reached into his pocket. 'I don't need to pretend. I will pay for my mango. But I only have British coins.' He handed her one.

'We can take British coins,' she said. 'But this is a sixpence. That's far too much for a mango.'

'You keep the change,' he said, closing her hand around the coin.

'I can't believe you're going away again,' Adanna said sadly. 'When will you be back?'

'Soon,' Remmie promised. 'We call at Lagos at least once a month.' He glanced again at his watch. 'I wish I could kiss you.'

'I wish I could kiss you too,' she whispered.

'Let's both close our eyes for a moment,' Remmie said, 'and pretend we have.'

Adanna and Remmie stood on either side of the pile of mangoes and closed their eyes for a few moments, then opened them with a smile.

'How was it for you?' Remmie grinned.

'Take care of yourself, my love,' Adanna said.

He looked down at the mango in his hand with the address scribbled across the skin in black ink. 'You too, my love,' he said and slipped reluctantly back into the crowd.

CHAPTER THIRTEEN

Rom couldn't sleep. While his mother was working her night shift in the ambulance, he lay alone in the house where he had spent his childhood, listening to the creaks of the timber frame, the whistle of the wind in the chimney, the rustle from the line of poplar trees at the end of the back garden. It all seemed so familiar, yet somehow it was diabolically different — a warped mirror-image of the world he had known until this moment. It was a world in which Charlotte had betrayed him.

He stared at the ceiling in the darkness and tried to comprehend what she had told him. The child might be his or it might not. It might be the offspring of another man altogether. An officer, he had heard her say as he had walked away.

He walked to the bathroom, splashed his face with cold water, and gazed at his features in the shaving mirror. This was the fool who had believed Charlotte was at home awaiting his return, while he was out there risking his life on the high seas. This was the fool who had loved her so wholeheartedly, the fool who had longed to return to her. He needed answers. Who was this damned usurper who had taken his love from him?

He returned to his bedroom, dressed quickly, and rushed out of the house, his mind in a turmoil. The first flicker of dawn was just beginning to paint the suburban skies as he walked through the deserted streets and found his way onto a double-decker bus alongside a group of bleary-eyed commuters.

The city rumbled past the window as Rom looked out, uncertain what he was really doing. The semi-detached houses morphed into endless ranks of redbrick terraces, like rows of dirty teeth, broken up by the occasional extraction, where a bombsite now stood — grim piles of dust and rubble where a home should have been.

Rom stepped down off the back of the bus in the city centre with a nod to the conductor. The city was still waking up, with a whistling street sweeper brushing around an apparently immovable air-raid warden, who was sitting on the steps of St George's Hall, turning his steel helmet in his hands. Rom turned the corner, passing the Central Library with its protective coat of piled sandbags and looked down towards the sprawling city and the river beyond. It was shocking to see the extent of the damage caused by the May Blitz on this part of Liverpool; whole blocks of the financial district had been almost entirely removed from the landscape.

He carried on down the hill to Dale Street, passing more bombsites, before eventually finding The Mitre. It was a modern-looking place — solid, with pale stonework and fancy Art Deco windows. He banged on the door, but it was locked and nobody appeared to be inside. He banged again, then took a step back towards the kerb and looked up at the windows. Without realising he was doing it, he heard his own voice bellowing up towards them: 'Charlotte! Charlotte! Come down here. I need to talk to you!'

After a moment one of the windows from the upper storey opened and a woman's head appeared — dishevelled, as if the occupant had been woken from her sleep. But it wasn't Charlotte. Then Rom realised he recognised the face — it was Polly, whom he had met briefly months before in Plymouth.

'Oh, it's lover boy,' Polly said, grinning down at him. 'Aren't you looking handsome, sailor? Sadly, though, it's not me that brings you here, is it?'

'Is Charlotte there?' Rom called up.

'She's on the night shift. Mind you, she'll be due home soon. If you wander down to Exchange Flags, you'll probably bump into her on the way.'

Rom gave a wave. 'Thanks, Polly.'

Rom walked down Dale Street and reached the Town Hall, which was also surrounded by a thick, protective wall of sandbags. He turned and walked around the outside of the building, to the courtyard known as Exchange Flags beyond, overlooked by the austere-looking Derby House. *So, this is where Western Approaches Command is based?* Rom thought to himself. He had previously only had a vague notion, but it was clear from the gaggle of Royal Navy officers walking up the steps and into Derby House that he had found the place.

Rom stopped on the far side of the courtyard and waited, pretending to struggle to light a cigarette, but keeping his eyes on the door of the building opposite. Then Charlotte appeared, not from the door, but from around the corner of the building. She was walking with an officer. Rom spotted the stripes of a Royal Navy Commander on the man's jacket.

They stopped and were exchanging words. It looked as if the man was whispering to Charlotte, a look of concern on his face. It was a remarkably ordinary face, Rom realised. He had expected his rival to be young and handsome, but this man was short, middle-aged, balding and wore wire-rimmed spectacles. Hardly a likely object of Charlotte's affections, Rom thought, taking a silent step back into the shadows.

He watched them for a moment longer, as the man placed his cap on his head and with a cheerful wave walked off in the direction of Castle Street. Charlotte walked across Exchange Flags in the direction of Dale Street. Rom surprised himself by following the man towards the Castle Street side of the Town Hall, leaving Charlotte to disappear around the other corner.

Rom continued to follow the little officer as he made his way along Castle Street — close enough to confirm his rank from his epaulettes. He was a commander — a very senior officer, and he was trailing him through the streets of the city like a detective following a lead. Rom didn't really have a plan. The man let himself into a building through a door in a courtyard just off Castle Street. It seemed to lead to half a dozen flats above the offices of an insurance company. Rom waited outside for him. Half an hour passed. An hour. He glanced at his watch. He couldn't wait there all day.

Rom walked into town and got something to eat in a little Lyons' Tea Cornerhouse. He remained in the busy I long after he had eaten, and then walked aimlessly around the streets of the city centre, trying to decide what to do. By the time he had made up his mind to confront the officer, evening was fast approaching and he realised he had passed the entire day in a troubled daze. He returned to the man's flat. When he was a few yards from the door, it opened and the man came out. He appeared to be in a hurry.

Rom followed him at a discreet distance. The man moved remarkably nimbly and Rom struggled to keep up as he cut his way through the crowd. He turned the corner on to James Street, just in time to see the man heading towards the station. Rom ran a few paces to catch up, and stood behind him in the box office queue — close enough to hear the destination he asked for through the grille. When he moved aside, pausing to put his wallet back into the inside pocket of his jacket, Rom stepped forward and repeated the man's request: 'A return to Hamilton Square, please.'

Rom kept his distance as best he could on the platform, getting on the underground train in the neighbouring carriage from the one the man had entered. The train rumbled into life, plunging into the darkness of the tunnel beneath the river. Rom took a seat and nervously played with the ticket in his fingers. After just a few minutes, the train pulled into the underground platform beneath Hamilton Square on the Birkenhead side of the Mersey.

Outside the station, the man approached the taxi rank. Rom hovered nearby and listened to the destination the man gave to the driver. He watched as the cab moved off towards the town centre, then approached the next cab in the rank. 'The Shrewsbury Arms, Oxton, please,' he told the driver, who put his cigarette to his lips, nodded and pulled away.

The pub was in a village on the very edge of the town. The cab moved uphill, away from the river, passing rows of redbrick terraces, pockmarked with the occasional bombsites like those he had seen in Liverpool. The cab pulled up ten minutes later in a leafy lane, beside a whitewashed pub. He paid the driver and climbed the steep steps that led into the bar. It was dark and musty, with a fire burning in the grate. He approached the bar and ordered a pint of beer, then chose his seat carefully, having spotted the officer he was trailing sitting in a quiet alcove nearby. He was drinking a little glass of whisky and Rom noticed that he had a second lined up. Then the door creaked open again and another Royal Navy commander strode in. The man pushed the second whisky across the table and the second commander accepted the drink.

Rom listened carefully to the conversation while sipping at his beer. They talked for a while about convoys. A successful Atlantic escort here, a less lucky one there. Then they talked about the weather for the month ahead, and for an inconceivably long time, they talked about how much they missed the test cricket. Then, much to Rom's confusion, they seemed to talk about a "beaver". He could only imagine it was some sort of codeword.

'Bad business about Beaver,' the taller officer seemed to say.

'Mansfield has me investigating the chap, despite his death. I suspect that more than one of the girls fell victim to him.'

'Bad business,' the taller man said again. 'Given that the chap is dead, who does it benefit to investigate it?'

'Well, my thought exactly,' the shorter man said. 'There is a bloody war on.'

After a while the taller man returned to the bar and ordered two more whiskies. More than an hour had passed when the first officer reached into his pocket and handed the second officer a document. 'Well, here it is, Whittle. Mansfield wanted me to hand it to you in person.'

'Good man,' Whittle said, receiving the folded document and putting it in his own jacket pocket. 'I'll fill it in as comprehensively as possible, but I hardly knew the chap. I'd only served with him for a short period last year. Six months at most.'

'Still, it all helps to build the bigger picture.'

Whittle nodded. 'Anyway, it's been good to catch up, Walters, old boy. It seems such a long time since I last saw you in Plymouth.'

'It must be two years since we shared a drink,' Walters said, shaking Whittle's hand. 'I'd better head off. I'm going to walk back down to Hamilton Square. The exercise will do me good.'

'There speaks a pen pusher, if ever I heard one,' Whittle said, laughing.

'I barely see the outside world these days,' Walters said, replacing his cap and giving his fellow officer a cheery wave before departing through the door.

Rom finished the last mouthful of his beer and followed him outside. He walked a few paces behind him before calling out, 'Commander Walters, is it?'

The man turned around. He looked surprised, but not unduly alarmed. He clearly recognised the outline of Rom's naval uniform.

'I'm sorry, dear boy, I can't quite recognise you in this damned blackout.'

There was a brief moment of silence, broken only by the rustling of the trees that lined the avenue, as the two men faced each other in the darkness.

'You don't know me, sir,' Rom said at last. He immediately regretted the respectful use of the word "sir" — it had slipped out automatically. 'But I have a sweetheart. I believe you know her. In fact, I suspect you have been screwing her, *sir*, while I have been out there putting my life on the line, doing the real work of the Royal Navy — taking on the enemy, being torpedoed by U-boats and attacked by dive bombers.'

Walters made an astonished little noise and then walked closer to Rom. He looked up at his face in the half light. 'I'm pleased to tell you, Lieutenant, that you are very much mistaken,' Walters hissed. 'And I'll thank you to remember who you're speaking to. Now, who the hell is this sweetheart of yours?'

'Charlotte Burton,' Rom said. 'And don't try to tell me you don't know her — I saw you both whispering sweet nothings to each other in Liverpool.'

Walters gave a mirthless little laugh. 'Now I understand,' he said. 'The pregnant girl?'

Rom felt his fists clench. It was all he could do to not swing a punch. If the man in front of him hadn't been a commander, he certainly would have hit him by now.

'It's complicated, she told me,' Rom said. 'Now I know why. The damned baby is yours, isn't it?'

'You've got hold of the wrong end of the stick, I'm afraid, young man,' Walters said. 'Now, calm yourself. You're going to have to take my word for one thing — I have had no involvement with your Charlotte. She's a dear girl, but I am a happily married man.'

In a moment of crippling embarrassment, Rom realised that the man was telling the truth. There was a clear honesty in his eyes. This was simply Charlotte's commanding officer that he was lambasting in the street.

'Without being too indelicate, Lieutenant, could the child be yours?'

Rom looked at the floor, feeling suddenly ashamed. 'Yes, it could be, sir. But she said something about an officer at headquarters.'

'Did she?' Walters said, suddenly more interested. 'Listen, you have a right to know. We are investigating a chap. We believe he may have been acting inappropriately with the Wrens. You shouldn't blame Charlotte.'

'What do you mean, I shouldn't blame Charlotte? Surely it takes two to tango?'

'Not always, I'm afraid, Lieutenant,' Walters said, with a shrug of his epaulettes. 'Not always.' He turned to walk away. Rom reached out and put a hand on his shoulder to stop him. 'Take your hands off me, son, or you'll be up before a court-martial. I've told you all I'm prepared to. I suggest you speak calmly to Charlotte herself. She's not at fault in any of this.'

*

Rom returned to Liverpool and found his way onto the Overhead Railway. He watched the docks passing by beneath the line in the darkness — ships silhouetted against the moonlight glistening on the silent river. He had never felt so bereft. Was the child his or another man's? Should he care? Couldn't he bring up another man's child as if it was his own? The questions raced through his mind.

Within a couple of hours, he was back on Dale Street, knocking at the side door to The Mitre. The door opened a little and Charlotte's face appeared in the gloom. She was still wearing her dressing gown and looked dishevelled, as if she hadn't had much sleep.

'It's you,' she said. 'Come in.'

He followed her up the drab staircase to the little flat. Polly was in full uniform, downing the last dregs of her cup of tea. 'Don't mind me, lover boy,' she said. 'I'm just on my way out.' She paused to give Charlotte a comforting touch on her forearm, then left.

'She's quite a character,' Rom said.

'Heart of gold,' Charlotte said. 'Do you want a cup of tea? There's some in the pot.'

'That would be nice.'

Charlotte moved into the little kitchen and started to clatter crockery.

'I thought we should talk about all of this,' Rom called through to her. 'I'm sorry about the other day. It was a lot to take in.'

'Tell me about it,' Charlotte said, as she returned in the doorway. 'This was the last thing I'd been planning.'

'How about you tell me about it?' Rom said, taking a seat at the little table as Charlotte placed the teacup down. 'Let's start with who the officer is. The man you had an affair with.'

Charlotte gave a bitter little laugh. 'I wouldn't call it an affair. I didn't have any choice in the matter.'

'What do you mean, no choice?'

'Christ, do I need to spell this out, Rom?' Charlotte ran her fingers through her hair. 'He raped me, Rom. Belvoir was a nasty, greasy little lieutenant who grabbed me in the corridor, pulled me into a cupboard and forced himself upon me. I had no choice.'

Rom got to his feet, the chair clattering to the floor behind him. 'I'll kill the bastard!' he hissed.

'You can't,' Charlotte said, leaning forward to place a calming hand on his.

'I bloody well can, and what's more, I damned well will!' Rom snarled.

'You can't kill him,' she said again. 'Because he's already dead.'

'Dead?' Rom repeated. He looked towards the open window, through which he could hear the noises of Dale Street waking up. 'He's dead?' He slowly picked up his chair and sat back down.

'He's dead,' Charlotte said firmly. 'Car crash in the blackout. The bastard got his comeuppance all right.'

'Dear God,' Rom said, reaching into his inside pocket for his cigarettes and lighter. He offered one to Charlotte, then gave her a light. He lit his own and took a long, slow draw on it, releasing a cloud of smoke that drifted up towards the ceiling as the implications of what had happened settled in his mind.

'God, I'm so sorry, Charlotte,' he said, rubbing his eyes wearily. 'Why didn't you tell me?'

'I didn't know how to tell anybody.'

'He attacked you just the once?'

Charlotte nodded.

'Well then, I think the child is unlikely to be his,' he said. 'And as far as I'm concerned, it's mine. We are having a baby. But you should tell your superiors about what happened to you.'

'I don't want to ever speak of it again,' she said, gazing at Rom through the smoke now hanging over the table. 'He's dead. What more can they do to him? No, you said it yourself, Rom — it never happened. We both need to forget about it.'

'Let's get married, Charlotte,' Rom said.

'I don't know,' she said. 'I don't want to get married because we feel forced to.'

'I don't feel forced. I wanted to marry you anyway,' he whispered, holding out a hand.

'Can I think about it?' Charlotte asked, getting to her feet.

'I'll probably be back on a ship next week. Why don't we just do it now, while I'm here?'

Charlotte shook her head. 'I don't care what people think of me anymore,' she said. 'Ask me again next time you're home. Give me time to think it through, Rom.'

'All right,' Rom said with a shrug. The two sat in silence for a long moment, before Rom got to his feet. 'Why don't you get dressed? My mother said I have to take you somewhere nice while I'm here.'

Charlotte smiled. 'I always liked your mother.' She stubbed out her cigarette in a little silver ashtray and walked slowly around the table. She took Rom's face in her hands and kissed him.

Remmie stood on the deck of the SS *John Holt* as she pulled back out of the Lagos Lagoon. He looked out as the city moved into the distance — what he would do to be able to stay and make a life with Adanna, rather than this constant travelling.

'Why so glum, chum?'

He turned to see Scaggs approaching.

Remmie shrugged. 'Just thinking about how I like being on land.'

'Ah yes, she can be a treacherous temptress, the sea,' Scaggs said. 'You're right to be wary of her. But don't be fooled. Life on land can be seriously dull. Imagine a world that didn't keep moving — that didn't keep showing you new places every day. I'm not sure I can even contemplate it. But then, I've been doing this job a long time. This is my world now.'

'Do you not miss people?' Remmie asked. 'Is there not a Mrs Scarisbrick out there, waiting for you to return?'

'Oh no, nothing like that,' Scaggs said. 'I'm too much of a loner for all that. There nearly was once. But it wasn't to be.'

'What happened? Did she give you the heave-ho in the end?'

'No. Life gave her the heave-ho, I'm sorry to say. Consumption,' Scaggs said, matter-of-factly. 'There was nothing of her, anyway — my poor little dove. She was a slight thing. The TB knocked her for six. She was dead within a week.'

'Jesus, Scaggs, that's awful,' Remmie said.

The big man shrugged. 'You have to take the hand you're dealt in this life. No good moping about it.'

'That's true enough,' Remmie said, placing a hand on the older man's shoulder. 'Still, it must be tough.'

'No soul is ever alone, who has the sea for company.' Scaggs turned his gaze out towards the ocean and breathed in a deep lungful of the salty air. 'Stop looking back to Lagos. She's not on this ship, but you are — and the bosun will be looking for you.'

*

Remmie's fingers were getting faster. His banjo-playing had started to draw a little crowd whenever he played on deck, and Scaggs watched on, nodding appreciatively, with all the quiet pride of a good teacher. He was fast developing his own style — it was more joyous and pluckier than Scaggs' playing, which always seemed somehow mournful, even when he was performing the most upbeat of jigs.

'You have a real natural talent, lad,' Scaggs told him, when he finished his impromptu performance, and his crew mates had wandered away with smiles on their faces.

'You've taught me everything I know, pal,' Remmie said.

But Scaggs shook his head. 'No, you can't teach what you have. It's more intuitive. It's something that was always inside you. I just put the instrument in your hand and showed you its arse from its elbow.'

Remmie laughed. 'Well, that's the first time anyone has ever told me that I actually do know one from the other!'

Scaggs hunkered down next to Remmie, leaning against the deck rail. Remmie started playing again — a calmer tune this time. Scaggs lit a cigarette, then offered the open packet to Remmie, who declined. The older man blew a cloud of smoke into the breeze and listened to each note being played. 'You know,' he said at last, 'if anything happens to me, I want you to make sure you get hold of this banjo. It's meant a lot to me over the years, and I'd want it to go to someone who will actually play it, when I'm gone. There's nothing quite so sad as a silent instrument.'

'You're not going anywhere, Scaggs, don't worry,' Remmie said.

'I don't know. I'm getting on a bit, and my old smoker's cough is worse than ever. My old man died when he was ten years younger than I am now.'

Remmie nodded. 'I suppose none of us really know when it will happen,' he said.

'Aye, certainly in this war,' Scaggs added, taking another lungful of smoke, then releasing it through his nose. 'You have to remember — with Fritz out there in his U-boat, dead-set on taking down any ship that moves on this ocean, you can hardly take your life for granted.'

'I suppose we just have to take every day as it comes,' Remmie said.

'That's as sound a philosophy as any,' the older man said. 'Now, do me a favour. Play that one for me again.'

CHAPTER FOURTEEN

Rom's uniform was ironed to a crisp ahead of his medical assessment. His boots were polished. His cap was brushed. He had never gleamed quite so handsomely. But the dour-faced Royal Navy doctor couldn't have looked less impressed. 'Take a seat, Lieutenant,' he muttered, watching Rom's every move over the top of pince-nez glasses. 'How are you feeling in yourself?'

It was a question they always seemed to ask, but it made little sense to Rom. 'I'm feeling fine,' he said with a smile.

The doctor looked through Rom's notes. 'Because it looks like you had a little bit of trouble readjusting the last time your boat was sunk in action.'

'Yes, but HMS *Defender* wasn't really sunk by the Germans,' Rom attempted to explain. 'It was damaged, badly damaged, but it was sunk by our own chaps. It was scuttled. We were on the ship firing the torpedo that sunk her. We weren't on *Defender* when she went down. It's quite a different sensation, I can assure you, doctor.'

'How are you sleeping?'

'Never better.'

'Any concerns? Any worries?'

Rom thought about the anxiety that had consumed him since he'd returned, as a result of Charlotte's condition. 'Not really,' he said. 'Certainly nothing relevant to my service.'

'Really?' The doctor sounded unconvinced. '"Not really" doesn't sound like a no to me.'

'It's complicated,' Rom said.

'Is it?' the doctor muttered, examining him more carefully over his spectacles. 'Well, move on to the next room. The nurse is going to take you through some forms that we need to complete. Then we will report back on our considerations, and this will be fed back to you via the normal channels. Do you understand?'

'I do, thank you, doctor.' Rom got to his feet, then paused. 'But I want you to know, I'm perfectly capable of getting back on the bridge of a destroyer.'

The doctor gave a quiet "Mmm" sound, which Rom could not interpret, and then nodded towards the door.

Rom received his orders the following day — he had been assigned a new ship, but it wasn't quite what he'd expected. He groaned as he read the letter: *Following the considerable strain of recent weeks, it has been deemed beneficial for you to spend some time on a smaller vessel, which should offer you some respite from the stresses of constant action experienced aboard a destroyer.*

Rom turned the page. He had been assigned a position on HMS *Gorleston*, a cutter active in the 40th Escort Group.

'They've assigned me to a cutter — a tiny little vessel that will flit around the outside of Atlantic convoys on the route between Liverpool and Freetown in West Africa,' he told his mother gloomily.

'Well, that doesn't sound too bad,' she said. 'You may cross paths with your father and brother out there.'

'You don't understand,' he said. 'They think I can't cope with being on a destroyer at the heart of a battle.'

'Why would they think that?'

'I didn't mention it, Mother, but I had some treatment last year for a kind of shock, after the sinking of HMS *Grenade*.'

Eileen sat down opposite him at the kitchen table. 'What do you mean, shock? Are you saying you had shellshock, Rom?'

'No, I don't think so,' he said. 'I just struggled to sleep, that's all. I kept reliving what had happened and thinking it would happen again. They put me in hospital for a few weeks in Belfast.'

'Why didn't you tell us?'

Rom shrugged. 'I didn't want to worry anyone. I wasn't physically injured.'

'But I should have known about this, Rom,' Eileen said.

He reached out and laid a reassuring hand on her arm. 'I'm absolutely fine now. That's what's so damned frustrating. I'm perfectly capable of getting back to another destroyer. I don't want to serve on a bloody toy boat.'

'You don't get to dictate where you serve, Rom,' she said. 'It may only be for a few months, and then once you have shown them that you're right as rain, you could put in for a transfer to a bigger ship again.'

Rom nodded. 'I suppose so. She's in Gladstone Dock having a fit-out, so I need to go and introduce myself to the captain tomorrow. But I don't expect he'll need me aboard for another week or so.'

'Well, that is good news,' Eileen said, beaming. 'You need to get all the rest you can, Rom, after everything you've been through.'

'Oh, please, Mother, don't you start,' he said, sinking his head into his hands in mock despair. 'I'm absolutely fine, as I keep saying.'

'Good, well, you'll be even more absolutely fine after another week of your mother's home cooking, won't you?'

*

Rom's expectations of another week at home were quickly dashed. His new captain told him he was needed aboard the very next day to help oversee the completion of the fit-out.

HMS *Gorleston* was a compact little vessel, and its captain was a compact little man. Commander Ronald Keymer frowned perpetually and seemed to take an unhealthy interest in the little ship's heritage. But he was certainly filled with energy.

'She's a Banff Class Escort Sloop, originally acquired from the US Navy under the Lend Lease programme, you understand?' Keymer said as he gave Rom a tour of the ship. 'She was built as a Coast Guard cutter in 1930. Lake Class — quite an improvement on earlier designs, certainly better suited to the rough North Atlantic. But she served for a time in the Pacific. In fact, she was one of the ships involved in the search for Amelia Earhart back in thirty-seven. Now we're tasked with convoy escort duties to and from West Africa and through Gibraltar for the foreseeable. Have you been to Gib?'

Rom raised an eyebrow. 'Yes, a couple of times. Strange place.'

Keymer nodded sombrely. 'Yes, it is rather.' He moved on swiftly to introduce three officers who were busily working on the bridge of the stationary ship, each with a clipboard, pencil and reams of papers. 'May I introduce Lieutenant John Smith, the ship's first lieutenant, Sub-Lieutenant Robert Wilson, our navigation officer, and Lieutenant Charles Brown, our chief armourer.'

Rom shook each man's hand in turn. The chief armourer gave him a friendly smile and offered the more informal "Charlie".

'Good to meet you all,' Rom said. He could see from their uniforms that they were a mixed bunch — Royal Navy, in the case of the first lieutenant, and RNVR and RNR in the case of the other two men. 'I'm looking forward to joining you,' he added, a little awkwardly.

The captain led him gently away by the elbow. 'How are you really feeling about joining us, Hutchinson?' he asked.

Rom gave a noncommittal gesture.

'Bit of a kick in the teeth, after serving on the bridge of a destroyer, what?'

'Perhaps a little,' Rom admitted.

'Don't take it to heart. She's a good ship, and you'll like the crew. They're a friendly bunch. Sometimes it's better to be a big fish in a small pond, you know?'

'Yes, sir,' Rom said. 'Thank you, sir.'

Later that day, Rom said his goodbyes to Charlotte over a bowl of soup back at one of the new "British Restaurants" opened by the Ministry of Food. It was a dour setting, and under the circumstances, only seemed to add to their misery. Charlotte's face was creased with sadness.

'You will take care of yourself, won't you?' Rom fretted. 'It's important that you eat — for both of you. Have you thought any more about my proposal?'

'Was it really a proposal?'

'Of course it was,' Rom said, leaning across the table. 'I want to marry you, Charlotte.'

'That's because you always do the right thing, Rom,' she whispered. 'I'm not sure that's the reason to get married.'

Rom looked perplexed. 'Your logic is lost on me, I'm afraid.' He leaned forward once again. 'I love you, Charlotte. You do know that much, don't you?'

'I love you, too,' Charlotte said, wiping the corners of her glistening eyes.

*

The ship was having a boiler clean and being fitted with the Type 286M radar equipment, and despite what Captain Keymer had said, there really wasn't much for Rom to do over the next few days other than settle himself into his rather cramped cabin and get to know the other crew members as they came back from their shore leave. The captain was right — they did seem to be a friendly bunch. He got on particularly well with a midshipman named Alec Lewis, with whom he found himself sharing his cabin. Lewis was the sort of chap who was always cheerful, and Rom passed seemingly endless evenings with him playing cribbage with a mangled old deck of cards.

Rom also spent some time getting his head around the *Gorleston*'s capabilities. The little ship was surprisingly well kitted-out when it came to armaments, which Charlie Brown was more than happy to show him. She had a 5in and a 3in gun, two six-pounders, and then a further four 20mm guns that had been added when she was taken over by the Royal Navy. She also packed two stern racks that held eight depth charges.

'They're obviously expecting us to see some action on the convoys,' Rom said.

'I expect there'll be a little skirmish here and there. You know how it is,' Charlie agreed.

Exactly a week after Rom's arrival on the ship, her fit-out was signed off and she was formally assigned to the 40th Escort Group. They set sail and met their first convoy a few miles off the Irish coast. They would be supporting the OS Series convoys to West Africa and inward SL Series return convoys to Liverpool, working closely alongside other HM Cutters *Landguard*, *Lulworth*, the little sloop HMS *Bideford* and the destroyer HMS *Stanley*.

As the convoy formed up ahead of the passage to Freetown, Rom couldn't help but look across at HMS *Stanley* with envious eyes. The destroyer looked huge and imperious alongside HMS *Gorleston*. That was the sort of bridge he was supposed to be serving on, he thought to himself. However pleasant the atmosphere might be on *Gorleston*, however friendly everyone might be, there was no doubt that Keymer had hit the nail square on the head — simply being there felt like a kick in the teeth.

The convoy escort that Rom was now a part of had grown into a mighty protective force as it mustered off the Irish coast. They had been joined by the destroyers HMS *Wanderer* and HMS *Witch*, the Flower-class corvettes HMS *Campanula* and HMS *Clematis*, and the armed merchant cruiser HMS *Cathay*. But the ship that brought a smile to Rom's face was the appearance of HMS *Vanoc* — the destroyer that had, with its new-fangled radar equipment, played such a major part in taking out those prolific killing machines U-99 and U-100, alongside HMS *Walker*, earlier in the year.

But within days, the euphoria of being back at sea had passed and Rom's first experience of escorting a convoy on HMS *Gorleston* quickly descended into chaos. Just a few hundred miles into the voyage, with the cold waters of the North Atlantic offering an ominous grey landscape in every direction, the U-boats began to strike, picking off ships one by one. For Rom, it felt very much like the work of a wolfpack, working in co-ordinated parries, passing silently beneath the escort to choose their prey. The SS *Segundo* was the first to fall victim to the sleek, deathly dart of the U-boat's torpedo. She had barely slipped beneath the waves, when the SS *Saugor* was similarly hit — a blast and a devastating fireball left a plume of acrid black smoke that reached towards the sky like the waving arm of a drowning sailor. Later, the SS *Tremoda* and the SS *Embassage* also met the same fate.

Gorleston was a flurry of activity as she progressed from one disaster scene to the next, desperately pulling injured sailors from the water and plucking the luckier men from the crowded lifeboats. The decks of the little ship quickly became crowded with miserable-looking merchant sailors, sitting silently for most of the time, lost in their thoughts. Until a change in regulations three months earlier, the merchant crew members' pay stopped the moment a ship sank. They no longer had that to worry about. So Rom imagined they must simply be replaying the attack in their minds, allowing it to sink in properly, coming to terms with the loss of close friends or perhaps sombrely considering just how close they had come to dying that day. Rom and the other officers of the bridge didn't have time to offer consolation. They had far too much on their hands, firefighting the impact of the repeated attacks.

'There must be more than one of them down there,' Rom said to Keymer after the *Embassage* was struck.

'Either that or the U-boat captain is damned handy at twisting around the convoy and attacking it from every direction,' Keymer said. 'There must be at least two of them, if not more.'

Every attempt by the convoy escort to hunt them down proved fruitless — the U-boats seemed able to vanish like ghosts whenever ASDIC caught any trace of them and the *Gorleston*'s depth charge rack remained fully stacked.

The following day, the British cargo ship SS *Otaio* went down 330 miles west by north of the Fastnet Rock. All 10,000 tons of her slipped beneath the waves in moments, and of the seventy-one crew, fifty-eight were saved. The majority, including the stricken ship's captain, were picked up by *Vanoc*.

Once again, it gave Rom a strange feeling of nostalgia to watch the hard-edged silhouette of *Vanoc* at work.

A game of cat and mouse soon ensued between the convoy's destroyers and the pair of hunting U-boats. But once again, by the time the sun had set, the attackers had slipped away unseen.

The further south the convoy reached, the quieter things became. As the temperatures began to rise and the clouds began to clear, to be replaced by sapphire skies, the waters became more peaceful. It seemed they had left the U-boats behind, content with their kills.

By the time the lush coast of Sierra Leone appeared on the horizon, Rom was relieved to be delivering the remains of the convoy safely to its destination. Freetown offered a crowded skyline of ramshackle shoulder-to-shoulder buildings, and when they came up alongside, Rom was taken aback by the bustle of the seething streets below. It seemed a long way removed from the gloomy misery he had left behind in the shell-shocked streets of Liverpool. He looked out and wished he could step ashore and experience it for himself. This was the kind of landscape that his father and brother must have seen at Lagos.

But there could be no shore leave for Rom. *Gorleston* had to be turned around swiftly. Within a couple of days, she would be setting out to accompany the homeward-bound convoy. They would be back out there amid the grey expanse of sea and with the ever-present threat lurking beneath the waves. As he breathed deeply and took the warm African air into his lungs, Rom consoled himself with being safely here in the harbour, for the moment at least — a brief respite from all they faced out there on the ocean. His mind inevitably went back home. He pined for Charlotte's touch and wondered how she was coping, whether she was coming to terms with the idea of being a mother, whether she had been reassured by his acceptance of the situation. Then he thought of his own mother. She would have opened his letter long before, and perhaps she too would by now be coming to terms with the idea of being a grandmother in her mid-forties.

Rom reached for his cigarettes and smoked languorously as he looked out across the sprawling African city, wishing he could be at home.

Charlotte arrived for her night shift amid the perpetual gloom of the network of corridors that surrounded the operations room at Western Approaches HQ. She couldn't walk down these flickering corridors now without feeling a constant unease, despite knowing her attacker was dead and buried in his grave. She paused to hang her coat on her usual hook, took a moment to straighten her skirt and gave her hair a habitual pat to push down any curls disturbed by the wind and rain. Then she took a deep breath and walked through the little door into the great sprawling chasm of the busy operations room. As she walked towards her usual desk, ahead of the enormous floor-to-ceiling map of the Atlantic, she was beckoned by the curling index finger of Nan Currie.

'Yes, ma'am?' she queried, as she moved towards the superintendent's desk.

'Can you come with me, dear?'

Nan Currie led her back across the operations room and up the little narrow steps that led to the Commander-in-Chief's office. Charlotte felt as if her heart was in her mouth. Suddenly she knew with a devastating certainty what this was all about.

Jack Walters walked out of the boss's office and passed her without making eye contact. Nan Currie gave a gentle knock and was called inside. Charlotte could hear her making an obsequious noise of agreement, before she returned to the door and called Charlotte inside.

Sir Percy was sitting at his desk, his golden admiral stripes gleaming on the wrist of his navy-blue jacket, his tie knotted neatly below his pointed chin. His hair was combed back and glinting with Brylcreem, but his eyes were heavy with exhaustion. 'Come on in, my dear,' he said, putting more tenderness into the word "dear" than Nan Currie had managed. 'Come and take a seat.'

Charlotte sat nervously opposite as Sir Percy lit a cigarette, flipped the lid back down on the silver lighter and cast it aside onto the pile of papers on the desk before him. Charlotte could feel the presence of Nan Currie hovering behind her seat.

'I expect you know why I need to see you, don't you, Burton?' Sir Percy said, raising his eyebrows a little as he spoke.

Charlotte didn't speak, but nodded slowly and cast her eyes towards her hands, which were twisted in her lap.

'Yes,' Sir Percy mused distractedly. 'Now, listen, we all know these things happen. 'But of course, you understand that this is no place for an expectant mother.'

Charlotte looked out through the window that ran for the whole length of the office, giving the commander a cinematic view of the activity down in the operations room and the plotters charting the movement of the convoys on the wall map.

'How long can I stay?' Charlotte asked, feeling a rising sense of panic at the idea of having to leave the job she had grown to love.

Sir Percy reached for a folder on his desk and opened it. 'I have here your discharge papers, Miss Burton.' He handed them across the desk with a strained smile. Charlotte took the papers and looked at them. 'The superintendent here tells me you were a very good worker,' he added. 'So, I wanted to thank you for your service.' Sir Percy got to his feet and placed his cigarette down on the edge of a silver ashtray that was perched on the corner of his desk. Charlotte took this as a cue to get to her feet.

'Thank you, sir,' she whispered, and moved towards the door, sensing Nan Currie's presence close behind her.

Polly and some of the other plotters looked across with concerned expressions as Currie led Charlotte back across the operations room, towards the door and her coat hanging on the peg in the corridor beyond. Once they were alone in the dimly lit corridor, Currie muttered something that Charlotte didn't quite catch.

'I'm sorry, Superintendent? What was that?'

Currie glowered at her with disgust. 'Your pass.'

Charlotte handed it to her.

'You're a disgrace to the Wrens,' the older woman said, and held out a hand to indicate the direction of the exit staircase at the end of the corridor.

'Oh, go to hell, you old witch,' Charlotte managed to spit back at her, before turning on her heel and marching angrily towards the door. It was only when she stepped outside and felt the cold night air hit her, that she crumpled, cupping her face in her hands and sobbing as the door to Derby House slammed behind her.

Eileen picked up the letter from the doormat after a long night shift. Her eyes were so bleary, she could barely read her own name on the envelope. She tore it open and was surprised to ecognize the writing as being in Rom's hand. He must have posted this as he was boarding the ship, she thought. A thank you note? She carried it into the kitchen and took a seat at the table to read it.

Dear Mother,

By the time you receive this, I should be a few hundred miles out into the Atlantic Ocean, in the little bathtub that is HMS Gorleston, *squeezed into my little cabin or eating the cook's stew. Thank you for feeding me up so well during this shore leave! Hopefully I won't be hungry for some time.*

There's no easy way to tell you this, Mother. I wanted to let you know that Charlotte is pregnant with my child. I intend to marry her. Her mother has kicked her out. She's living with one of her workmates in a flat above a pub in Dale Street — The Mitre. Keep an eye on her for me, would you?

So, it looks like you're going to be a grandmother rather sooner than you'd expected. I hope you're not too cross with me. Maybe you could break the news gently to Father?

Love,
Rom

Eileen placed the letter carefully down on the table and took a deep breath, staring into the middle distance as she attempted to take in what she had just read. 'Oh Rom…' she whispered into the empty kitchen, before wearily getting to her feet, filling the kettle with water and putting it onto the hob with a lonely clatter. As the steam began to rise she felt light-headed, as though her world was falling apart around her.

Two days later, Eileen got off the train and made her way up from the Overhead, along James Street, Castle Street and Dale Street. It was Sunday morning and the city's commercial district was much quieter than it would normally be during the week. Children were playing on some of the older bombsites, with rubble piled into "dens", where "cowboys" were noisily waiting to ambush "Indians". Eileen smiled. It only seemed like five minutes ago that Rom and Remmie were playing like that, without a care in the world. *Now look at them*, she thought to herself.

She continued walking along the pavement and eventually came upon The Mitre. It was closed, but she found a door at the side with a doorbell for the apartment above. She rang the bell and waited. After a moment a young woman opened the door. She had bleached blonde hair pulled back in a short ponytail, and was still dressed in a garish pink silk dressing gown.

'You are?' she asked, a hint of aggression in her voice.

'I'm here to see Charlotte,' Eileen said.

'And you are?' the young woman repeated.

'Who are you? Her keeper?' Eileen said, pushing past the woman and striding confidently up the staircase.

'Oi! Where d'you think you're going?'

Eileen walked straight through the only open door on the landing. Charlotte was sitting in a little armchair. It was clear from the redness of her eyes that she'd been crying.

'Mrs Hutchinson!' she said, clearly alarmed. 'What are you doing here?'

'I came to see you, Charlotte,' she said. 'Can I come in?'

'Do you know this woman?' the blonde woman shouted across to Charlotte, pointing at Eileen.

'Yes, it's fine,' Charlotte said. 'She's Rom's mother.'

'Eileen,' said Eileen, holding out her hand towards the blonde girl frowning before her.

'I'm Charlotte's flatmate, Polly. Have you ever thought to wait to be invited before barging your way into people's homes?'

'I needed to see Charlotte urgently,' Eileen said. 'Would you mind giving us a bit of privacy?'

'Oh, now I've got to make myself scarce in my own flat, have I?'

'Polly, please,' Charlotte said.

'All right.' Polly shrugged. 'I know where I'm not wanted. I'll be in my room if you need me.'

Charlotte gestured for Eileen to join her on the other armchair. 'Would you like a cup of tea?'

'Don't worry, love. I'm fine,' Eileen said. 'You stay there. You need to get all the rest you can, in your condition.'

'Ah, so he's told you.'

Eileen nodded. 'That's my grandchild you're carrying.'

Charlotte raised her eyebrows involuntarily, but didn't attempt to tell Rom's mother that it was "complicated", as she had done with Rom. 'Is that why you've come to see me?'

'Rom mentioned you'd had a little falling-out with your own mother. I thought you might need some help. Or just someone to talk to, perhaps?'

'You're not angry with us? About all this?'

'I was worried at first, I'll admit that. But I know these things can happen.'

'And Rom's father?'

'I've not told him yet,' Eileen said. 'I've not had an opportunity. He's at sea. I'm just here to check you're all right.'

'That's kind of you, Mrs Hutchinson,' Charlotte said, her eyes glinting with tears. 'They kicked me out of the Wrens. Inevitable, I suppose. But it came as quite a shock.' The tears finally burst their banks, and she rummaged in the pocket of her dressing gown for a handkerchief. She dabbed at her eyes for a moment, then added, 'Well, I suppose I've made my bed and now I need to lie in it. That's what they say, isn't it, Mrs Hutchinson?'

'Please, Charlotte, would you call me Eileen?'

Charlotte nodded, her fingers playing with the corners of the handkerchief she was clutching.

'But you're right about one thing, my love,' Eileen went on. 'You do need to stay in bed and rest. You'll be glad of it in a few months' time. Now, how are you fixed for rations? You should be on a green ration book, you know. Pregnant women get extra milk, orange juice, cod liver oil — all the things you need to keep your baby healthy.'

Charlotte crumpled once again into her handkerchief. 'What am I going to do? This baby has ruined everything.'

Eileen reached out and put a hand on Charlotte's arm. 'Life is never what we dream it's going to be, my love. But you and Rom need to get married. Before you're too big to get down the aisle, I'd say. You're both so young. There will be plenty of time for romance. Right now, with this war on and the —' she gestured awkwardly towards Charlotte's abdomen — 'the situation in which you find yourself, well, I think you both just need to concentrate on doing the right thing.'

Charlotte turned towards her. 'Do you really think so?'

'Yes,' Eileen said. 'Now, we need to start packing your case.'

'My case?' Charlotte sounded confused.

'Yes, your case. You're coming to live with me, at least until the baby's born. You need someone who knows what they're doing looking after you. Trust me, love, Jean Harlow in there may be a good pal, but she's not going to know what to do when your waters break.'

'I can't leave Polly on her own,' Charlotte said.

'Oh, I don't get the impression that Pretty Polly is the type of girl who will be alone for very long,' Eileen said. 'Listen, you need to think about yourself now, Charlotte — it's all about you and that baby, do you understand?'

Charlotte nodded.

Despite seeming out of place when he first joined the crew of SS *John Holt*, Corporal Eddie Crabtree, the young Royal Artillery gunner from the Maritime Anti-Aircraft Regiment, had now become a familiar figure on the ship. Remmie liked Crabtree, with his dry sense of humour and self-contained ways. He was often to be found servicing the 4-in deck gun that was now mounted at the stern of the ship.

The sun was shining as they headed north, sailing just west of Madeira, some 350 nautical miles off the coast of Morocco.

'Tell me something, Crabtree,' Remmie said to the young corporal as the ship cut through the azure waters. 'How effective do you think you would be with that thing, in the event of our being attacked by a German dive bomber?'

'How do you mean?' Crabtree asked, his shoulders tightening defensively.

'Well, say a Stuka was to swoop down towards us now, all set to drop its deadly payload on the quarterdeck and send us all plummeting towards Davy Jones' locker…'

'I don't know. I reckon I could take him down, with a bit of luck.'

'What odds would you give yourself?'

'Odds?'

'Yes, you know — if you were a gambling man. What odds would you give yourself for taking down a Stuka dive bomber that was attacking us — sinking down at a ninety-degree angle, going at, say, three hundred and fifty miles per hour?'

'I don't know. Maybe twenty to one.' Crabtree shrugged. 'Maybe twenty-five to one.'

'Christ, not exactly a solid bet then.'

'Well, there's a certain degree of luck involved, I'd say.'

Scaggs appeared behind Remmie. 'You wouldn't be teasing this young corporal now, would you, Hutchinson?'

'It wouldn't be in my nature to do any such a thing, Leading Seaman Scarisbrick,' Remmie said with a wink.

'Anyway, who is Davy Jones?' Crabtree said, clearly glad to be changing the subject.

'Don't be saying that name out loud on the deck,' Scaggs grumbled.

'Why not?' Crabtree asked, looking baffled.

'Bad luck, of course.'

'It strikes me that almost everything is considered bad luck on a ship,' Crabtree observed, then returned his attention to servicing the weapon. 'I'm sorry I asked.'

'Well, you should be, lad,' Scaggs said with a frown. 'For no good comes of that kind of talk.'

Remmie leaned on the deck rail and looked out to the east, the island of Madeira a mere smudge of green on the horizon. A moment later, his eyes caught the V-shape of an enormous bird, riding the thermals overhead. 'What the hell is that?' Remmie asked.

Scaggs turned and followed the young deckhand's gaze. 'Ye Gods...' he muttered. 'First you mention the name of that fiend of the deep and now this.'

'What is it, Scaggs?' Crabtree asked.

'It's a damned albatross,' Scaggs replied with a groan.

'Don't tell me it's bad luck to see one of those too,' Crabtree said.

'It's more than bad luck, boy,' Scaggs whispered, gazing at him with a wild, fearful glare. 'It means we're done for — for sure.' He turned to Remmie and then back to Crabtree. 'We're dead men,' he whispered, then turned to walk away back along the deck.

Remmie looked up at the enormous bird that was soaring overhead. 'Well, that's cheery news,' he muttered. 'You'd better get that gun back together, Crabtree.'

'Yes, I reckon I better had.'

CHAPTER FIFTEEN

The convoy that formed up off the west African coast was a ragtag collection of merchant vessels that were heading back to Liverpool from Lagos, Freetown and half a dozen smaller ports. They were carrying all kinds of produce — from palm oil to peanuts, from cocoa to rubber and timber. From the cramped bridge of HMS *Gorleston*, Rom watched the ships move benignly into the familiar column-based formation, with the convoy escort ships slipping into their protective places on either side, the destroyers dominant, like oversized swans keeping a watchful eye on their young. It was a strangely peaceful scene — silent and spectacular.

But the peace did not last long. Just a few days into the voyage, as the convoy steamed west-northwest of the Canary Islands, the first torpedo struck, not long after midnight. Until that moment the menacing presence of a U-boat beneath the waves had gone entirely unnoticed. Nobody even saw the distinctive line of white foam moving towards the SS *St Clair II*. The first anyone knew of the attack was the moment of detonation itself, when the torpedo struck the little merchant ship and sent up a blast of seawater and shrapnel.

'She's going to be lost for sure,' Rom said as he attempted to study the gaping wound left in the ship's side through his binoculars in the darkness. 'It looks like she's taking on water rapidly.'

'Thank you, Hutchinson,' Captain Keymer said calmly. 'Can you kindly inform our friends on HMS *Lulworth* that we are initiating a rescue mission? We will pick up as many men as we can, but if they are able to assist, that would be marvellous.'

'Yes, sir,' Rom said, lowering his binoculars and heading across to the radio set.

Gorleston was quickly manoeuvred up alongside the stricken ship, and a group of lifeboats that had already been launched moved towards the scrambling nets being lowered from the starboard deck. HMS *Lulworth* also turned towards the wounded ship, which was already beginning to lurch perilously in the dark waters. There was little light from the waxing moon and the stars glimmered in the heavens — a great swirling expanse of them, with the Milky Way twisting like a strand of deep blue ribbon above the grim scene. Rom could just about make out the *Lulworth*'s crew pulling men from the water. In little more than half an hour, the deck of HMS *Gorleston* was packed with rescued sailors, shivering beneath grey woollen blankets, despite the mildness of the night.

One young sailor looked particularly shaken-up. Rom perched beside him where he was sprawled, leaning against the bulwark.

'You all right, chap?' Rom asked.

'He was there one minute and the next he was just completely gone, sir,' the young man whispered with wild eyes.

'Who was, sailor?'

'One of our gunners, sir. He had a baby, he did. He'd barely seen him, being away at sea, like. Anyway, this chap, he walked past me on the deck, just before the torpedo struck. He was just in the wrong place at the wrong time. He was there one moment and gone the next. Completely gone.'

Rom nodded. The sailor was still staring forward towards the deck. Rom knew that the best thing he could do was listen.

'There one moment and gone the next,' the sailor repeated.

'Best way to go,' Rom said at last. 'He wouldn't have known a damned thing about it.'

'Do you think so, sir?' The youngster turned towards Rom's face for the first time.

'I'm sure of it, pal. Now, stay here. I'm going to get you some tea.'

Rom had similar conversations with half a dozen of the rescued men. They all had those same staring eyes, as if they couldn't quite believe what they had seen and were watching the moment of impact being played out over and over again. Eventually, Rom returned to the bridge, sighing heavily as he stepped into the pilothouse.

'We have twenty-six of the *St Clair II*'s crew onboard now, sir, including the master,' Rom told Keymer. '*Lulworth* has a further five men. She had a complement of forty-four, so we believe thirteen men have been lost.'

Keymer looked out at the burning remains of the merchant ship. A plume of dirty black smoke was rising skywards. The lurching keel now meant the stricken ship was almost lying on her side. She bore a striking resemblance to a dead whale, Rom thought. He had seen one once, washed up on the beach at Crosby. It had been a fetid hulk by the time he had seen it, with gulls picking at its flesh. He had only been eight or nine years old and the melancholy sight had had a profound impact on his young mind. The whale had remained there for much of that summer, gradually decaying, until Rom and Remmie had been able to see its ribcage. Rom had been struck by how finely they were structured, like the wooden roof joists of an old barn. With the first storm of the autumn, the grisly relic was washed back out to sea, leaving behind a ghostly indent in the sand that had remained for another week.

'She'll be going down in the next half hour, I would imagine,' Keymer said, snapping Rom from his reverie. 'Saving thirty-one souls from a complement of forty-four doesn't seem like too bad a return, given the sheer size of the blast hole. I think we need to leave her to slip below alone, and catch up with the convoy. We need to consider the other ships.'

'Yes, sir,' the first lieutenant, Smith, agreed, before turning to the quartermaster and barking out an order to increase *Gorleston*'s speed.

'Aye aye, sir!' the quartermaster barked back. 'Taking her up to fifteen knots.'

'The deck is hellish, sir,' Rom said.

Keymer nodded. 'They're being looked after?'

'Yes, sir,' Rom said. 'I've assigned some men to brewing up and handing out blankets. None of them seem badly injured. But they're in shock.'

The captain looked ahead at the ocean pensively. The first glimmer of the dawn was edging above the eastern horizon. 'Poor chaps. They've taken quite a beating, no doubt,' he said. 'We will need to call into Ponta Delgada with them. We simply don't have the space or provisions to get them all the way home with us.'

Rom nodded. 'It is rather cramped on deck.'

'Not like being on a destroyer, eh, Hutchinson?'

'Not really, sir, no.'

A mile further up the convoy, the SS *John Holt* steamed on. Remmie had seen the plume of black smoke behind them to the south when he came on deck at first light. He knew what it must mean, but tried not to pay it too much attention. It was part of daily life when sailing in a convoy. If you stopped to ponder the devastating reality of every sinking ship, you would quickly be discharged as a nervous wreck. So Remmie, like all the other sailors on all the other ships, simply got on with his own job.

The atmosphere onboard the *John Holt* had been tenser than usual, since the convoy commodore, the imposing Commander Alexander MacRae, had chosen the *John Holt* as the ship from which he was to command the voyage. Like so many convoy commodores, the wiry old man had come out of retirement to fill the role. He barked his orders from the starboard wing of the pilothouse as he worked tirelessly to keep the columns of the convoy in line and the gaps between the ships evenly spaced. It struck Remmie that he was like a Victorian admiral, dug up, dusted down and placed on the bridge of a modern merchant vessel. Remmie didn't know how the captain coped with his constant presence. Hime was a calm and considered man, but even he must be feeling uncomfortable about this usurpation of his dominance on the bridge.

The morning light was watery. Remmie had more than an hour before his shift would begin, and he knew he should be in bed asleep. But he hadn't been able to settle and so had taken a silent stroll around the deck. He leaned on the starboard deck rail, fumbling with his packet of cigarettes, trying to decide whether or not he wanted to smoke. He heard steps moving along the deck behind him and turned to see Scaggs shuffling along. He gave Remmie a wave.

'Morning, Remmie! Just taking my morning constitutional!'

Remmie waved at his friend and watched him for a moment as he walked on towards the fo'c's'le.

Remmie looked back down at his cigarettes. After a while, he replaced them in his pocket and gazed towards the sun, rising like an enormous orange in the east. It was casting its beams out in great misty shafts of light. There weren't many moments of pure peace onboard the *John Holt*, so he was determined to enjoy the tranquillity of the hour. There was nothing to break the calmness — only the constant drone of the ship's engines far below the deck and the buffeting of the breeze. He closed his eyes for a few seconds, enjoying the feel of the early morning light on his face.

Everything changed in an instant.

A torpedo struck the *John Holt*'s fo'c's'le on the port side, rocking the entire vessel and sending Remmie tumbling onto the deck. It seemed like he was on his back for a long time, gazing up at the sky, which was being consumed by the rapidly growing plume of smoke rising from the front of the ship. In fact, he was probably only down for a few seconds. He instinctively checked his limbs, as if they might have been lost without him realising it. Then he scrambled to his feet and was struck by the hellish inferno that had so rapidly engulfed the front of the ship.

'Scaggs!' Remmie cried out as he started to run forward towards the blast site. But he already knew it was hopeless. His friend could never have survived that blast. He must have been right in the middle of it. Yet still Remmie's legs carried him forward towards the heat of the flames. He only stopped when he felt a firm hand grabbing his upper arm.

'Get back!' a voice cried. He turned to see the chief engineer pulling him away from the blast site. 'Get yourself to one of the lifeboats, now!' Clensy ordered before running on towards the engine room door.

Remmie did as he was told, turning and moving towards the nearest lifeboat. The deck around him filled with noise and frantic movement as dozens of sailors emerged from their cabins to get themselves off the stricken ship.

Hime had already called for them to abandon ship. An alarm was ringing out loudly and a group of sailors was beginning to winch down the first of the lifeboats under the extraordinarily calm supervision of the chief mate and the third officer.

Remmie stood still for a moment as the men rushed around him. It was as if he couldn't lift his feet from the deck, as if his brain had been consumed by the confusion and horror of the moment. He didn't even see who it was who grabbed him by the shoulder, thrust a lifejacket into his hand and pushed him towards a lifeboat.

The lifeboat had already been half swung out beneath the davits, so he could look down and see the broiling sea below as he lunged into the little boat and took his seat. The winch crew continued to lower her down towards the surface of the water, giving Remmie a strangely angled view of the exterior of the ship. He reached around his body and strapped on his kapok lifejacket at the very moment the lifeboat's keel touched the waves and began to be tossed around.

The winch was disconnected, and a group of the men lifted the oars and began to pull away from the ship. Even as he gazed up at it in a sort of stunned fixation, he could see the *John Holt* beginning to slope forwards into the water.

'Dear God,' he whispered. 'She's going to go down.'

Once they had pulled a little way clear, the oars were lifted, and the boat was allowed to bob around with the rise and fall of the waves. Remmie watched as more lifeboats were lowered, and all the time the ship sloped more perilously forward. At last, the final lifeboat descended, containing the captain, chief engineer, some of the senior officers of the bridge, the bosun and the convoy commodore, Macrae.

The ship let out an agonising groan then slipped swiftly down, gaining momentum as she went, like a carriage on a rollercoaster cresting the apex of its tracks, before plummeting down. The ship growled and then gasped as her stern deck rail was finally consumed by the sea and enormous globes of air bubbled to the surface, delivering a curious mishmash of items that floated in the enormous absence where the ship had been. Anything that could float and had not been tied down on the deck now littered the waves.

Remmie could not quite believe what had happened to them in the space of just a quarter of an hour. It felt as though his world had collapsed around him. How had a warm, gentle morning in the ocean southwest of Madeira descended into such chaos? A morning when he had simply been leaning on the deck rail and enjoying the rising sun on his face — now that deck rail was sinking through the murky depths to find its place with the shipwrecks of old on the ocean bed.

To his astonishment, a burly-looking stoker who was seated beside him in the boat began to cry. Remmie put an arm around the man's back and attempted to give him a comforting pat, but then realised he was only patting the solid cork board of the man's lifejacket.

'I'm sorry. It's just the shock,' the stoker said, turning to Remmie.

'That's all right, pal,' Remmie said. He turned his head quickly, having spotted something moving alongside the boat. He twisted himself into a kneeling position and leaned out to take a swipe at it. A couple of the men around him grumbled as he caused the lifeboat to rock. Remmie turned around and retook his seat, holding a dripping banjo by its neck.

'It's Scaggs's banjo,' he said, emotion breaking his voice.

'Scaggs will be grateful to you for rescuing that,' a voice opposite said.

Remmie looked up. It was the ship's cook. He had his lips pressed together and was nodding emphatically.

'I don't think Scaggs made it,' Remmie said, still gazing at the banjo. 'He had just walked up to the fo'c's'le when the torpedo struck.'

The men around him cast their eyes down towards the bottom of the lifeboat. The stoker beside him, who had now regained his composure, added, 'I think that young anti-aircraft gunner was up front too. He was servicing his gun. I'd seen him a few minutes before.'

'Crabtree?' Remmie said.

The stoker nodded sombrely. 'Yes, that's it. Crabtree. Little bloke.'

'I wonder who else we lost,' the cook added after a moment, turning to gaze back towards the void where the ship had last been seen.

Remmie ran his hands across the fingerboard of the banjo. The strings hummed as he moved his fingers over them. 'Scaggs knew,' Remmie said. 'He said to me recently that if anything happened to him, he wanted me to have his banjo. He knew what was going to happen.'

The men turned to look across at another of the merchant ships in the convoy, a tanker, which was passing nearby. The column they had been sailing in had shifted a few hundred feet to the west to avoid the sinking ship and its floating remnants. Men on the deck of the tanker stood and watched them in their lifeboats. They were little more than stickmen from this distance, but Remmie could see the despair in the way they stood, their drooped shoulders as they leaned on the deck rail of their own ship. Once it had passed, one of the Royal Navy's escort ships cut across the column to approach them.

'Ah, the cavalry is here,' the stoker laughed bitterly.

'Well, I for one am just grateful somebody is here to rescue us,' the cook muttered. 'I've had enough of this little boat already.'

The ship that edged towards them looked almost like a miniature warship. Remmie recognised it as a cutter — a

Banff-class sloop. There had been a few of them in recent convoy escorts. But as it approached them, he was aware just how compact the little ship was. She can't have been more than two hundred and fifty feet long. He guessed she was a little under two thousand tons. Maybe less. She was probably half the size of the *John Holt*. It was going to be a cramped passage home, he thought to himself, as the ship came up alongside and began to lower her scramble nets.

Remmie was one of the last to make it up the net and onto the deck of HMS *Gorleston*. He removed his lifejacket and hung the strap of the banjo across his chest, so the instrument clung to his back as he made the climb.

'Silly fool,' one of the Royal Navy ratings grumbled when he reached the top. 'You'd be better served wearing the lifejacket than the damned banjo.'

But Remmie ignored him. He was simply relieved to have finally got himself and the banjo up there in one piece. He slumped down on the deck, propped up against the edge of a metal staircase amidships. He lay the instrument beside him and looked down at it. Scaggs was alive in those strings, Remmie thought. He would make sure they kept singing out their tunes — just as Scaggs had taught him. He felt a wave of emotion sweep through his body as the tears came.

Although he had lost friends — real flesh-and-blood friends like Scaggs and Crabtree — it was also impossible to not be moved by the loss of the ship herself. She had had a character all of her own — her quirks, her movements, her familiar sounds and smells. How many miles had they covered together? She had cut through the expanse of the oceans and opened the world up to Remmie and countless other sailors in her time. Now she was sleeping in the deep, undisturbed by the shimmering schools of fish exploring her decks. The thought of it was almost more than Remmie could bear. He cast his head down towards the deck and took long, slow, deep breaths until he regained his composure.

'I don't believe it.' A familiar voice stood out suddenly above the chatter of the other men, interrupting his contemplations. 'They said it was the *John Holt* and I couldn't believe it. But it is you!'

Remmie turned to see his twin brother grinning down at him from halfway up the steps. 'Rom?' he gasped.

'Remmie! Christ, I'm relieved you're in one piece,' Rom said. 'Mother would kill me if you'd met your end on a convoy I was escorting.'

'Jesus, Rom, we need to stop meeting like this,' Remmie said, rising to his feet and clutching his head in disbelief. Now he was laughing, though he didn't really know what the great joke was.

Rom stepped down and Remmie took a step forward. The brothers embraced. Another of the deckhands from the *John Holt*, who was known to be something of a comedian, called out, 'Take me to the sick bay! I'm seeing double!'

Somehow, in spite of the horrors they had seen that morning, the men standing on the deck around them laughed.

Within a few hours, the rescued sailors had all found makeshift accommodation around HMS *Gorleston* — a bench here, a table there, a blanket rolled out at the end of a corridor. Remmie was one of the lucky ones — he was given a pile of blankets alongside the bunk bed in the cabin that Rom shared with Alec Lewis.

'Look at this,' Lewis joked. 'Talk about it's not what you know, it's who you know!'

'This is more comfortable than my cabin on the *John Holt*,' Remmie said.

'The least we can do is to make sure you actually get some sleep between here and the Azores,' Rom said.

'The Azores?' Remmie looked up. 'You mean we're not getting transported all the way home?'

'Not on *Gorleston*,' Rom said. 'There simply isn't room. There are men asleep on every square inch of the deck. It's one thing down here, where it's hot. Imagine what it would be like when we get up into the North Atlantic.'

'So, we're being dumped on an island in the middle of the ocean?'

'It's hardly a desert island,' Rom said. 'Don't get any ideas that you're going to be the next Robinson Crusoe. You'll be taken to Ponta Delgada. It's a nice place, from what I've heard. It'll have a hospital and everything. Think of it as a little holiday.'

'Then what happens?'

'You wait to be picked up. A troop ship will be diverted this way, the SS *Oronsay*, and they'll take you and the chaps from *St Clair II* back up to England. You'll probably be in Liverpool just a few days behind us.'

'Fair enough, I suppose.' Remmie shrugged. 'I'd just got the idea that you'd be taking us all the way back.' He returned his attention to positioning the blankets on the floor in the most comfortable position. He picked up the banjo he had been clutching all day and laid it carefully down beside the place where he would be sleeping.

'What's with that thing?' Rom said. 'Since when did you play the banjo?'

'I've been learning to play. One of my mates on the *John Holt*, Scaggs, he was teaching me.'

'So that's Scaggs's banjo?'

Remmie nodded.

Lewis looked across the cabin at Remmie and posed the question that hung in the air. 'Did Scaggs not make it then?'

Remmie shook his head. 'He was right there, where the torpedo struck. He didn't have a chance, poor chap.'

'It's tough losing a pal like that,' Rom said, leaning over the side of his bunk. 'It's happened to me. My cabin mate on HMS *Grenade* was killed before my eyes. He was such a nice young lad. Chubby, we called him.'

There was a poignant silence for a few moments, before Rom redirected the conversation in an attempt to lift the mood.

'Wait until Mother finds out that we brought you in,' he said.

'I brought him home last time, when *Grenade* went down at Dunkirk,' Remmie explained to Lewis.

'No!' Lewis gasped. 'What are the bleedin' chances?'

'Oh, it's a funny old world, when you're a twin,' Rom said, leaning back against his pillow, as if this enigmatic statement explained everything.

'It certainly is,' Remmie agreed, as he settled beneath his grey woollen blanket.

The three men lay in the darkness, lost in their thoughts for a while, before Rom sat up again and leaned over the edge of the bunk. 'This mate of yours, Scaggs,' he whispered.

'Yes?' Remmie looked up into the darkness.

'He'll still be around, you know. You think you've lost him now, but he'll still be there, if you need him.'

'Really?' Remmie said. 'Is that really what you think?'

'I don't think it,' Rom said. 'I know it. He'll be about.'

'Well, I certainly hope you're right,' Remmie whispered back.

*

The next morning, Remmie and Rom stood together on the deck of HMS *Gorleston* as the Azores came into view. Before long they could see Ponta Delgada itself. It was a pretty place, with a grand-looking harbour, fronted by colonnaded buildings, an ornate clock tower and the city sprawling beyond in clusters of white-painted houses that seemed to glisten in the sun.

'It doesn't look too bad at all,' Remmie said.

'You sound surprised,' Rom said. 'Didn't I tell you it was a nice place to be shipwrecked? I could certainly think of worse. We called at Freetown recently. I got a glimpse of the kind of places you and Father have to put up with on the west coast of Africa.'

'Actually, I love Lagos. It has an energy to it that we just don't get back home.'

'Is that right?' Rom asked.

'I met someone out there, actually,' Remmie added. 'A girl. She's really something else, Rom.'

'Oh, Christ, you're not smitten, are you?' Rom said. 'Not with one of the natives? What will Father say?'

'He already knows and he isn't happy about it,' Remmie said. 'She's lovely, though, she really is, and she's had such a terribly hard time. Her whole family was killed when a group of thugs burnt down the bar her father ran.'

'Jesus, Remmie — it doesn't sound like the kind of family you should be getting involved with.'

'You don't understand,' Remmie said, with a dismissive gesture. 'But you would if you met her. Trust me, if you met her, you'd know what I was talking about. Anyway, I shouldn't have mentioned it. Father thinks it's all over, so not a word to our parents.'

Rom held his palms up. 'Not a word, Remmie. Your secret's safe with me,' he said. He briefly considered telling him about Charlotte's pregnancy, while they were sharing confessions. But he couldn't find the words. The twins looked out at the approaching city for a moment, before Rom added, 'Do you get to go home much?'

'Quite often. We're in and out of Liverpool every few weeks. I don't always get shore leave, but sometimes I do.'

'I've been home a few times. Normally when the Germans sink another of my ships.'

'Yes, I heard your run of bad luck continued after HMS *Grenade*.'

'Oh yes,' Rom said nonchalantly. 'I was on HMS *Defender* at Tobruk when she was dive bombed and we had to scuttle her.'

'I never thought I'd see the *John Holt* go down,' Remmie said, shaking his head. 'I still can't believe it.'

'Well, you're in one piece. That's the main thing,' Rom said. 'And now you get to put your feet up here and wait for your ship to come in.'

'Did you hear Dad's been given command of the *Remus II*?'

'Yes, Mother wrote to me,' Rom said. 'What are the chances?'

'I know — talk about keeping him on my back,' Remmie quipped as he watched the berthing lines being cast out to the waiting dockers. The dozens of rescued sailors from both the *John Holt* and the *St Clair II* were bustling about the deck expectantly. 'Well, I suppose I'd better go and get my things,' he said. 'We'll be disembarking any minute.'

'What things?' Rom said. 'You've only got the clothes you're standing up in.'

'The banjo,' Remmie reminded him. 'It's down in your cabin.'

'Of course.' Rom reached into his pocket. He took some banknotes out of his wallet and put them into his brother's hand. 'In case you need something.'

'Thanks,' Remmie said. 'That's good of you. I'll pay you back, when I can.'

'Don't worry about it,' Rom said, and the twins gave each other a brief, back-slapping embrace.

'Look after yourself,' Remmie said. 'Watch out for them Germans.'

'You too,' Rom said. 'But what am I saying — you'll have the banjo to defend yourself with.'

Remmie laughed in spite of himself, and, after giving his brother a final slap on the shoulder, he headed down to collect the instrument before the gangplanks were lowered.

Below decks, he said his goodbyes to Lewis, who was playing solitaire with his deck of cards on his bunk. 'Thanks for putting up with another Hutchinson in your cabin,' Remmie said.

'You're welcome any time.' Lewis grinned and gave him a playful wink as Remmie grabbed the banjo and headed out into the mass of men who were shuffling towards the exits.

When he eventually reached the quayside, he looked up and saw Rom waving down at him.

'See you back in Liverpool!' Remmie bellowed up towards the deck. He stopped for just long enough to wave the banjo in the air, before he was swept away by the crowd.

Ponta Delgada seemed alive with colour and activity. The Portuguese attempt at maintaining neutrality gave the city a strange shroud of normality. There would be no death raining from the skies here, Remmie realised. He made his way along the harbourside, surrounded by his crewmates, as HMS

Gorleston immediately began to slip back out towards the ocean.

They were led to a nearby US naval base — Naval Base 13, which had been built during the previous world war and was looking flaky around the edges. It wasn't the hospital accommodation that Rom had imagined, but Remmie was happy enough to be given a springy bed in a large and spartan dormitory.

He carefully laid the banjo beneath his bed and strolled outside. The idea of getting some rest on dry land appealed to him in that moment. But he also wanted to be outside in the open air. It was warm, but not oppressively so, as in Lagos. Here the sun was shining down like on the finest English summer days, and there was an almost constant sea breeze. Remmie was grateful for it and spent hours sitting on a strip of yellowed grass outside the dormitory, taking in the enormous dome of the blue sky.

Rumour was that they were to be picked up by a troop ship within a couple of days, but Remmie could have happily stayed for longer in this peaceful place. He watched the goldfinches with the clown-like red on their faces and the yellow flashes on their wings. They were bustling around in the branches of a mulberry tree, feasting on the rich, purplish-black berries and chattering to each other. He lay back on the grass and closed his eyes, feeling the sunshine warm his face as the birds twittered. It felt as if he had died and was now in a kind of heaven.

Would it be like this if he had gone down with the *John Holt*? Was this the sort of thing that poor old Scaggs would now be doing, lying somewhere beautiful with the sun on his face? He doubted it, somehow. Scaggs's heaven would be more watery — an expanse of ocean, and his own ship to sail across it for all eternity.

In the evening, the men were given permission to walk to the nearest bar, and the cash Rom had given Remmie came in handy. The bartender was more than happy to accept the US dollar bills and Remmie was able to line up the drinks for a few of his shipmates. He hardly knew any of them. Most were stokers, who had lived a more hidden existence on the *John Holt*, working their shifts below decks in the ship's growling engine room. They had a reputation among the deckhands as violent ne'er-do-wells, but after a few glasses of beer — almost exclusively on Rom — Remmie found himself quickly making new friends.

When the troop ship, the SS *Oronsay*, appeared ahead of its expected schedule in the harbour the very next morning, they were marched down to the quayside nursing their hangovers, with Remmie carrying the banjo strapped on his back. He walked wearily up the gangplank of yet another ship and realised they would only be a day behind HMS *Gorleston* enroute to Liverpool. They might even both catch the convoy up as it steamed up through the North Atlantic. Remmie certainly hoped so. The idea of being on a solitary troop ship on the great, ominous expanse of the ocean filled him with dread. After all, the very U-boat that had sunk the *John Holt* was still out there hunting.

CHAPTER SIXTEEN

HMS *Gorleston* had managed to catch up with the stragglers at the back of the convoy within thirty-six hours. She had taken on three passengers at Ponta Delgada — two Royal Navy lieutenants and a Royal Navy commander, who were being relocated following another ship sinking off Madeira. The rest of their crew were to travel on the troop ship that Remmie would be joining out of Ponta Delgada. Drinking while at sea was ordinarily frowned upon amongst the officers, but in the interests of hospitality, the wardroom was opened that evening with an inviting row of gin bottles displayed on the side tables.

'Don't mind if I do,' Rom said, when the captain lifted the bottle and shook it at him. He took the drink from Keymer's hand and was helping himself to tonic, when the first of the ship's guests arrived. To Rom's amazement, he recognised the senior officer at once.

Commander Richard Courtenay-Boyle RN had been Rom's first captain, back on HMS *Grenade*. They had been through a lot together during that first year of the war. He had last set eyes on Courtenay-Boyle in a guesthouse in Ramsgate, after they had been repatriated following *Grenade*'s sinking at Dunkirk. Both men did a comical double-take as their eyes met across the room.

'Hutchinson?' the commander said at last with a gasp. 'What the bloody hell are you doing here?'

'Sir!' Rom beamed. 'How wonderful to see you again.'

'Didn't I tell you it was a small world in the Royal Navy?' Courtenay-Boyle grinned. 'But what are you doing here?'

'I'm serving on *Gorleston*, sir.'

'You're serving on a cutter?' Courtenay-Boyle failed to mask his surprise.

'I was sorry to hear about your ship, sir.'

'Oh, never mind that.' Courtenay-Boyle shrugged. 'Nothing we haven't been through before, eh, Hutchinson?' He gave Rom an affectionate slap on the back.

Keymer wandered across. 'Gin and tonic, Courtenay-Boyle?'

'Jolly decent of you, Keymer. I won't say no.'

Keymer smiled and wandered back towards the row of bottles to pour his opposite number a drink.

'I say, Hutchinson, this will never do,' Courtenay-Boyle went on, once Keymer was out of earshot.

'What will never do, sir?'

'This!' he said, with an exasperated gesture that encompassed the whole wardroom. 'You're a destroyer man, Hutchinson. We can't have you serving on a little tub like this.'

'I was on HMS *Defender* when she was hit at Tobruk,' Rom explained. 'It was felt that I would benefit from some time on a smaller vessel. They seemed to think losing a second ship might put a strain on me.'

'Nonsense!' Courtenay-Boyle hissed. 'What utter nonsense!' He seemed enraged by the indignity of it. 'No, no, no. The first thing I'll be doing when I get back to Blighty is having a word in a few ears at the Admiralty. This will never do.'

By the time HMS *Gorleston* had peeled off from the convoy in Liverpool Bay and made her way back in towards Gladstone Dock, the sun was setting. The SS *Remus II* was edging back out in the opposite direction, towards the widening expanse of the Irish Sea. He had heard of his father's new command in a letter from his mother, and he couldn't resist smiling when he saw the ship — as he had done when he had read the letter.

The idea that his father had another Remus to worry about was a comical coincidence. But to see her now, moving out with the Liverpool skyline in her wake, he imagined his father must be proud to be at the helm of such a ship. She must be nearly twice the size of the SS *Robert Holt* and the SS *John Holt*. It seemed he had steamed to the head of the *John Holt* company's little fleet. Rom couldn't resist giving a pointless, invisible wave out towards the bridge of the SS *Remus II*.

'Once again, Father,' he muttered, 'we are ships that pass in the night.'

'What's that, Hutchinson?' Keymer asked.

'Nothing, sir.' Rom smiled. 'I was just acknowledging my Father — that's his ship heading out of the river now.'

'Yes, of course.' The captain nodded, turning his head towards the merchant ship. 'It seems you've just missed each other.'

'It happens more often than you might think, sir.'

'Still, it must have been a tough voyage for you, Hutchinson, with your brother's ship being torpedoed.'

'He was fine. At least we're all in one piece, sir. I heard that my father's previous ship, the *Robert Holt*, went down too, not long after he handed over command. So, I can't complain. We've been remarkably lucky.'

'It's not an easy time to be a merchant seaman or to be related to one. I'm sorry you won't be getting any shore leave on this visit, Hutchinson. I'm afraid we'll be turning around rather quickly.'

Rom shrugged. 'That's all right, sir. It's the nature of serving with your home city as your home port.'

'Yes, frustrating, I'm sure.'

'Can't be helped, sir.'

'Good man,' Keymer said. 'We need to get *Gorleston* across to Belfast. But then she's going to be in dry dock for a couple of weeks at least. You can jump on a ferry home and see your family.'

'Thank you, sir,' Rom said. 'That would be good.'

Once they were up alongside, Rom was dismissed from the bridge, so he could go and say his goodbyes to Courtenay-Boyle. He found his former captain waiting impatiently on the deck as the gangplank was lowered. 'It's been good to catch up, sir,' Rom said as Courtenay-Boyle shook his hand.

'I meant what I said, Hutchinson,' the commander replied. 'I will be putting in a word for you at the Admiralty. This little ship is no place for a lieutenant of your calibre and experience.'

'Thank you, sir,' Rom said, instinctively lowering his voice, although the two men were a long way out of earshot of Keymer and the other *Gorleston* officers. 'I do miss being part of a destroyer's crew. It's a different level, if you know what I mean, sir.'

'Of course, I completely understand that, Hutchinson. Leave it with me.'

'Good luck with your next command, sir.'

'Thank you, Hutchinson.' Courtenay-Boyle gave him a pat on the arm. 'It's been good to have an opportunity to catch up. God speed, young man.' With that, he stepped down the gangplank onto the quayside. He turned briefly to wave up at Rom, before being consumed by the crowd of dockers and sailors.

In the early hours of the following morning, as HMS *Gorleston* moved back out into Liverpool Bay and dawn was breaking behind them, Rom caught sight of a troopship steaming towards the mouth of the river. Even from that distance, he knew it was the SS *Oronsay*, carrying his twin brother home. He raised his binoculars and took a closer look.

'Good man, Remmie,' he muttered. 'So, you made it home in one piece in the end.'

As *Gorleston* turned to head towards the north-west, he caught a final glimpse of the troopship growing ever bigger on the horizon. 'It's the story of our whole family,' Rom said once again to himself. 'We're all just ships that pass in the night.'

Rom's memories of Belfast were not happy ones. The last time he had spent any real time in the city, he had been in a psychiatric hospital under observation. But with HMS *Gorleston* delivered across the Irish Sea for its fit-out work, he busily emptied the contents of his cabin wardrobe into his bag. He then began emptying his locker. He wouldn't normally take all his possessions from his cabin when he took a period of shore leave. But somehow this felt different. He believed that Courtenay-Boyle was serious when he said he would put a word in for him at the Admiralty. Something made him think this wouldn't just be a couple of weeks away from the ship; he believed he would not be setting foot aboard *Gorleston* again.

He shook Lewis's hand. 'I'm off then, old chap.'

'You are planning on coming back, though, Lieutenant?'

'Oh yes, of course.' Rom flashed him a smile, then looked to his bag. 'I just thought I'd get everything properly washed, while I had an opportunity.' Rom took one more look around the cabin. 'You've been good company, Lewis. Thanks for that.'

'That's quite all right.' The midshipman sounded surprised by the compliment.

Rom pulled the bag onto his shoulder.

Lewis smiled. 'Enjoy your leave.'

'You too, pal.'

He said quick and chirpy goodbyes to Keymer, Smith, Wilson and Brown as he passed each of them in turn in the corridor and on the deck. But he then stepped down the gangplank and made his way off the quayside and down towards the ferry terminal without looking back.

For Remmie, it felt peculiar to arrive back into Liverpool's Canada Dock with no welcome party awaiting their return. No officials from the John Holt Company. No families gathered on the quayside. No press men wanting to capture a picture of the fearless shipwrecked sailors. He was simply told by Captain Hime to take some shore leave, and that head office would be in touch with him about his next posting. Rom had given him a change of clothing and had even lent him a heavy RNVR blue overcoat, insisting it was a spare. One thing about being a twin was that their clothes had always been interchangeable. It had irritated the hell out of Remmie when he was a child, but now, as he wrapped the coat around him against the Mersey chill, he was more than grateful.

He wandered down the gangplank alone, clinging on to Scaggs's banjo, with an eye to the gathering storm clouds, hoping it wasn't going to rain before he made it home.

He felt around in his pockets and found some sterling notes that Rom had given him alongside the US dollars. He had just about enough to take a cab, but frugality got the better of him and he wandered along the dock road to the nearest Overhead Railway station. It was only when he was changing trains at Seaforth, that he realised that his mother probably had no idea the *John Holt* had gone down. She could well be out of the house on a long shift behind the wheel of an ambulance. He didn't know where his house key was. He felt around hopelessly in his pockets, but he knew it was probably still in his cabin on the SS *John Holt*, deep beneath the Atlantic waves.

When he finally made it to the family home, he was relieved to see a lamp on in the front room in the darkening autumnal afternoon. But it wasn't his mother who answered the door. To his surprise, it was Rom's girl.

'Rom!' she cried, tears welling in her eyes.

'I'm sorry, Charlotte, I'm afraid it's Remmie.'

'Remmie?' she said, as if she didn't quite believe him. 'But the coat...'

Remmie looked down. 'Oh, yes, sorry. It's a long story — do you think I could come in?'

Charlotte laughed. 'Of course, Remmie, it's your home. Come on in. We heard about the *John Holt*. Are you all right?'

'I'm fine,' Remmie said. 'Not so much as a scratch.'

'What's with the banjo?'

'Another long story,' he replied. 'How about we get the kettle on? What are you doing here?' he added, as Charlotte stepped back and finally allowed him into the hall.

Charlotte smiled weakly. 'You're going to be an uncle, Remmie.'

'Rom didn't say a word,' he muttered, more to himself than to Charlotte.

'You've seen Rom?'

'Yes!' He smiled. 'It was his ship — HMS *Gorleston* — that came to our rescue, when the *John Holt* sank.'

'It never was!'

'Not a word of a lie,' Remmie said. 'Cross my heart and hope to die.'

The accidental reference to death fell heavily, and the grin dropped from Remmie's face.

'Come on through and sit in the kitchen. It strikes me that we've both got lots of stories to tell.'

'You can certainly say that again, Charlotte,' Remmie said.

CHAPTER SEVENTEEN

It had been a long shift in the ambulance for Eileen. There had been no further bombing raids, but it didn't take the Luftwaffe to create chaos in a city like Liverpool. Sometimes the residents could do it for themselves. In that one night alone, she had been out to patch up wounds after a pub brawl, rush an elderly man having a suspected heart attack to hospital, and then, just as she thought things had settled down, she had attended a horrendous scene in the city centre. A woman had killed herself by jumping in front of an express train as it went through Edge Hill Station. There was nothing they could do for her, of course. But while they waited for the authorities to clear the tracks of her remains, she and May had proved useful in calming the poor little man from the ticket office, who had seen the whole thing and was beside himself with the trauma of what he had witnessed.

It had, in short, been a dreadful night. But nothing could have prepared her for what she saw as she turned her key in the front door and walked into the hallway. Closing the door behind her, she reached for the light switch. The bulb flickered into a glow and revealed a swathe of deep red blood across the hall floor.

'Charlotte! Are you all right?'

'Mother!' The voice that called back from the kitchen was Remmie's.

'Remmie? You're home! What's happened? Where's all that blood come from?'

But as she stood in the kitchen doorway, she immediately knew. Charlotte was on the floor, her knees up by her head, sitting in a pool of blood.

'Dear God, Remmie,' Eileen muttered, springing towards the girl.

'I didn't know what to do, Mother,' Remmie said, staring at Charlotte with wild eyes. 'She was fine earlier. Then I went for a wash and when I came back down, she was like this. I can't get any sense out of her. What's happened?'

Eileen was already on her knees beside the girl, embracing her. 'Deep breaths, love, take deep breaths. We're going to get you help. Run to Doctor Stringer on the corner, Remmie. Tell him she's had a miscarriage.'

Remmie dashed out of the front door and ran down the street.

Rom found his house key in his pocket and opened the door as quietly as he could manage. It was late and he knew his mother would either be fast asleep in bed or out on a night shift with the ambulance. But there was a light on in the kitchen, so he dropped his bag on the hall floor and walked through. Remmie was on his hands and knees with a pail of water and a scrubbing brush.

'Has it become habitual then, holystoning the decks?' Rom grinned at his brother as he removed his cap.

'You're home,' Remmie said looking up.

'So are you. Good voyage back?'

'Not bad,' Remmie said, looking up at him. He was still on his knees, and his face was creased with concern.

'What's wrong, Remmie? Where's Mother? Is she working?'

'No, she went in the ambulance.'

'So, she is working then.'

'You need to listen to me, Rom.'

'All right. Can I put the kettle on while I do? I hate that ferry journey from Belfast. I'm exhausted.' Rom stepped around his brother and began to fill the kettle.

'It's Charlotte.'

'Charlotte was here?'

Remmie nodded.

'Ah, so you know then?' Rom said, lighting the gas hob with a match. 'Is that disapproval I see on your face?'

'No, not at all,' Remmie said, putting down the brush and getting to his feet. 'Look, sit down, will you?'

Rom took a seat at the kitchen table. 'What's the matter?'

'We think Charlotte has lost the baby. I'm sorry, Rom.'

'Lost it? What are you talking about?'

'There was blood everywhere,' Remmie said, with a sweeping gesture around the kitchen.

'Are you telling me she's had a miscarriage?'

Remmie nodded.

'Is she ok?'

'Yes, I think so.'

Rom looked up, tears were welling in his eyes. 'I'm still going to marry her.'

Remmie nodded.

'Where is she now?'

'I don't know. Sefton General, I suppose? But maybe they would have taken her into the Royal. Best to wait for Mother to get home. Then we'll know more.'

'I can't just sit here, Remmie,' Rom said, getting to his feet and making for the front door. 'I need to find her.'

Rom walked as far as the main Liverpool Road, and then turned and began walking towards the city. After half an hour, he saw a hackney cab coming in the opposite direction and was relieved when the cabbie spotted him hailing from the far pavement in the darkness. The roads were empty and the cab motored along at a decent pace, but it still took half an hour to make it through the city's sprawling suburbs. It was half an hour for Rom to sit in the darkness on the springy leather seat and think about all that had happened.

He felt as if his life had been upturned into a mixing bowl ever since that day back in 1939 when he and Remmie had sat with their parents listening to the Prime Minister on the wireless announcing the outbreak of war. He had battled the Germans, the elements and the fates to get to where he was today — a burnt-out wreck at the age of 18, with the creases of anxiety painted into his face like a middle-aged man. It was as though he had suffered the slings and arrows of half-a-dozen lifetimes in these past two years. But now this.

He hadn't exactly been overjoyed to find out he was to become a father at first. But the idea had grown on him. He had seen a bright future for him and Charlotte, with the little one on the way. Now what would the future hold? He reached into his pocket and pulled out the small black leather box he had been carrying around with him for weeks — since he had visited Boodle and Dunthorne the jewellers on his last shore leave in the city.

The cab was arriving at Pembroke Place. He replaced the little box back in his pocket and stepped out into the night, reaching back in through the front window to pay the fare. As the driver pulled away in a twisting U-turn, Rom turned and looked up at the imposing red-brick hospital building. As he walked towards the main entrance, he was surprised to see his mother leaning against the wall, a cigarette in her fingers, the tip glowing in the night like a tiny beacon amid the blackout.

'We don't often see you smoking, Mother,' he said.

Eileen looked up. 'You're home?' She turned her eyes down towards the cigarette. 'I don't smoke much anymore. But on days like these, we all need something to steady our nerves.' She held the cigarette out to one side as she reached forward to embrace her son. 'I'm glad you're home, Rom. I'd offer you a cigarette, but I don't have a packet. One of the doctors gave me this. You're welcome to it if you like.'

'It's all right, Mother,' Rom said, reaching into his pocket. 'I have my own.'

'Did Remmie tell you what happened?'

Rom nodded as he lit the cigarette. 'How is she? Can I see her?'

'She's sad, Rom. But she'll be all right. There's a procedure. It's not pleasant.'

'Poor Charlotte,' Rom muttered, looking to the floor and taking a long drag on the cigarette.

'You're both young,' Eileen said. 'You'll be all right.'

'I want to see her,' Rom said.

'No, Rom, they won't let you. Stay here. Let me go and speak with the sister.'

Rom waited alone in the darkness and smoked. Moments later, Eileen reappeared.

'They said you can have a few minutes with her, love,' she whispered, holding out her hand, as if to invite him inside.

A stern-faced nurse met him at the reception desk and led him through the quiet corridors of the hospital, before finally leading him through another heavy door into the casualty department. It was more brightly lit, and he could hear doctors and nurses talking and patients groaning behind the different sets of privacy curtains. Eventually she opened one of the curtains and stepped back to invite Rom inside. 'You can have five minutes, Lieutenant, no more.'

The curtain was closed behind him. Charlotte looked pale and small where she lay on the bed, beneath a woollen blanket.

'How are you feeling, sweetheart?' he said, rushing towards her and taking hold of her shoulders as he leaned forward to kiss her forehead.

Charlotte's eyes rolled up towards him, her pupils dilated widely. It was clear she was on some heavy medication. But there was a twinkle of recognition in them when they finally focused on Rom's face. 'This time it really is you?' she whispered.

'It's me. I'm home, Charlotte. I'm so sorry I wasn't here.'

'It's all right, Rom,' she said, her voice fragile as she attempted to drag herself up into a sitting position. Rom attempted to help by moving her pillows to support her.

'I'm so sorry, Rom,' she said, tears welling in her eyes. 'There was nothing I could do.'

'I know, I know. Don't upset yourself. You're going to be all right — that's the main thing.'

Charlotte turned her face away.

He reached into his pocket and produced the little black leather box. He opened it and held it out to her. 'I wanted you to have this for your finger,' he said.

Charlotte looked at the ring for a moment. Then her eyes turned back to Rom. 'I think my finger would like that,' she said with a weak smile.

'So you've made your mind up? You will marry me?' Rom said breathlessly. 'Even now?'

Charlotte reached up and took the ring out of the box. She carefully placed it on the fourth finger of her left hand. 'Especially now,' she said softly.

Rom felt his eyes dampening as he leaned forward to kiss Charlotte's pale lips. 'We'll be all right, won't we?' he asked.

Charlotte looked at him for a long moment and nodded. 'Yes, Rom,' she whispered. 'We'll be all right.'

Back outside his mother was waiting for him.

'We're going to get married,' Rom said.

'Good lad.' She smiled. 'Now let's get you home to get some sleep. You can see her again in the morning.'

But Rom was woken early the next morning by a knock on the front door. By the time he had made it down to the hall, Remmie was holding a small card, which he handed to his brother.

'It's a telegram, for you,' he said.

Rom turned it over and tried to take in the message through his bleary eyes. 'It's from Commander Keymer,' he said. 'I'm being reassigned a new ship with immediate effect. I'm not to go back to Belfast to *Gorleston*. I'm to join HMS *Fury* at Gladstone Dock at 8am on Monday morning.'

'This Monday? As in tomorrow morning?' Remmie said.

Rom nodded. 'HMS *Fury* is a destroyer. Old Courtenay-Boyle said he was going to put a word in for me with the Admiralty. Christ, Remmie, I didn't think they'd listen to him.'

'Are you pleased?' Remmie asked tentatively.

'I'll be back on a destroyer, Remmie. Of course I'm pleased,' Rom said. 'But what about Charlotte? I can't leave her alone in this state.'

Their mother, who was standing at the kitchen door, stepped forward. 'She won't be alone. I'll look after Charlotte. You need to go and do your duty.'

After a hasty breakfast, Rom made his way back into the city centre. This time he was allowed a little longer with Charlotte and she seemed much more her usual self. Her eyes were back to normal, but there was no denying the sadness that was etched into her brow.

He told her about his new posting and she smiled. 'You need to be back on a destroyer,' she said softly. 'Don't worry about me, I'll be all right.'

'But next time I'm home, Charlotte, shall we get it done?' He reached for her hand and his fingers played with the engagement ring. 'If something was to happen to me now,' he added disjointedly. 'We should get married as soon as we can. That is, if it wasn't just the drugs talking last night.'

'It wasn't the drugs,' she said. 'Let's get married just as soon as we can.'

'We're really going to do this, Charlotte, aren't we?'

'We are,' she said. 'Of course, we are.'

The following morning, Gladstone Dock was bathed in an amber glow as the sun rose over the city. HMS *Fury* loomed large, like a granite cliff face at the quayside. Rom saw the captain ambling down the gangplank and made his way along the quayside to meet him.

Lieutenant Commander Terence Corin Robinson RN, was a tall, wiry man, with chiselled, handsome features and piercing eyes. He had a presence about him that let Rom know straightaway that this was a man with long years of experience in the Royal Navy. He turned his aquiline features towards Rom and smiled. There was something in the smile that told Rom that this was a captain he could happily serve.

He dropped his pack, stood to attention with a stamping of a shiny shoe, as his right hand moved mechanically to his forehead to give a crisp salute.

'Lieutenant Romulus Hutchinson reporting for duty, sir!'

HISTORICAL NOTES

In the first week of May 1941, Liverpool endured one of the most intense and destructive bombing campaigns of the Second World War. Known as the May Blitz, this seven-day assault by the German Luftwaffe left the city scarred, its people shaken, and its role in the war effort more vital than ever.

Liverpool had long been a strategic target. As Britain's principal transatlantic port, it was the gateway for supplies, troops, and equipment from North America. The city's docks handled the majority of war material entering the country, making it indispensable to the Allied cause. The Germans knew this, and they struck with brutal precision.

Between the first and seventh of May, the city was bombed almost every night. The raids were relentless, with hundreds of aircraft dropping thousands of high explosive bombs and tens of thousands of incendiaries. The Luftwaffe's aim was clear: to cripple the port, disrupt the flow of supplies, and break the spirit of the people. But Liverpool, though battered, refused to buckle.

The damage was staggering. Nearly 1,900 people were killed, 1,450 seriously injured, and around 70,000 made homeless. Bootle, a district just north of the city centre, was particularly hard hit. Of its 17,000 houses, nearly half were destroyed or damaged. Fires raged across the city, fuelled by incendiaries and the flammable cargoes stored in dockside warehouses. One of the most devastating incidents occurred when the SS *Malakand*, loaded with munitions, exploded in Huskisson Dock. The blast was so powerful that the ship's anchor was hurled more than a mile away, landing near Bootle General Hospital.

The city's emergency services were stretched to their limits. Air Raid Precautions wardens, firefighters, and volunteers worked tirelessly to rescue survivors, extinguish fires, and maintain order. Many of them paid the ultimate price. Twenty-eight ARP wardens and members of the Women's Voluntary Services were killed during the raids, with many more injured.

Communal air raid shelters, hastily constructed in the early months of the war, were overwhelmed. Conditions inside were described as intolerable, with overcrowding, poor sanitation, and the constant threat of collapse. Yet these shelters became places of solidarity, where neighbours supported each other through the terror of the night.

Despite the destruction, the May Blitz failed to achieve its strategic aims. The docks, though damaged, continued to operate. Ships still arrived, cargoes were unloaded, and the lifeline to North America remained intact. The resilience of Liverpool's people was as vital as any military defence. Their determination ensured that the city remained a cornerstone of Britain's war effort.

Some of you may leave the book wondering what happened to Bridget, the lady bombed out of her Birkenhead home a few months earlier, in March 1941. I can tell you with confidence that she went on to have a happy and fulfilled family life. I know, because she was my maternal grandmother, my Nan. I grew up hearing her reminiscences of life during the war. Bridget's son, Les, is still with us today. Not so long ago, I sat with my Uncle Les as he celebrated his ninetieth birthday and he told me about that day, long ago, when the roof was blown off the family home.

Another real individual who is fictionalised in this novel, is Kapitänleutnant Otto Kretschmer, one of Germany's star U-boat aces in 1941. I have kept as closely as possible to the real incidents of his capture, even down to the tussle on the deck over a pair of binoculars. In fact, the pair of high-powered Zeiss binoculars he tried to throw back into the sea had been a gift from Admiral Donitz himself. He didn't want them to get into enemy hands.

Throughout the early years of the Battle of the Atlantic, few names struck fear into Allied convoys like that of Lieutenant Otto Kretschmer. Known as "Silent Otto" for his preference to avoid radio transmissions and his mastery of stealth, Kretschmer became the most successful U-boat commander of the war in terms of tonnage sunk. His exploits aboard U-99 earned him fame back home and notoriety around the world.

Before joining the Reichsmarine in 1930, he spent time studying in Britain, which gave him a deep understanding of English culture and language. This experience would later influence his conduct during the war, particularly in his interactions with British captors.

Kretschmer's wartime career began in earnest with command of U-23, a small Type II submarine. His early patrols in the North Sea and off the Scottish coast were marked by precision and daring. He laid mines in Moray Firth and sank several merchant vessels, including the Danish tanker *Danmark* and the British destroyer HMS *Daring*. But it was with U-99, a Type VIIB submarine, that Kretschmer truly made his mark.

His tactics were revolutionary. Rather than relying on submerged attacks, Kretschmer preferred to strike on the surface under cover of darkness. His motto, "one torpedo, one ship", reflected his emphasis on accuracy and conservation of resources. This approach proved devastatingly effective.

Between April 1940 and March 1941, Kretschmer sank 47 ships, totalling more than 274,000 tons. Among his most notable victims were three British Armed Merchant Cruisers, *Laurentic*, *Patroclus*, and *Forfar*, all sunk in November 1940. These successes earned him the Knight's Cross of the Iron Cross with Oak Leaves and Swords, one of Nazi Germany's highest military honours.

Despite his fame, Kretschmer remained a reserved figure. He shunned propaganda and avoided the limelight at home, preferring to focus on his crew and mission. His quiet demeanour and tactical brilliance earned him the respect of both allies and adversaries.

In March 1941, while escorting Convoy HX 112, British destroyers HMS *Walker* and HMS *Vanoc* detected U-99 using ASDIC, an early sonar system, which is where Rom and the crew of Walker dramatically come into contact with this towering figure of the Kriegsmarine in my fictionalised account.

His capture marked a turning point in the Battle of the Atlantic. Alongside the loss of fellow U-boat aces Günther Prien and Joachim Schepke (the U-boat captain that Rom witnesses slipping beneath the waves before the capture of U-99) the event dealt a significant blow to the Kriegsmarine's morale and operational capability.

Kretschmer spent the remainder of the war as a prisoner, first in Britain and then in Canada. He was held at Bowmanville POW camp, where he remained in contact with German naval command and was even the subject of a failed rescue plot in 1943. After the war, he returned to Germany and joined the Bundesmarine, eventually rising to the rank of Flottillenadmiral and serving as Chief of Staff at NATO's Baltic Command before retiring in 1970.

A NOTE TO THE READER

Dear Reader,

This is a piece of fiction. Some of the characters are based on real people, others are complete fabrications of my imagination. Where real names are used, please be aware that I merely present fictionalised versions of their real lives, a process I have approached with great respect and care for the dignity of their memory.

I am grateful for the works of countless historians and writers who came before me in informing this fictionalised account, but I would particularly point the reader to two memoirs. Captain Donald Macintyre wrote about his actual experiences on HMS *Walker* in his firsthand account *U-Boat Killer* (1956), while the exploits of Otto Kretschmer, captain of U-99, were recorded in *The Golden Horseshoe* (1955), for which Kretschmer worked closely with writer Terence Robertson.

Wherever possible I have clung closely to the real events and the actions of real ships, but have sometimes deviated in the cause of storytelling, either to increase the dramatic impact on the lives of the fictional and fictionalised characters, or to amalgamate disparate real-life incidents in a manner that allows them to be recounted as a coherent narrative.

The John Holt Line's ships tended to be named after members of the Holt family. The Alfred Holt Line (or Blue Funnel Line) which also ran out of Liverpool had been founded in the previous century from within the same family, but was operated independently as a separate business. This line tended to give its ships names from classical history and literature with the likes of the SS *Agammemnon*, the SS *Titan* and the SS *Prometheus*. While there was a G.B. Wadsworth ship called the SS *Remus*, which sailed out of Goole during the First World War, to my knowledge there was never a ship named the SS *Remus II* as part of the merchant fleet. It is the only fictional ship in this novel.

I hope you have enjoyed spending time with my fictional twins, Romulus and Remus Hutchinson, who will reappear in further adventures. Reviews are important for authors, so if you enjoyed *In Danger's Hour*, I would be really grateful if you could take a moment to review the book on **Amazon** or **Goodreads**. You can sign up to my newsletter and find out more about what I'm working on by visiting my website: **www.davidclensy.com**.

David Clensy

Sapere Books is an exciting new publisher of brilliant fiction and popular history.

To find out more about our latest releases and our monthly bargain books visit our website: **saperebooks.com**

Printed in Dunstable, United Kingdom

75035734R00143